STOP AT NOTHING

George Squire and his wife Gertrude are visiting New Orleans, where his spouse insists on staying at an old "haunted" mansion that's been renovated into a hotel. When Gertrude's jewels are stolen, the proprietor, Monsieur Favreau, insists that one of the many ghosts associated with the structure's past has been at work. But George doesn't believe in the supernatural, and sets out to prove that a more mundane force is involved. Only THE MYSTERIOUS MIRROR can provide an answer!

Here are a dozen scintillating tales of murder, mayhem, and urban insanity, ripped from the steamy pages of the 1950s and '60s pulp magazines!

Borgo Press Books by MORRIS HERSHMAN/LIONEL WEBB

The Blackbirder
A Knife for My Love and Further Mayhem
Rogue Slave
Sebastian
Seeing Is Deceiving: A Gail Brevard Mystery
Silent Treatment and Other Stories
Sparhawk
Stop at Nothing: Classic Crime Stories
Vicious Circles: Classic Crime Stories

STOP AT NOTHING

CLASSIC CRIME STORIES

MORRIS HERSHMAN

THE BORGO PRESS
MMXIII

STOP AT NOTHING

FIRST EDITION

Published by Wildside Press LLC

www.wildsidebooks.com

STOP AT NOTHING

CONTENTS

DANGEROUS TO KNOW

Yes, I'm still alive, as you can see and hear. Since I sent for the two of you, nothing bad has happened to me.

Won't be long, though, before it does. Doctor Siegel told me a little sneakily only a while ago that I'll never get up from this bed for long.

Which is why I asked you two, my son and daughter, to come out here. Not to say goodbye or anything so sticky-sentimental. We all said goodbye when you left home. I accepted it then, and at my age I'm grateful that the two of you aren't living in my pockets any longer. You both have to make your own mistakes, to sometimes help and too often hurt the people you love, just as I did.

But I was able to make life a lot pleasanter, financially, at least, by making a good living. I never played the miser with either of you. My work and skills made it possible for both of you to marry well and spend your time among the rich and powerful.

And now, my son, my daughter, I feel justified in calling in your debts. It's time for you to do something very important to me so I can die—not pass away or pass over, if you please, but die, which is a nasty business—with the certain knowledge that a promise I made to myself has been kept, a promise that had been the breath of life to me.

Both of you are looking a little unsettled now. I suppose that there are a hundred and one foolish questions you want to ask before either of you will stir to do what I need done at this of all times.

I'll make a deal with both of you. I'll give a straight statement of my reasons. In return, if anything bad starts to happen while I'm talking, I want an agreement that you'll follow my instructions without stopping to think. I know I never could stop myself from making deals but it means a lot, though this one will certainly be my last.

Here goes, then. The whole story, the whole truth.

* * * * * * *

"Let's get away from our homes," Lillian said to me on that rain-washed morning as she hurried out of her parents' place. The light wind ruffled her shiny red hair and brought glints to what she herself called her Rita Hayworth eyes. That was an appropriate description for her to use because she often buried herself in a movie magazine. She was called Lil for short and sometimes Lillums, after a comic strip character. At sixteen, I was sure she could be the most willing girl that ever drew breath.

I grinned while starting the car, not at all surprised. We had previously agreed to spend this Saturday on a picnic for two. I was so glad at getting her to myself that I forgot to notice she wasn't carrying a food basket, but I sure realized that for once she had kept an appointment early. That last point I took for a promising sign.

"The Hill ought to be a good place," I said, naming what might have been the quietest spot in all Wyoming.

"No, I meant it, Dwight! Let's do something on impulse for once, go far away, just you and me out of town."

It sounded fine for a few hours. "I'll just take time to write a note to my father, so he won't worry."

"Either we go now or I leave, and I mean it."

"I have to stop off and get gas for the car."

I drew up a few yards from a public phone booth.

"You ought to call your folks and tell 'em we'll be gone for a while, Lil. You've got two parents to worry for you."

"I'll phone while you're away." She touched me affectionately, I thought. "Don't waste time."

I didn't intend to. In the house, I wrote out a short note telling my father I'd be home later than usual tonight. Then I went to the garage for a couple of gallons of gas. My father kept them out there because gas was an object of wartime rationing at the pumps, and he had managed to squirrel some of the stuff away in case of an emergency.

And to a horny sixteen-year-old boy, this was an emergency. Lil hadn't yet gone all the way with me—actually I hadn't done it with any girl yet—and my high school buddies said confidently that she was hot stuff who'd do it for anybody.

She hadn't left the car when I got back and put the gas cans in the truck, not expecting to use more than one for this trip. I didn't plan to do much driving.

"Go on," she said urgently when I slowed down just before the Hill. "We're driving to the moon if we have to."

"I've only got a couple of cans if you want to cover distance, Lillums, but no coupon book to buy gas at the pump."

"I took my—my folks' coupon book," she said after a second, giving what looked like a friendly smile if you didn't notice the eyes. "I thought I'd forgot, but here it is."

I signaled her to move closer if I was going to drive. She did, resting her head lightly against a shoulder. I was reaching for her at a traffic stop when she turned the car radio on to a music station. I'd hoped for a romantic number but we heard *Comin' in on a Wing and a Prayer.* I perked up when the news came on, wondering if our soldiers had done any fresh damage to Hitler or Tojo, but Lil snapped it off.

"None of that miserable war news, honey. Let's spend our first full day without the world being here."

We were out of good old Barnley and in Idaho, on US 85 when my teen-aged appetite caught up with me. The nearest diner served its idea of a Dagwood sandwich while Lil picked up half a dozen movie magazines for herself. I remember spilling some vinegar across one copy, making Lil look murder at me. (Funny how I can remember that incident over fifty years ago, but I couldn't tell you what I had for my miserable lunch this miserable afternoon.)

I was feeling bitterly disappointed by the time the sun started to weaken. We had stopped only so that I could eat and for the needs of traffic. Lil had snuggled close to me every so often, and even brushed my body in certain strategic places when I seemed tired, but she hadn't gone further.

Swallowing my disappointment, I decided to make a left turn now and a little afterwards a right. That way, she wouldn't protest at my taking us home until too late.

She opened those matchless eyes as soon as I made the second turn, having been snuggled against me. Deftly, she raised herself.

"You're probably too tired to drive much longer," she said softly. "We'll have to stay overnight somewhere."

I had to shrug, even though my interest had perked up considerably at the idea of rooming with her. "I can't afford a hotel."

"We'll go to a boarding house, honey."

"I suppose I've got enough for tonight."

The boarding house lady sniffed suspiciously at us, but agreed to put us up when money was offered in advance. I never will forget my hand quivering when I locked the door on the two of us.

"I'm a good girl," Lil whispered. "Really."

And that night, in a room with brown wallpaper, shoddy furniture and a lingering smell of disinfectant, in that room the two of us (don't smile now, whatever else you do) went all the way.

I was groggy when I woke up on Monday morning. Leaving Lil fast asleep, I weaved my way down to the nearest diner for breakfast and some sports news on the radio. I was an avid fan of the New York Giants baseball team, and we were in the toilet that year because so many players had been drafted. It was one sad session, but the food gave me energy.

I called home, intending to let my father know I'd be back very soon and to suggest he tell Lil's folks the same about her. My father must have left for work earlier than usual. There was no answer.

Lil was half-dressed when I got back.

"Soon as you have your breakfast," I said, looking away with difficulty from the trim and unforgettably beautiful flesh, "we'll leave."

"Good. I can stand to see some other states."

"Leave for home is what I mean," I explained as a shadow crossed her face. "Our people must be worried about us."

"Who cares?"

"Do you care that we've got just about enough money to get home on?"

Lil reached into her pocketbook. "I was able to bring some extra before I left. With that and the gas coupon book, which I'll put in this drawer, we ought to be all right."

"Two hundred dollars," I said thinly after counting with the help of a wet thumb, "isn't going to last long now we're on our own."

"Then we stay in this town—what's it called? Argo, yes—we stay until we've got enough to scram out."

"We'll have to get jobs."

"Sure, and we live together all the time."

I was breathing a little harder at the notion of having a girl around and doing things together.

She had been carrying the gas coupon book in a hand, but now she put it into a drawer and covered it with a kerchief over the envelope in which she had deposited it.

"It's going to send us as far as we want to go," she said happily, smiling down at it. "We'll remember that coupon book forever, sort of like *Back Street*, honey. Very romantic."

I didn't know what she meant about romance, whatever that might be. I was so excited I hardly cared.

It was easy for us to settle in: Every business needed workers, and nobody was inclined to ask more questions than strictly necessary. Names had to be given, but we made them up. We were ready to invent Social Security numbers if asked, but the bosses were just as glad to pay us off the books. There weren't any computers to track down strangers and you didn't need identification to use the men's room at a restaurant.

The other side of wartime employment became clear to me when I tried to reach my father. I wanted to leave a message at his headquarters because he traveled a lot and could be away for weeks at a time. On several occasions I called his central office, but always got hold of the same idiot who was in charge of the switchboard and I could only hope she understood some of what I was saying.

I took a liking to Idaho while I was out there, sometimes driving along the Clearwater River—and the water *was* clear— or inspecting Douglas fir trees as if I hadn't seen others. When Lil was riding with me, the two of us would stop and play, so that my nature studies were rewarding in different ways.

On the trip back to our boarding house, Lil would slather her lips with Tangee lipstick and stop at a stationery store for a new load of movie magazines. We could afford movies themselves about twice a week, and although it was dark and not every seat around was always taken, she allowed no fooling around during a romantic movie and always criticized the leading lady's acting ability or looks afterwards.

"*She* isn't much," Lil would say about whatever it was. "Don't you think I look as good as she does?"

"Better," I'd tell her.

Movie-going always caused her to ask how much money we had saved up. One weekday night, after she won five dollars at Screen-O, the theatre lottery game, she said, "I think we've got enough money altogether to blow this town."

I was amused, for some reason. "Do you want to go to New York and see the Stork Club?"

She had talked wistfully about New York City, but now she shook her head. "South, honey. South is the direction I'm going in."

"That covers a lot of territory from here."

"We'll go as far as we can and when our money runs out we'll stop in another town and work until we can afford to—well, to go further."

"Do you expect me to throw my life away on the road?"

"In a couple of years you'll be old enough for the Army and heading for war, so you might as well have a good time before you've got to go."

"Driving all day for God knows how long isn't my idea of a good time."

She shook her head, turning away. "You don't have to come with me if you don't want to. I can make it to as far as I'm going."

The idea of being without her was enough to make me anxious. "Let's take one more week and then go."

"I can't see how one week will make much difference, Dwight, but if you promise you'll go South in another week, I'll compromise and wait."

"Swell," I said, and forgot anything as soon as I touched the warm buttons of her dress....

I hadn't been cutting another deal for its own sake, you understand. What I wanted was the time to decide on a new maneuver for getting a message to my father. Common sense insisted he already heard from his office that I was safe, but it couldn't hurt to make doubly sure. Lil had extracted a promise that I wouldn't write him because a note might be traced, but I hadn't been asked to swear not to contact her own people instead and requests them to leave a message for my father if he wasn't available. The trouble was that I didn't feel sure what sort of reception I might get from them. Antagonism was certainly flourishing on Lil's side and was most likely returned in spades to her and anybody she liked. Believe it, kids, I didn't want to step into a hornet's nest.

While trying to make up my mind during the next days, I actually started to dial the long distance operator, but gave it up and decided not to anything else about that.

Well, we took the one valise with the clothes each of us had bought, and we started off. I told myself that I just wanted a few more good times with her and then I'd turn around for home.

We fetched up in a little Nevada town called Radden, which was closer to Reno than Las Vegas. Reno was the best-known city in the state because rich people travelled out there for quick divorces, with only a month-long residence requirement, I think. I don't' recall seeing public gamboling while we lived and worked out there.

I do remember the first time we saw our boarding house room, and holding hands around the double bed, then falling on top of it. A good time was had by all.

We went dancing that night, which isn't really important in itself, although Lil was one of those girls shrewd enough to wear only a trace of perfume and who can melt against her partner on the dance floor. One of the songs played that night was the super-romantic *People Will Say We're in Love*, with its inferences about a community made up of persons knowing each other well enough to exchange gossip. It gave me the idea that would have come to me a long time ago, I'm sure, if I hadn't been so happily groggy in these last weeks. In spite of her closeness on the dance floor, that song's words caused me to use my head. All I had to do was to phone my best friend back in Barnley and ask him to leave a message for my father. Simple, of course.

I waited until late afternoon of the next day, stopped in for coffee, and refused a chance to take my change in war stamps. At the public phone booth I called Floyd Walsh's home. Floyd, answering, sounded surprised as hell to hear me.

"Your father? Dwight, I hate to be the one who tells this, but your father is in jail."

"He's—what?"

"Your father is supposed to go on trial very soon. The police are saying that he set fire to the Waterson house and killed Mr. and Mrs. Waterson."

"Lil's parents, you mean?"

"Well, step-parents, you know. The police think that Lil died in the fire, too, but there isn't evidence that scientists are able to identify to say for sure; those people don't know as much as we think they do. And the police think you were with Lil, too, and you're also—you know."

My father had never liked the Watersons and didn't go for the idea of my seeing Lil. He claimed that with a girl as easy as her, I might catch some disease. Plenty of people knew how he felt. You might say that there was a motive, but only if you thought my father was irrational.

"And how about my father's car, Floyd? What do the police think happened to that?"

"I don't know. I haven't heard anything about it on radio or seen anything in the paper. I don't think anybody knows."

"Okay, Floyd," I said after a long painful pause. "I'll get back to Barnley soon as I can."

It meant going to the boarding house garage for the car as a beginning. While I circled it, Lil came around the corner and hailed me.

"I've got good news." She grinned expansively. "Let's go up and I'll tell you."

There was no point to starting a discussion that would turn into our first real argument. I followed her up to the room where she exulted about having landed a job as cashier for (of all places) the local movie house. Wasn't that a break for such a movie fan?

Lil, who was nobody's dummy, of course, saw that my thoughts were on something besides her. She looked unbelieving, then smiled and settled own on the double bed, gesturing for me to join her and forget everything else.

I think I did it mainly because it would be a goodbye between us, goodbye to the best time I'd ever had. A big part of my youth would be gone soon after I had found it.

She turned away eventually, as she always did first when we were on a bed and had got finished. Her beautiful eyes were already half-shut, again as usual, by the time she covered herself. I had been counting on her usual reactions to make my departure easier, and she hadn't disappointed me yet.

"Wake me for supper, honey," she said, again as before. Her breath was soon coming evenly.

I got up, took my clothes, and tiptoed into the bathroom. There was some trouble putting on shoes without a horn and I called out at the stab of unexpected pain in a forefinger which turned out to be a bad substitute.

Lil stirred.

Tiptoeing out, I stopped very briefly. Leaving my new clothes behind wasn't a wrench, but I wanted to take the gas coupon book to help get home. Valuable seconds were wasted while I reminded myself that I'd have been committing theft. I didn't know just how I could get home in the car, but the idea of my possibly being responsible for a crime shocked me for the first time in my life. And, as it happened, the last time.

As I was looking thoughtfully at the car and wondering how far I'd get before having to ditch it, I heard her voice raised slightly but in anger. "Where are you sneaking the hell off to?"

She had come running after me, clothes straggling on that wonderful, maybe flashy, body, red hair tumbling down. By the light of a rising moon her eyes glittered furiously.

"I'm going home, Lillums. My father is in jail and I want to be near him when he goes on trial."

"No, you're coming with me," she insisted, clearly surprised that I wouldn't rather be where I could make love to her almost any time I wanted to.

I hadn't intended to break bad news to her, but she was being so insensitive I went right ahead. "My father is accused of killing your parents."

She gestured dismissively, although the Watersons had adopted her as an infant. "You're driving me out to California, damn it, to L.A."

She hadn't told me before that there was a clear-cut goal in her mind, a place where she wanted us to stop for however long, maybe to stay. It seemed like one more of the vital matters I hadn't known about. Everything was happening too quick.

"Listen to me," she said urgently, leaning forward. "I'm as good-looking as any actress in Hollywood. I know I'll be even better with the right make-up and lighting. I'll end up being famous everywhere in the world and you can be my manager. I don't intend to strike it good, Dwight, and forget all about the one who helped me most on the way up."

My insides were churning by this time. I had to accept it that the girl I loved had set fire to her parents' home with both of them inside, then hurried out of there to join me so I could take her to California, to L.A., to Hollywood and the movie studios.

She was still talking quickly and quietly, but with desperation. "I took care of those stupid people because they wouldn't stake me. Do you think I'm going to let you stop me from becoming famous in the movies? Do you?"

She was coming nearer to the car.

I turned, raising a hand to keep her from getting closer. She looked angry, then bent over and came up with a heavy cord of fireplace wood and raised it over her head, prepared to kill me. She was ready to sacrifice another human life, a third, so she could have a car taking her quickly and comfortably to that location where she felt so passionately she belonged.

I reached for the weapon and she suddenly lowered the wood with youthful energy, bringing it down to strike forcefully against my left thigh. Gasping in pain, I lost my balance.

Lil took the brunt of that loss, dropping the wood to help keep herself upright and falling back, stumbling before she dropped heavily. There was a squashing sound as she struck her head against the wood that had damaged me. She lay at my shaky feet, where she remained still. Very still.

Only one word described her condition, as I realized through advancing and receding waves of pain. I couldn't bring myself to think that word, let alone say it. In self-defense, nothing but self-defense, I had done—this.

Very soon now I'm going to make it plain exactly what favor I called you here to the hospital lto do for me. Two well-off young people like yourselves, with comfortable lives, might be asking if it's worthy helping a man who would commit such an act on the body of another human being, even if it wasn't done on purpose, even if the killer is your father. Wait just a while longer, put your critical judgments in the freezer and I should be able to convince you at least of the depth of my powerful regrets over what took place.

At the immediate moment, though, it didn't matter. What I had to do was to get away from there in such a way that I'd be safe from the consequences of that horrible deed.

It was, all things considered, easier done than said.

I drove the car out to a corner of the wide street where few people lived and nobody was in sight. Putting Lil next to the driver's seat was a cinch.

The landlady of this boarding house hadn't seen me in a good light, so I took a chance and went back to the room. I left a day's rent and took away what was necessary.

Returning to the car, I drove out of town. I stopped, got out and put Lil behind the wheel. After the license plates were in my light suitcase, I crushed her fingers so that no prints could be taken; police scientists in those days couldn't do full reconstructions. The teeth posed no problem for identification because Lil's dentist had been drafted recently and no one would be asking about his records.

There was one other thing I did for I-don't-really-know-what reason. She'd had beautiful eyes, had called them Rita Hayworth eyes, and I opened them. It made no sense, but I didn't want to not do it, if you know what I mean.

Then it was a question of going out to the highway and hitching a ride, not unusual in those wartime days when drivers didn't flinch and pick up speed at sight of a hitchhiker.

You understand that the decade in which this happened as well as general wartime conditions helped me get away with what I did. None of my actions would be successful today, and I'd have been locked up in minutes.

...well, *what* about the car? There had been a cliff nearby and much as I hated doing it, I sent the car over. The gas tank was exploding when I turned away.

I got back to my home town just a day before my father's trial for murder got under way. His lawyer talked to me in detail before going into court. I made a good impression on the witness stand, being an A student with a lot of friends and nothing against me. My father was a respectable widower who was bringing up his son responsibly, and I would think that half of Wyoming knew us. Add that to the lawyer pointing to the apparent disappearance of the Waterson's adopted daughter at the time of the fire, and the Not Guilty verdict was a foregone conclusion.

There isn't too much else about me that you never knew before. In summary, I never got into the Armed Forces when I turned eighteen, largely on account of residual damage from that wound across the left thigh that Lil had inflicted on me. It hadn't been a problem to me after the first weeks, though, and it's possible my father's friends wanted to keep me out of danger as I was his one living relative. I doubt if anything along that line would happen today, and it must've been unusual even then, if that's the answer, of course.

I stayed in the U.S., drifting from one foolish job to another. At twenty I started college in Laramie and met the girl who would become your mother. We got married in the third year, and I was in such a hurry to establish myself I didn't graduate.

A bad mistake as a rule, especially in these days when it seems you can't have enough higher education. But not a bad mistake for me at that particular time.

Television was a brand-new business, with everybody in it starting from scratch. Along with Henry Simonowicz, a long-time friend, I raised money for a syndicate which acquired a franchise for a local station. Your mother once said that I was interested most of all because I could never forget not having known about my father's trial until almost too late, and I wanted to be sure news got more quickly to more people.

Eventually, Henry joined me in buying out the other members

of the syndicate. After a few more years, I bought out Henry and later I let the Preferred Broadcasting people buy me out for a lot of money. Doesn't it all remind you of the old saying about the little fish and the big fish?

I expected to pyramid my money in another business, but my interest wasn't caught. (Even you two, self-absorbed as you've always been, must recall how damned restless I was for a long time afterwards.) From the day I sold out I was retired.

Which brings me directly to this very day, and the urgent favor I must have from you. First, you're to help me sit up on the right side of the bed. I have to be in a position to take out something from the far end of the drawer, where I put it when I was first hospitalized. And then I'm going to take that something out of the drawer. While your backs are turned, I'll rip it in half and in quarters and, if my strength allows, into eighths.

No, I won't let either of you do any part of the chore. I touch it and nobody else. After I drop those shreds into this hospital waste bag, you'll leave. Don't tell. Don't look back.

Can't you realize what it is? Why, it's all that's left to me of her. Yes, I know Lil wasn't smart enough to realize she'd be suspected of two arson murders she couldn't avoid committing, and was eventually ready to murder me, too. And I know, none better, that in no way was she the woman my wife was. Truly, I know those things very well.

All I have left of her is a faded envelope holding a gas ration coupon book from World War II, a book she had touched and that is tangible proof that for a short time my Lillums and I were together. Of course, it was an episode of prolonged youthful lust that ended badly. But I didn't live with her for every day into old age, and to a dying old man who sees so clearly through that boy's eyes and remembers with that boy's heart, it was first love. And, you see, one of the few things that the old have learned is that first love is true love.

THE LADY CONFESSES

Thomas Reed, Assistant District Attorney, knew the neighborhood well. Now it seemed unusually quiet as he walked through it during the early part of the evening. He brushed what might have been some lint off his gray tweed sport jacket and walked past the rundown tenements, and the dull looking old storefronts.

He could feel that people's eyes were on him as he walked, but he shrugged and crossed the street. There was a shuttered butcher shop on the corner and as he came to the front of it somebody whispered: "Murderer!"

Tom Reed whirled, but he couldn't see anybody. Then he noticed that people were gathering at the corner of Holley and Pine, almost in front of him. They were small in number, not more than three or four to a group. Some children were included, most of them so small that they had to be held in their mothers' arms.

A man appeared from the Pine end of the street and pulled a woman forward. She was a mall thin woman and as she ran she called out: "I'm the one! I killed him. Stoska is innocent of...."

Her words trailed off as the man came to a stop in front of Tom Reed. The man was dressed better than most men in this section. He wore a close-fitting blue suit, and handkerchief points peeped out of a breast pocket. He was tall and heavy, and seemed very sure of himself.

"Something's come up, Mr. Reed, and it's got to be taken care of as soon as possible," he said loudly, glancing back to see that the audience was paying attention. "I'm a friend of these people. Whatever interests them, it interests me, too. My name is Arthur Lade."

The time-serving political hatchet man," Reed said flatly. "Your party is out of power, and a dirty scandal in this neighborhood is sure to help them get votes at the next election. I know who you are, Mr. Lade. I know plenty about you."

"The point is," Arthur Lade said quickly, "that this woman has something important to say to you. She came to me a little while ago in the hope that maybe I could do something, but with another political party in power all I can do is urge her to tell the truth in hopes of getting justice for a man who needs it desperately—tonight."

The weak scrawny woman drew a long breath through her nose and asked, "This Herman Stoska—are they going to kill him?"

"He's been sentenced to die in the electric chair," Reed said, his eyes narrowing. "He dies tonight for having shot his wife and her lover when he found them together. What about it?"

"Stoska is innocent," the woman bawled, waving one arm no thicker than a pipe. "I am ready to tell the truth!"

Reed stared down at her for a moment, his face becoming hard. Then he turned, and ordered the crowd to stand back in a voice that carried the steely ring of authority.

Slowly the crowd obeyed. A woman pushed her child forward, cursed in a foreign language and finally picked up the child in her arms. She crossed the street and stood staring.

Reed swung back just as Arthur Lade said, "This woman is Mrs. Alvar. You must remember the name. You tried the case."

Tom Reed did remember it. Luther Alvar had been murdered along with Mrs. Herman Stoska.

Mrs. Alvar was crying loudly. "Stoska is not guilty!" she got out between sobs. "I can prove this, you hear?"

The crowd halted in mid-motion. From a sullenly hostile group, they became angrily alert and very still. More than one man who had retreated a few paces now came back slowly.

Reed was disturbingly aware that to annoy them at this time could bring on a small-sized riot.

Mrs. Alvar sniffled. Lade's fingers worked at the handkerchief-points rising out of a breast pocket. "This woman is entitled to a chance to save the life of an innocent man," he said. "I was told you walk through this neighborhood nearly every night on your way home. I took the precaution of making sure by having you tailed."

Muttering rose in the crowd, whose members didn't know that all of them were being victimized by Lade and the woman who had probably been bribed. She looked acutely uncomfortable.

"Mrs. Alvar," Reed said coldly, "you'd have told me all this a long time ago, if there was any truth in it."

"No!" The woman was tearful. "I figure something will happen, somebody will find truth. A man who is innocent, a man like Stoska, he won't be killed that way."

"This present administration is railroading an innocent butcher to the chair," Lade said, gesturing back of him at the closed butcher shop. "And you were the one who made it stick in court."

The crowd, many of whose members had been Stoska's customers, looked at other crowd members and nodded sympathetically.

"I got proof," Mrs. Alvar added. "I can prove what I say. Let me prove it now."

"All right, Mrs. Alvar," Reed said, realizing that he had given ground. "What's your proof that Stoska is innocent? Let me see it."

The woman nodded and opened her purse on a heavy, black .45 automatic. The audience seemed to hold its breath as Reed took the gun out, turned it around in his hand, and sniffed at the cold barrel.

"That is the gun I did it with," Mrs. Alvar said listlessly, holding one slim hand in another. "I followed my husband and Mrs. Stoska to her place, shot them, and left."

The murder weapon had never been found, a circumstance which had been the only weakness in the prosecution's case against Herman Stoska. The man had been discovered in his apartment with the two dead bodies.

"Where was this gun?" Reed asked, trying to make himself sound skeptical.

"I take it away with me after I did the two bad things," Mrs. Alvar said tonelessly. "Then I keep it. No one ever searches me at all."

Arthur Lade thundered. "Positive proof! The wrong person has been put in danger of his life, a victim of dirty politics and religious prejudice. "What are you going to do about this new evidence, Mr. Reed?"

"Well, this gun is of the same caliber as the one that did the killing and may well be the murder weapon," Reed admitted. "But that doesn't mean Stoska wasn't able to get the gun to you, Lade. You simply kept it till the last minute. Now you want to create enough momentary confusion to get Stoska a reprieve and yourself an election issue."

"Herman Stoska is scheduled to die in the electric chair in three hours," Lade trumpeted. "There's plenty of time to call the Governor. What will you do about it?"

"I'll check something first," Tom Reed said levelly. "You say, Mrs. Alvar, that you discovered your husband with Mrs. Stoska at her apartment and you shot both of them and left, taking the gun with you. When you saw Stoska was under arrest you kept quiet, but now you have to talk. Is that right?"

"Y-yes."

"Take the .45 back," Tom Reed said coldly, watching as he managed to deposit the huge gun in Mrs. Alvar's hands and the woman sighed as if her back was broken before dropping the heavy weapon to the sidewalk. Lade picked up the gun and placed it back in her purse.

"You know as well as I do that Herman Stoska killed them and the crime he'll pay the penalty for is the one he committed," Reed went on. "You can leave, Mrs. Alvar, unless you want to be arrested on a false evidence charge."

The woman turned and started to shuffle away. Lade, her protector, said: "Mrs. Alvar and I are taking this gun downtown and to a newspaper office and I'll see that it's given appropriate publicity. The whole city will know that this administration railroaded a man. The whole country will know about it."

"It won't do you any good," Tom Reed said firmly.

* * * * * * *

"Herman Stoska confessed his guilt before he was electrocuted," the police commissioner told Reed later that evening. "How did you know Stoska was guilty and the woman was innocent?"

"The gun told me," Tom Reed said. "The precious gun that was supposed to 'prove' Stoska's innocence long enough for a reprieve; but could never have proved that Mrs. Alvar was guilty. And I'm sure she knew she'd never be a serious suspect in any other investigation."

"How do you mean?" the police commissioner asked.

"That gun was too heavy for her," Reed said. "She couldn't possibly have lifted that huge .45 and fired it, because I proved conclusively that the gun was too heavy for this frail woman to hold."

PAYBACK TIME

Felix Clarke was perfectly at ease until just before the end of this family visit with his mother-in-law. He and his wife were already on their feet, and he had deftly rounded up the sullen children when Vivian, embracing her mother before leaving, said softly but tautly, "Don't worry, everything will be all right."

He had been talking happily about his and Vivian's shiny duplex apartment in a shiny new co-op on East Thirty-Fourth Street, above one of Manhattan's gold coasts, and had been on the verge of inviting "Mother," as he called her, too, at her sunny insistence, for a long visit. He would have meant every word. Mrs. Adelaide Budge had certainly done more for his happiness than the real parents he had never known, let alone those foster parents who scorned but envied his youth, who only used him to gouge money from their city. Will power and hard work allied to a happy marriage had put him into the position to take Colorado skiing vacations, to send his children to good private schools, and to live better than three-quarters of the struggling residents in New York City. No wonder he considered himself among the blessed, and that it was the family of Adelaide Budge, taking him to themselves as one of their own, who had blessed him.

Now, concerned for the old lady's welfare, dread thoughts of some medical emergency winging through his brain, Felix asked quickly, "What's wrong, Mother?"

Vivian, separating herself from the fragile old lady, looked gratified by her husband's worry, but said, "We'll talk about it later."

And, to Mother, she said soothingly, "We won't let him go near you."

At least no medical horror was involved, thank God. Whatever was wrong, it could definitely be fixed by somebody.

Vivian didn't say much until she and Felix and the children had climbed back into the snazzy Lexus 400 and were halfway done with the forty-mile drive to her sister's place in Chatterton, the closest town. The car handled so well that he was glad for enough silence so that he could revel in it, if only for a few minutes, in the pleasure of using such fine machinery. But he was worried about Mother's continued happiness, and he turned anxiously toward his wife.

"It's on account of Barney," Vivian finally told him, having made certain that the children were dozing.

"Your adopted brother, you mean?" Of course Felix knew the family history backwards and forwards. Weren't they part of one larger family, after all? "He hasn't hurt you or your sister in years, not since he turned sixteen and ran away from home. Nobody has ever talked to him since then."

"That's because he hasn't tried to reach us." Her eyes wandered fitfully over the landscape's summer greenery under appropriately ink-dipped clouds. "And for the last dozen years, he's been in prison for robbery with violence, but he'll be coming out very soon now and he's bound to see us and raise hell, as he always does when he can. As for Mother, she couldn't take it any more; not after two heart attacks."

They were interrupted by their six-year-old, Corey, who sat up and moved two parallel near-fists, as if he was the one who was driving. Any talk about the subject would have to be done cryptically, almost in code.

"If B does anything, Viv, I'll take him on."

Felix was being offered a chance to give a return after several years of good living over and above what a freelance journalist's income might have covered. Remembering how much he owed Addie Budge for her kindness, he and Vivian as well, he wanted to be hailed as the rescuer, to feel that his actions had entitled him to a place at the family councils. Having taken, he would be able to give from a full heart.

It was always a little surprising to see that his sister-in-law didn't look much like Vivian, especially not in Viv's ramrod carriage and carefully-tended features. Sharon was a friendly woman whose presence graced the fieldstone house in which she lived with her family. She didn't often show that sharp intelligence which was hers, and Felix suspected she would want to own the horse's breath in a bottle if she made a horse trade. Felix liked and respected her.

Sharon nodded in relief at hearing that Mother was taking everything in stride, and that Mrs. Dax, the housekeeper hired after Mother's first heart attack, was still efficiently at her post. Before Felix could complain at not having been given bad news in advance, Sharon was congratulating him on having arrived before the rain, and adding that dinner would be on the table in minutes. Felix always suspected that Sharon cooked elaborate twenty-ingredient dishes for family and friends, but served only simple, hearty fare to visitors from the city. Only to Sharon, he felt certain, did he owe his current dislike for cold milk....

"All our friends had braces when we were little girls," she grinned at one point, making the smallest of small talk over hot roast beef and mashed potatoes drenched in butter. "Mother wouldn't let me have braces like the others—what did I care if all Viv's friends and mine had teeth like iron—oh damn it!"

The phone was shrilling. Sharon's husband, Zack Dunbar, started for the kitchen, but she got there first. Zack had been a diabetic since late childhood, with added high blood pressure, and Sharon tried to save him from as much stress as possible. Come to think of it, Zack wouldn't be much of an ally against a rampaging ex-convict.

Sharon didn't resume the anecdote when she came back, and deftly deflected questions about why her face had suddenly been bleached with tension.

"Felix, I'm going to ask you for a favor," she said levelly at meal's end. "Will you and Zack put all the children to bed and then join me and Viv in the living room?"

Felix did his part with difficulty. Four-year-old Penny was going into one of those activity jags which perversely came upon her after a meal. As for Corey, he had to be told severely that he couldn't eat cookies and pizza after that healthful roast beef, to which he had only given a few pecks under duress.

Felix's mood turned somber when he walked briskly along the uncluttered ground floor hallway and into the airy living room.

"Barney has been set free and he's coming here," Sharon started, while a watery-eyed Zack ws closing the door behind himself. "I couldn't keep him away."

The bell rang harshly at the back door as she was speaking. "If this is him, dear," she warned Zack just before taking it on herself to answer, "Let me do the talking."

Zack shrugged, knowing that his health had reduced him to the status of a consultant in almost any difficulty. It was no surprise that he compensated by an avid interest in shoot-'em-up movies and expensive cars, the latter being a hobby he shared with Felix.

Vivian drew out a hand, reassuring her husband.

Felix noticed the TV set behind her, reminding him of an incident before they got married. They had been seeing each other steadily for months, having discovered the sort of mutual interests that only single people make a point of cultivating. Vivian had come to Manhattan for this meeting. She had already irrevocably planned to live in Manhattan as long as she lived at all. Watching the TV news on Channel Eleven one night, because she wanted to see a City Hall ceremony at the end, Viv suddenly let out a gasp. She had recognized her adopted brother, even though she hadn't seen him in years. That look of concentrated meanness in his face was unmistakable, she said, better than a signature. Having been convicted of robbery with violence in stealing a mint of money that had recently been re-taken, he had been filmed on his way to prison in Illinois.

Of course, Vivian had phoned her sister right away. The

night was ruined and, instead of watching the Jets game and following that with lovemaking, he'd had to hear all about her wicked adopted brother. But he loved Vivian and knew even then that the two of them would eventually more than make up for lost time....

"You're a good guy," she said softly to Felix, who had encouragingly taken his wife's hand. "Too good to be any part of a rotten set-up like this, with Barney."

"Nobody can really choose what happens to them, honey, but I'm glad I'm with you."

She suddenly withdrew and he followed her eyes, looking up to see that Barney Whatever-His-Current-Last-Name-Was was in the room.

He glanced at Felix, then at Vivian, and nodded negligently at Zack. He looked paler now than in those years-ago television pictures, but every bit as mean, his face frozen into lines of eternal anger.

Sharon shut the door firmly on them. "I can guess why you've come, but you might as well spit it out, just the same."

There weren't going to be any prelims to this fight, not even the ritual courtesy of touching heavy gloves.

"Okay. Before I got let out of Joliet early for keeping my nose clean, I was told I had a good chance to come in on a sweet deal, a business proposition that could make a lot of money for me."

"And you want a lot of money now for this proposition which even my cats probably know doesn't exist."

Barney didn't bother to make denials. His was the bearing of a man used to violence, a man perpetually wary, eyes hooded and body wire-taut. But he spoke softly, as if telling a fairy tale to children.

"Fifty thousand is what I need. You give me a fat five-oh, and you never see me again."

Did anybody in the room believe that?

"I don't know for sure that Zack and I have got that much in the bank, but I'll go over and try to get it for you, even if I have to take out a loan."

Barney nodded. He was sullen, looking for a chance to blow his cool, but he accepted Sharon's poison-tipped words.

Felix, like the others, he was sure, felt grateful that the vermin hadn't mentioned going out to get what he wanted from Mother. All the same, he would have given something to challenge Barney, to knock him down and stand with a foot on that burly body while Viv raised his right hand and proudly proclaimed that he was the winner. But it was the fantasy of a freelance crime reporter with notes for an unwritten novel in a desk drawer at home, and he stayed in place.

"Well, I'm not gonna make a tin dime 'til tomorrow." Barney nodded at his own wisdom, relaxing enough to start a yawn. "Been on the road for hours; three miles from that nothing railroad station of yours, and I'm tired enough to grab some Z's where I'm standing."

"We've got a room that'll be free for one night only."

Barney gestured her rudely out of her own living room, and when she was on the other side of the door, he strode to it without looking behind him. Zack, eyes downcast, turned in the opposite direction. Vivian suddenly stood. "I'm going upstairs to put the kids in with us tonight, Felix, just like we all used to travel when they were younger."

He joined her, rather than stay in the room with his desperately unhappy brother-in-law. He went downstairs again afterwards, wondering if Sharon wanted to talk to him about this grim situation. He found nobody except for the somber tabby cat, which he nearly tripped across. Sharon must have gone to bed, if not to sleep, realizing that talk alone wasn't likely to help. He went upstairs himself.

In his and Viv's room, he spent time looking out the curved window with its view of dark, snaking roads and still-wet grass under a fingernail of moonlight. At long last, he joined Viv in bed, remembering one of the many foster fathers in his past, this one in Wichita, who cruelly insisted that the boy sleep in the same bed with him and his wife. (As a grown man, a crime reporter, he had written anonymously about that social crime.)

Viv reached out a hand for him. Smiling, he took it, but made no move toward her.

He surprised himself again the next morning. Waking up about half-past nine, he realized he had slept like a top.

It was a cry of distress that woke him. Felix made sure that his wife and children were in the same room and sleeping deeply. He almost hurled himself into a country outfit, as he called it, and rushed softly to the front stairs. When he looked down, he saw Zack and his and Sharon's children, the sickly accountant trying to get to his feet and falling back, the children's pudding faces imprinted with fear.

The sound of Sharon's voice through the part-open living room nearly pulled Felix back in shock. His normally self-possessed sister-in-law sounded weak, and the familiar boisterous tones had been replaced by a note of pleading.

"Mother told me more than once that she doesn't want to see you again, ever, and she did enough for you over the years so that her wishes ought to be respected."

And Barney sure of himself, in control, cracking the whip, snapping, "That's tough!"

"She's had two heart attacks already, and you can't let her risk having another that might be the last. You can't do that, Barney, not even you!"

"There won't be no trouble when she does what I tell her and loans me the money.... Here are the keys!"

He surged out of the living room by the back door. Felix, not having been able to reach Barney, opened the front door and would have hurried past the grim sight of Sharon sitting up slowly from the shiny floor, but she drew out a shaky hand for his help. Her face was the dull red of somebody who had been physically struck, her eyes narrowed in naked hate.

"I have to stop him," Felix said when she was on her feet.

"There are a few minutes before he can find his way to the garage." She paused for a deep breath, calling silently on her reserves. "I was leaving for the bank and he said he'd come with me. I figured it would be better to have him staying where you could keep an eye on him, Felix—I'd have waked you up, of course—so I told him pretty sharply that I'd go alone. He got the idea fixed in his head that I would be going to the police instead. He was furious, and for no real reason. He swore he'd go directly to Mother for the blackmail money—that's what it is, of course, blackmail to leave us alone until he wants more—and he knocked me down and took the keys to my car, the Taurus."

She was justifying herself needlessly, taking valuable time to prove that her behavior hadn't been provoking.

"I'll get on his case right now."

The wind seemed to have been knocked out of her. "He's stronger, Felix. Any fight that takes place, you'll lose."

"No fighting, no biting." He had already opened the burnished panel under the sparsely appointed bookcase. Beneath a row of fitted sheets on the bottom shelf, she insisted on keeping the gun that he had taught her and Zack to use, giving instruction that they respected because he wrote mostly about all sorts of crime and its sordid accessories. He should have remembered the gun-and-silencer much earlier, but he didn't like to think about weaponry. His particular work had helped to make him more law-abiding.

"I'll sit on him while you phone the police, Sharon. I can charge him with making threats and he'll be out of circulation."

"But he'll come back. Then it's the same business all over again, and you may not be here next time."

"By then, I'll have thought of something else."

"I don't want the police coming here." Never mind any added danger to him. Think of the children's sensibilities, Zachary's condition.

"No, I don't suppose you do." He spoke carefully, like a housewife purring over apples, rejecting plums. "I'll take him into the cop shop."

Later in life, whenever he came to think back to the extraordinary morning that changed so much for him, his first recollection was of the short while it took to do what had become absolutely necessary. From start to finish of the basic chore, he needed about ten minutes. Less time than researching and writing a crime article, then having a meal at some expensive restaurant, less time than traveling from Thirty-Fourth Street in Manhattan over to his book publisher's on Forty-Eighth during a busy day. Ten minutes to change the patterns of six lives. And at least five of those minutes were taken by running out to the slope-roofed garage behind the house and hidden in part by a cluster of huge stones, making sure that Barney was inside—actually opening the door of the gray Taurus—and approaching him.

After which, it was a matter of seeing Barney turn alertly, growing even more tense than usual this time at the sight of the pitch-black nine-millimeter semiautomatic in Felix's taut right hand....

That ten minutes didn't include time needed to deal with Barney and drive out of the garage with his burden, as he took to referring to the bitter ex-convict.

Nothing was likely to go wrong up at the house in the meantime. Sharon could be depended to keep a sharp eye on her two-male brood, and send Zack to do some errand. Vivian had almost certainly been told to supervise a lethargic Penny and an unconcerned Corey, whose idea of spending a morning in any visit to the country was to sit in his room and listen vacantly to his Walkman.

When Felix got back to the garage, he noticed that Zack's favorite car was out. Leave it to Sharon to make sure that every angle was covered. Without much more training, his sister-in-law could have worked well as a world-class executive.

He was halfway to the house when he heard a car approaching, and turned to see Zachary's silver Aston Martin Volante swerve on its way into the garage. Felix hardly ever noticed his brother-in-law being active behind that wheel without thinking that it took a sickly accountant to drive an expensive classic car like a mad dog in heat.

Zachary was taking an unusually long time leaving the garage. As soon as he appeared, Felix knew the reason for that delay. Mother, Mrs. Adelaide Budge, was walking tentatively at his side, strong-mindedly annoyed with herself for having to lean on somebody else's arm. A family of iron-willed women. Sharon had come by her inflexible determination absolutely honestly and so, to a certain extent, had Felix's wife.

His mind remained otherwise free of thought while waiting for them to draw closer. The old woman's eyes roamed speculatively across his impassive features as she advanced, paying more attention to his expression than to her path.

With the cool reserve of a man who once interviewed a Mafia godfather over a three-day period, he said, "Barney won't be coming back. Not if he has any idea of what's good for him."

"Thank you." The old lady moved her lips without being able to speak. "I'm very grateful."

"It's the only thing I've ever been asked to do in exchange for your accepting me into a caring family unit. During so many years of foster homes, that's what I wanted most of all, and you gave it to me."

"I understand you had him arrested," Zachary complained.

Dinner had been eaten silently, and the kids had trotted off to watch one of his action movies. "If nothing else, Mother will have to testify, and she can't hold up under an ordeal."

Felix's head turned swiftly, causing Vivian, who was gathering the dishes on his and the kids' side of the table, to drop a fork. "I didn't have time to tell you about that. I realized that if I had him taken in, there was a small chance he might come back. A much better idea hit me on my way to the garage, and now I'm sure as can be that none of us will ever see him again."

"What's this idea?" Sharon's brows soared in her perplexity. "What did you do?"

"I simply put a proposition to Barney—let me finish. What I offered him was a solid chance to make contact with a Mafia leader in Kansas, where he'd be settled."

"And he agreed to that?" Sharon leaned forward, a fanatic hypnotist trying to obtain the desired reaction from her subject. "And he won't be back, ever?"

"Barney took a little persuading, I won't say no, but he finally saw it my way and he'll stay where he's put. If he goes anywhere against orders, his godfather will get out a paper on him."

"You mean what they call a 'contract hit?'" Zack, the fan of action movies, was ready to swoop down on facts or die trying.

"I'm owed enough by those people to be sure it'd get done. Barney would satisfy himself about that before cutting up, so he'll be a good solder from now on."

Zack accepted it, and Mother Budge looked at his expression and those of the younger women before officially changing the subject. She said that Felix and Vivian and the children were expected to make another visit during Christmas week, as usual. Vivian spoke before he could, saying happily that they'd all be on the scene unless an urgent assignment came up for Felix and he had to go far away.

All well and good, but he wished that Sharon wasn't so reserved, so unrelievedly somber.

She walked over to him just as he was easing the last Louis Vuitton into the best place in the car, like a baseball manager urging an injured player to the day's lineup. This visit was coming to its end on schedule the morning after what he now called "that trouble." Hardly a serious word had been spoken to him by anybody in the family since last night, but he had noticed silently questioning side glances from Sharon.

Zack had been talking eagerly about road reconstruction to watch for during the coming trip, and mentioned at least two speed traps. Sharon, coming over, urged her husband to help Mother, who had stayed overnight to say goodbyes to Felix and Vivian and their children. Mother finally appeared, escorted by Zack on one hand and Sharon's oldest on the other. Behind her came Vivian with Corey and Penny and Sharon's tabby bringing up the rear. It was a family scene that Norman Rockwell might have happily painted.

He was a little surprised to see Sharon looking so serious as she came close and glanced around to make sure that everybody else remained at a narrowing distance. Certainly she didn't want to be overheard.

"I've been waiting to find out something, Felix. By the time you game ma back that gun late last night, it surely didn't stink as if it had been fired, but there was one less bullet inside."

It was his turn to throw a swift look over a shoulder, making sure that the family remained at a little distance away, but he said nothing.

Sharon certainly recognized a silent admission. "Where did you put him...it?"

He raised his head, looking pointedly beyond the rough circle of trees at the end of the property. He wouldn't speak now or ever about the grueling labor of digging and replacing sweet-smelling earth, returning pick and shovel to their dust-pocked places in the garage only after every inch had been clean thoroughly, checking the car floor to make sure there wasn't any trace of blood, and then checking again, brushing dirt clusters off pants and shoes with a maid's rigor. He might have told Sharon that everything was free of traces, but he wouldn't have added that the good news didn't apply to his teeming memory.

What he did next was to raise both hands in a circle, including himself with the whole family, under a symbolic tent. He had once talked to a Mafia wiseguy who used the phrase "Payback Time," and he had paid back the Family for taking in an emotionally parched young man raised by indifferent to bone-mean strangers, for welcoming him into the same tent.

"You're another one who knows about taking responsibility," she said a little sadly. "I can't let the others go on believing that pretty story you invented to keep them from a very bad shock. Eventually, they'll all hear what you did for us, the kids, too, including yours. If you don't tell Viv, I will...so be careful and drive like Zack told you, Felix. When it comes to driving around here, Zack wrote the book."

He was quiet during the homeward trip, making believe it had been an ordinary visit in the same way Barney had made believe that committing crimes meant nothing to him. In his briefly feverish brain, he put together a list of other similarities, each a man whose natural parents played no part in his upbringing, a man drawn to crime, a manipulator, a man obsessed by memories. And he realized that he would be coming back to the scene and back and back, never being allowed to forget. Payback Time was forever.

RUMBLE FOR A BLONDE

Roy Flecker stepped into the wide comfortable hall of his two-story home. His wife Marjorie was waiting for him, looking him up and down.

It happened almost every weekday, her nervous scrutiny when he got back from work.

"Nobody put a knife in me today," he said wryly.

Marjorie agreed and stood up on tiptoes to kiss his balding forehead. "Darling, I never know if you'll be home at all."

"Things aren't that bad." Her lack of confidence was annoying. "The kids won't go after me. They know it's my job to keep them out of trouble."

Over the dinner table, just as he was settling back for the first course, the phone rang. Marjorie looked accusingly at him. For some reason she always did that when the phone rang.

Roy felt compelled to say, "Maybe it's just a relative, honey."

Marjorie ran a hand through her dark hair and pattered away. She reappeared in the kitchen doorway and stood still as if to alert him.

"For you, dear. Sergeant Abrams."

In spite of sudden weariness, Roy emptied his shot glass before pushing back the chair and walking slowly to the phone. He still held a crumpled napkin in a hand.

"One of your little angels," the Sergeant said sourly. "Disturbing the peace. Says he wants to see you. Asked for you like you was his mouthpiece."

Roy nodded uselessly. "What's his name?"

"Henry Gerrard. Ring a bell?"

"I don't know him under his real name, no." Roy drew a hard breath. "Did you do anything to him?"

"So far, I haven't put a glove on him. He says he's got some red-hot info for you. One of your stoolies, I guess."

Roy winced at the word. He was, after all, a social worker with youth gangs and not a policeman.

"Where are you keeping the boy?"

"The hood's right where he belongs. Jail. Precinct house."

Roy said he'd be there as soon as possible. On his way back to tell his wife he was leaving, Roy stopped short. Marjorie was already standing in the doorway, a hand on the crown of his gray straw hat. As he approached she came toward him and fitted the hat on his head.

"If we have boys of our own," she asked moodily, "do you think you can get them into a really murderous gang?"

Roy shrugged it off. He reached the precinct house in less than twenty minutes. He found Sergeant Abrams in a small stuffy office and swearing, as he looked down at a paper-clogged desk. A fan hummed nearby, so loudly as to make the room hotter, somehow. Abrams was a tall man with a thick nose and narrow eyes. Roy hated to look at the Sergeant's bald head.

"I never get out from under paper work," Abrams sighed. "This kid of yours, Henry Gerrard, says he's got information you'll want to hear. He's willing to work a trade—the info for his getting out. Damned punk."

Roy said mildly, "We can't boil all the j.d.'s in oil, you know."

"We ought to." Abrams signaled Roy to follow him towards the jail section. "No difference between them and the older hoods, except they get Momma's little helpers to hold their hands." Abrams squinted sideways. "No hard feelings, Mr. Flecker, but I'm an old-line cop."

They were walking past rows of cells. Glances to one side or the other showed men in sullen, bitter positions. One man was spitting on the floor. Another, in a hopeless rage, kicked the cell fixtures. Only younger prisoners looked up as the two men passed.

They halted in front of the cell of a boy of fifteen. He was tall for his age, with a square-shaped face and wide brown eyes.

"Hello, Squarehead," Roy said affably, a professional smile stretching his lips. "Can I come in and talk?"

It was the sort of question asked in order to give a youngster the chance to say something sardonically friendly in return, and in that way to let down the mental barrier even slightly. Squarehead only nodded and sank back against the bed while a guard opened the cell door and closed it back of Roy.

On the outside, Abrams glared once at both of them and pounded down the hall. Roy, although he could leave at any time, caught himself counting the number of steps and listening intently to the echoes that they set up.

"I did something silly, Roy," Squarehead said. "I made a big stink about paying for something I didn't like. Thought there wouldn't be any trouble, but I was wrong. Can I get out of here soon, you think?"

"I'll do what I can, Squarehead. I heard you've got some information for me."

"Yeh, that's right," The boy added that talking about it might be as much as his life was worth. Roy simply waited, sitting back on the hard bed and glancing at some of the obscenities scratched on the walls. "It's about Kevin. Him and his broad."

"I'm listening."

"Well, you know what Kevin's like. He's a nice guy. He's fair. Not like some guys who boss gangs. And I ought to know because I've been in the Wizard gang for six months."

"You aren't telling me anything, so far." But Roy smile as he said it.

"Wait a minute. You know Kev's broad, Crystal. Blonde, a good figure. Well, like I say, she's Kevin's broad. A guy's got himself a broad, he don't want no messing around. Somebody messes around, it means trouble."

"Somebody else is after her, I suppose."

"Yeah. Crystal says a guy's been hot after her, but she hasn't given him the time of day. The guy is Duke Hardin."

Roy sat up straight. No longer did weariness show in him. He felt keen, sharp, and this in spite of the warning bells clanging in him.

For Duke Hardin was leader of the second gang with which Roy worked, the Dragons. A fight between two leaders would extend down to all the members and result in a mass fight, a rumble in which innocent bystanders as well as gang boys could be hurt and even killed.

"Duke Hardin, he's a born troublemaker like all the Dragons," Squarehead was saying. "Can't trust any of them for sour apples. I wouldn't be surprised if there was trouble."

"And I suppose you'll try to tell me before anything happens."

Squarehead hesitated. Roy added, "I can't ask the cops to cut out any charges against you unless there's a good reason."

"So that makes me a—a stool pigeon."

Roy shrugged. He seldom thought of himself any longer as a social worker with high ideals and ethics. He had been working with gangs long enough to know that his job was made up of holding back a flood of water by keeping a hand in the dike, as the legend has it about a Dutch child. Any equipment that could be used in getting the job done was worth using.

"You've got my home phone number if you need it," Roy said. All the boys had his home number. "Does anybody from the gang know you've been collared?"

"Nah."

"How long have you been here?"

"Only about two-three hours."

"Tell them why it happened," Roy decided, "but say that you were let out because there was no evidence against you."

Roy got to his feet and rapped on the bars. He managed to secure Squarehead's release from an unwilling Sergeant Abrams—"So they have a rumble and they all kill each other. Who cares?"—and made his way home. He had just reached his desk the next morning and, as always, pulled out a newspaper, when his phone rang.

"You got troubles," Abrams said coolly. "Couple of Wizards were beaten up and dumped in garbage cans near Hallidon Street. They don't know who did it, but the figuring is that some new men from the Dragons did the job."

Roy thought quickly. "Are the kids home? The ones who were worked over, I mean. Give me the names."

The first boy he went to see lived on Hallidon Street. Roy climbed the dirt-infested stairs. His knocking on a red door was answered by a heavy Puerto Rican woman. In Spanish, Roy asked for her son.

He was led into a clean living room which had to be kept lighted in late morning. The boy lay on a couch. Three other couches were set next to each other in the room as well as two cots. Next to the window was a television set with an indoor antenna on its metal top. A gold crucifix hung above one wall. The smell of spicy foods was all over the apartment; sometimes the smell lingered in Roy's clothes after he'd left.

"Hello, Hector," he said pleasantly and, resisting the impulse to stand, sat down on the cot next to him. "What happened?"

"You can see." Hector Gómez's face and hands were covered with bandages, except for slits at mouth and nostrils, and one watery blue eye. "Four guys came at two of us. They had knives and boards with nails at one end, broken bottles and leather straps like the barbers use. A guy kept swinging the strap between my legs while another guy hit me with the board."

"Who were they?"

"Never saw any of them before. Maybe they were from the other side of town, but Kevin's been having some trouble lately...."

"I know," Roy said. "With Duke Hardin."

Neither gang had much trust in Roy, if they hadn't wanted him to know. It was an accepted fact of social work to gain dislike and distrust from the people you tried to help.

"Is Kevin planning to do anything about it?" Roy asked softly. "I'll find out anyway, you know."

"I can't tell you. No idea." Hector tried to shrug, but winced with sudden pain. "Maybe. Kev, he's called a meeting for tonight."

Roy hesitated. "Are you going?"

"Sure."

"Don't you think you've had enough?"

Hector said grimly, "In this neighborhood you belong to a gang or you're nothing."

Roy said a few useless words and left. His next trip was to a rickety deserted shack that stood in the middle of a dirty block. On a summer morning like this one, heat waves rose from the sidewalk and bathed him in his own sweat.

He knocked slowly three times, then walked into the Wizards' clubhouse. A boy and girl were embracing. They were laying down on a rickety old sofa from which springs stuck out rakishly. The boy glanced up to see who had come in, and then sat up.

"Kevin. Crytstal. I'm glad you two are here."

"What can we do for you, Roy?" Kevin rubbed lipstick from his cheeks and quickly buttoned his shirt. He was a tall boy with thin, graceful hands. "Anything wrong?"

Roy tried to calm down both of them by smiling. He had an idea in the back of his head that if any member of the Wizards could grow up into a good citizen, it was Kevin. He often told himself that if only one of the boys in each gang worked ou all right, then his, Roy's, job was worthwhile. Lately, he had been repeating the thought to himself more often than ever before.

"It's about the Dragons," Roy said, glancing to Kevin's right. "Do you know anybody in that club, Crystal?"

"I've met one or two."

"Duke Hardin? You've met him?"

Kevin suddenly asked, "You know about it? Duke's made some passes at her. So far, I've tried to keep things peaceful, but I don't know if it can go on."

Crystal tossed her blonde head. "Duke ought to be put in his place, you know, Kev, taught a lesson. It's bad when a decent girl can hardly walk outside at night."

She fumbled with sweater edges, trying to tuck them into her black skirt. She was a well-dressed girl, and an unusually graceful one considering that she wasn't more than fifteen years old. Probably the grace was instinctive as if she wasn't aware of being on display every minute. She wore a minimum of make-up as a rule, but now she drew out a compact from a box purse and ornamented her lips with a thin red tracery.

"Duke deserves a lesson," she added, "after what happened last night."

For Roy's benefit, Kevin said, "Two of my men were beaten up last night. Probably new men from the Dragons did the job."

"You can't be sure." Roy forced himself to hide his temper. "You're running a meet tonight. Do you want me to bring Duke with me?"

Kevin paused. "Do you think he wants—?"

Roy glanced over at Crystal. She had stopped in mid-motion, and a small smile drifted over her half-painted lips.

"You mean, does he want a rumble?" Roy shrugged. "Do you?"

"If Duke wants a rumble, he can have one," Kevin said nervously.

Roy glanced down at the youngster's sensitive-looking hands. "Kev, do you play an instrument?"

He hadn't known that he was going to say it. Kevin finally nodded.

"Yeh. Piano. My old man, he says it's good for me. I play pretty good, too."

"I always wanted to play trumpet, but I didn't have the lip for it." Roy shrugged. "See you tonight."

When he walked back into the place a few minutes after 8 o'clock, it was crowded with boys. Probably ten of them. In one corner, a card game was going on. The others sat and smoked cigarettes rapidly. At sight of him, most of the boys stiffened and grew a little more silent. Roy only greeted the boys who spoke to him. It was impossible to come into a meeting without feeling like a known spy allowed into the enemy's camp.

At his side was big, black-browed Duke Hardin. Duke grinned at everyone, said "H'lo," in an offhand way and stood near a wall.

"If I lean against this thing, it'll fall down."

There was no chair for Roy. Probably someone had taken away an extra chair. He often suspected that some of the boys found pleasure in forcing him to stand up during a meeting.

Back of the one table in the room sat Kevin. His long thin pianist's hands were folded at first. Then he unfolded them and wiped his flat face with a dirty handkerchief.

Of course there was no sign of Crystal.

"We got one thing to talk about tonight," Kevin said finally. "That's about the way we stand with the Dragons."

"I say we have a rumble." It was Hector Gómez who had just walked in, supporting his weight on a thick old cane. "Rumble. Look what they do to me, those Dragons."

He turned to glare out of his one good eye at Duke Hardin, who smiled back and turned to Kevin.

"I don't know what he's talking about."

"You didn't have four guys ambush two of ours?"

"No. Were the guys recognized? If they weren't, how do you know they're Dragons? Besides, we've got a peace treaty."

Roy, standing off to one side, nodded. Getting the treaty written and signed had taken a month of hard negotiating.

"How do you know," Duke asked again, "that the guys who beat you up were Dragons?"

"No other crew has got a reason," Kevin blurted out. "We never have trouble with any other gang."

One of the Wizards said to Kevin, "Ask Duke Hardin about your broad!"

Kevin turned to Duke.

"I swear I think you're losing your head," Duke Hardin said, although the grin was set firmly on his swarthy face. "What broad/"

"All of a sudden," Kevin asked calmly, "you don't know Crystal?"

"I know her, sure. I've seen her around. But I wouldn't fool with anything of yours, Kev."

He was still grinning, as if about to add, *And if you don't like it—*. Roy sensed the words on the boy's lips, and tried to keep from imagining what would follow.

Kevin looked at his opposite number for a very long time. "As long as we know where we stand," he said heavily. "No hard feelings, Duke?"

"No hard feelings."

Roy's wandering glance took in the sight of Squarehead Gerrard, his so-called stool pigeon. Then he watched Duke Hardin leave and the Wizards follow. At his gesture, Kevin remained.

"He was lying," Kevin said moodily. "I could tell."

He hadn't left his seat back of the table, which gave him a certain psychological advantage.

It was surprising, then, that Kevin had accepted Duke Hardin's disclaimers. Probably Kevin was anxious to keep the peace for a reason Roy didn't know yet.

Roy asked carefully. "Are you stuck on Crystal? Do you dig her?"

"She's got a good body," Kevin said casually. "A sweet looker, you know what I mean?"

"Would you want to drop her?"

"No. Give me one good reason why I should."

"It's just an idea of mine," Roy said. "I've got no facts to base it on. Crystal looks to me like a troublemaker. She wouldn't mind seeing two gangs in a rumble on account of her. I think she's been attracting Duke, going out of her way to tease him."

Kevin said angrily, "I'd rip her apart for that!"

"And then she'd run to Duke and you'd be in a wingding for sure, anyhow."

"If I drop Crystal, that stops him," Kevin nodded, then looked up. "Until he wants something else."

It was true, of course. If the inevitable fight was delayed as long as possible, Roy thought, a miracle might happen in the meantime. Typical social worker's reasoning, Roy told himself wryly.

"I wouldn't mind dropping her if I had to," Kevin added slowly. "She's just a broad, she don't mean that much to me. But if I do it, the guys will think I'm running out on a fight."

He waved a hand around the clubroom. Stale cigarette smoke hung in the humid air.

"Anything else happens between us," Kevin said patiently, "and there's no choice about a rumble."

And of course it was perfectly clear that something else would happen. For either gang to stop now would mean a loss of prestige by the leaders.

Kevin sat looking down at his long thin hands, moving the fingers slowly and then speeding up the tempo.

Roy suddenly asked, "Do you figure on being a pianist? For a living, I mean."

"I'm thinking about it," Kevin said with sudden anger. "So what?"

"Don't get sore at me, kid," Roy smiled. "I'm not on your back."

Kevin did indeed have a stake in keeping the peace. In the event of a rumble, something might just possibly happen to his hands.

Roy was still moody when he got home for the night, not answering any of the questions Marjorie asked about gang members; she knew them all by name.

When the phone rang early the next morning, the usual look of accusation appeared on Marjorie's face. For once he scowled as she went to answer the phone. She talked briefly, then came back into the kitchen. Her thumb pointed toward the hall.

"Won't give me his name," she said. "Maybe he's in the Secret Service."

The name was finally whispered to Roy when he answered the phone in turn. It wa his stoolie, Squarehead Gerrard.

"Just got the message for a special meet this morning," Squarehead added. "Important."

"Thanks. I'm glad you're playing ball—for a change."

Roy drove out to the clubhouse as soon as possible, parking the car a block away. It was a muggy day, and as he walked he could feel the weather shortening his temper.

Several boys were standing around as he appeared. At first he thought they were disgusted at seeing him, but pained expressions caused him to look toward the table at the end of the room. Crystal was sitting close to it on a chair. She was bent over, sobbing bitterly.

"Look, honey, if you'll just hold it." Kevin stood at Crystal's right, patting her blonde hair.

Roy didn't ask questions. He might have been a member waiting to hear what was wrong. For once he found an empty chair.

Time and again the door opened on boys who were just arriving. They muttered something to one or two others, then glanced uncomfortably at Crystal.

Finally Kevin raised a hand for silence. "Men, this is a special meeting, like you know. In a few minutes, Duke Hardin and some of his men will be here."

Kevin glanced hesitantly at Roy, but saw no change of attitude on Roy's part.

Somebody asked, "What's it about? What's the poop on it, Kev?"

It was Crystal who answered. She looked up and tried to wipe away tears from her red-streaked face with the little finger of her left hand. Even now, she was graceful.

"Last night when I was coming home, Duke stopped me and asked me to go with him for a drink. He said he had some whiskey at the Dragons' clubhouse. I said I didn't want to do it because I'm Kev's girl. Duke, he twisted my arm."

The question that rose to Roy's lip was asked by somebody else. "Why didn't you scream?"

"No point to it. If you scream, everybody runs away and you're all alone. If you want a cop, he's never around. Besides, who wants a cop?"

To them, of course, cops were the enemy. Roy made an effort to keep from squirming in the hard chair that was too small for his seat.

"Get to the point," Kevin said. And a little more gently, "Please, honey."

"Well, I finally said I'd go along. Duke said we should walk down the alley on Hallidon Street."

A couple of the boys nodded wisely. The same street on which two Wizards had been beaten up a day ago.

"When we got there," Crystal said slowly, "Duke turned suddenly and threw me away from him. I fell against a wall. Then he ran to me and started to unbutton my blouse. I tried to scream, but he put up a hand to my mouth. I tried to bite the hand, and then I tried to scratch him. He hit me hard along the jaw."

Roy leaned forward to listen and for once cupped his right ear. Back of him one of the boys laughed, probably at Roy's listening so intently to this particular part of Crystal's story.

"Then Duke said he'd give me something to remember him by. All the time he had been smoking. Now he took the cigarette out of his mouth and he ripped—ripped—"

"Go on!" Kevin's breath came hard. His face was white.

"—ripped half of my blouse. Then he took the lighted end of the cigarette and put it to my skin."

Crystal was sobbing again. Head in hands, she rocked back and forth. The boys were muttering among themselves.

"Duke did it again and again. It burned every time. He covered my mouth with a hand. I scratched his face or tried to, and he'd put in a new burn a little lower down. And I couldn't scream. Then he said, 'Now Kev will know whose girl you are,' and suddenly let go. I fell down." Her voice grew in volume. "Look what he did to me, look!"

She undid part of the blouse, showing that she wore nothing underneath. Her stomach had at first sight, been hideously scarred. A black path had appeared, almost a circular path except that one side was a little more straight than the others.

Somebody whispered, "D! It's supposed to be a D!"

"D for Duke. That's what he meant when he said it."

The letter had been set so that her navel looked like a punctuation mark. Crystal covered her stomach with the blouse. Roy leaned back, folding his hands and pressing the finger-crotches against their mates.

"Well, men?" Kevin talked above sobs. "You know what we've got to do."

Two knocks sounded on the door. As they weren't the code knocks used by the Wizards and Roy, everyone in the room stiffened. Roy, against his will, found his fingers forming fists.

The door opened on Duke Hardin and two other boys. Duke wore a thin strip of adhesive just below his chin. The other two stood behind Duke to the right and left, as they'd surely been ordered to do.

"Well," Duke said. It wasn't a question. "I got an idea you Wizards want yourselves a little action."

Crystal looked up at him and spat.

"Your broad's annoyed." Duke ran a hand through his thick black hair, then touched the strip of tape. "Cut myself shaving and bled like a pig."

"That's what you are," one of the Wizards said.

Crystal took it up, chanting, "Pig, pig, pig!"

"Shut her up," Duke said quietly. "I'm tired of her yapping." His eyes took in Roy, and he blinked almost lazily. "Well, what do you want? Get with it, man, get on the stick!"

"She says you made a pass at her and then wrote your initial on her belly with the lighted end of a cigarette."

Duke's smile could have meant that he had done it or that he hadn't.

"Is it true?" Kevin prodded.

"Makes no difference," Duke said surprisingly. "I'm getting sick of being accused of everything that happens to any of you Wizards or your girls. Do you want to scrap the peace treaty?"

Roy let out a long slow breath.

"No help for it," Kevin said slowly. "What you did to her, it means a rumble."

"I don't admit nothing, but a rumble suits me." Duke's eyes swept the room. "Ten of us against ten of you."

"Eleven," Hector Gómez called out. "I'm okay, no matter what your goons did to me. I'm in good shape."

"I'll only have to pull in one of my men," Duke said. "Weapons can be every type. Tire chains is okay. So are pop bottles, zip guns, the works."

"No bullwhips," Kevin said sharply, after a quick look down at his thin graceful hands.

"Why the hell not? Bullwhips, too."

"All right." Kevin nodded after a pause. "No limit to how many weapons a man brings."

"The rules are that there's no rules." Duke looked around at the boys again, probably measuring each of them against one of the Dragons. "Any women to fight?"

"No," Kevin said firmly.

Crystal looked up. "I want to watch, I want to watch."

Like a child, repeating the same words in hopes of getting its way. She might as well have added, *You're fighting over me, so why can't I see it?*

"You bring her," Duke said, "I bring a broad, too. No weapons on them."

Kevin asked, "When do you want the rumble?"

"We can knock that around in a minute." He glanced toward Roy. "But don't let Johnny Law over here find out."

Duke said to one of his boys, "Spider, see to it that he don't listen from outside."

Roy shrugged. He always expected that gangs and cops both, would treat him as a probably enemy. He threw a meaningful glance at Squarehead Gerrard and walked to the door. He was aware of a boy's heavy footsteps back of him. Roy got into his car and drove down to the precinct house to see Sergeant Abrams.

He found the big cop deep in paper work again. The office fan grinding out warm air had forced Abrams to anchor most of the papers with various pens and pencils, and even a desk lamp.

"Any of your little angels acting up?" the sergeant asked.

"They're arranging a gang war among themselves." Roy gave details. "I need men to follow both leaders and report when the war's coming up. Can you spare anybody?"

"You're kidding." Abrams gestured at the wad of papers, their ends tip-tilted by blasts of warm air. "I'm up to the eyeballs in work and so's every man I've got."

Roy swore. "A formal request to your department would take about ten years, and that damn rumble has got to be stopped. If it goes through, thue kids will get hurt and God knows how many innocent people...."

"They'll pick a private place," Abrams said flatly. "Let 'em kill each other. What's the harm?"

"It'd be bad for business if I lost all my customers." Roy was grim. "Can you alert beat cops to be on the lookout?"

"I just made a note to do it."

Nothing else could be done here. At his own office, Roy talked to his superior, Mr. Jonas Malloy shook his gray head several times and mumbled into the hand in front of his mouth.

"Keep the worst from happening, if you can," he said. "I'll see what help I can get you from Abrams."

Roy nodded glumly and sat down at his desk. Images of the blonde, Crystal, rose before his mind. He saw the curious pleasure with which she'd behaved in sobbing about being branded.

It was possible that she could have previously persuaded four boys from another side of the city to beat up a couple of Wizards in hopes that blame would be put on the Dragons and a rumble come out of it. She'd have paid off the boys in the oldest way known to women. And when that failed to start a rumble, the branding had taken place.... Roy reached for the phone. When he put it down ten minutes later, after several calls, it rang.

"Hello, this is me, Squarehead. If I don't tell you where the rumble is, does that mean I'd still be in trouble with the cops on that old charge?"

"I'll have to tell the cops whether you've been cooperating,"

Roy said carefully, "or you haven't."

That was known as putting the screws on, but Roy felt as if his conscience was dead. In fact, hue was irritated by the delaying tactics. For one of the few times in his life, he could understand what makes a cop beat up a prisoner. Understand and suddenly shrug it off as something that wasn't really a part of him.

"Tonight, half-past seven," Squarehead mumbled. "At Wharton Park, right near the statue of Benjamin Franklin."

"Thanks, Squarehead."

When he hung up this time, he was a little more cheerful. He spent twenty minutes with Sergeant Abrams and then went home for a few hours. Marjorie, at the sight of him, shrugged.

"We were supposed to go out to Beverly and Vic Passy's house, tonight," she said irritably. "I guess you'll be working, instead."

"Right on the button, honey."

He took off all his clothes but underpants and had a long nap. Then he shaved, showered, shampooed his hair and put on a dark suit and black shoes. He forced himself to eat slowly.

Marjorie cautioned, "Don't do anything you shouldn't, tonight. I mean, let other people take the chances if it comes to that."

She often made provoking statements when Roy's mouth was full and he couldn't conveniently answer.

"Everything will be under control this time," he said finally. "I'll be with a dozen cops, maybe more."

"You won't get hurt?""

"I'm not figuring on it, no." As her face twisted with sudden pain, he said, "Nothing's going to go wrong, honey, believe me."

A few minutes later he was reveling in the long, slow comfortable drive to the precinct station. As soon as he reached it, of course, he tightened up. Quick steps took him to Abrams' office. The sergeant was strapping on a holster under one sweatband of a dark suit.

"Okay, Mr. Flecker. All set."

They rode in a police car out to the park. Roy was uncomfortable as always in a car driven by somebody else.

"You'll haul in about twenty kids," he said, "and they go smack off to jail and come out worse than they went in."

"Like I told you," Abrams began.

"I know what you told me: they belong in jail." Roy glanced out the rear window at the green-white police cars that were following. "The rumble's got to be stopped before it starts."

"How? Unless you go to every kid's house...."

Roy had considered it before, and decided that he could only manage effectively when both gangs were together. He hadn't wanted to take it on himself to ask for a special meeting because it was bad tactics to seem like a leader, himself.

"The rumble's about a girl. The girl's a teaser."

"She's been playing around with the other hood?"

Roy scowled at the mention of that word. "With Duke Hardin, of the Dragons. She says Duke Hardin made a play for her. When he couldn't stand any more teasing, he branded her by writing his initial on her belly with the tip of a cigarette."

"Little angels." Abrams threw up his hands. "We had rough kids in my day, too. I grew up in a hard neighborhood." He paused, glaring at Roy, and said hesitantly, "I think it's television that causes it all."

The cops left their cars a half-dozen blocks from the park entrance, and walked by two's to the appointed place. Roy with Abrams, had become moody. The backs of his hands tingled with ehat and the smell of greenery. Fireflies buzzed around old-fashioned lampposts.

"How would we stop it?" Abrams asked.

"Easy enough. As the kids come here your men grab them and disarm them, take away the weapons. When they're all here, I go into my spiel."

"Lecture, huh? Nobody ever reformed hoods with a lecture." Abrams scowled. "Besides, they go downtown to be booked for carrying weapons, anyhow."

There was no help for that, of course, but Roy guessed he

could talk to the judge who'd handle the case and arrange for suspended sentences. He'd had occasion to do it before, and a brush with the law might help to straighten out some of the boys.

"So, Flecker, what's the real gimmick?"

"I'll convince them they went off half-cocked and that the girl isn't worth a rumble. I'm sure I can prove something to them about the girl."

He had the brief satisfaction of seeing Abrams' eyes bug out.

"Not the way you're thinking," Roy said gently.

Above them now, was the statue of Benjamin Franklin, the head touched wituh green, and square-rimmed spectacles oddly glinting in the light from nearby lampposts. The statue fronted on a wide tree-rimmed path.

Abrams skillfully deployed his men, pointing out hiding places. The cops ran to them and took cover. Not a word was spoken. Hard white light caught the sheen of brown wood in the cops' nightsticks.

At Abrams' gesture, Roy walked with him directly back of the statue. Abrams spread out his handkerchief on the pedestal and sat down gingerly to wait.

It was 7:10. Roy had to control the impulse to walk around. He could imagine many things going wrong, but in this area of work the cops had far more experience.

"Don't worry," Abrams said quietly. "I've got orders to cooperate with you right here. There'll be...."

He broke off as footsteps were heard. But the steps had been made by a boy and girl walking arm-in-arm. Next came a boy with a portable radio on his right shoulder, walking as if mesmerized. A girl strolled back and forth briefly, her hips swinging as she looked around her.

Whenever anybody appeared who wasn't connected with the rumble, Abrams would whisper unpleasant remarks.

"That girl's going to find herself in a peck of trouble one of these days...you'd think people would have brains enough to keep out of a park at night. I mean these innocent people, these

Honest Johns."

A squirrel paused, sat up on its haunches, stared at them and ran. A car drove past not too many yards away, leaving a cloud of exhaust smoke that drifted toward the crouching men.

By 7:20, Roy was avoiding Abrams' eyes. The cop had already stood up and sat down a half dozen times.

"They usually get to the scene of a rumble half an hour early and wait around for the signal to start fighting." Abrams' voice was louder, now. "How good is your stool pigeon?"

"Reliable," Roy said thinly, "as a rule."

"Not this time. Looks to me like he was giving you stuff the gang wanted you to have. He told the gang what he owed you and they told him what to say."

Roy nodded slowly. "I can stop the whole business with a few words, so I have to get the shaft this way."

"You can't blame the punks for not trusting you."

Roy shrugged it off. "Where do we try next?"

"I don't get that." Abrams was sharp. "My orders were to stop the rumble here, not go chasing all over town."

"But they've got to be found before they kill each other."

"I don't agree with that, Flecker, but let's suppose you're right. Where do we start?" In the silence he added, "I can't spare so many cops to chase around town all night and not find anything."

Abrams was being perfectly reasonable now, and Roy's brain could only counter with the recollection of Kevin's long slim graceful musician's hands.

"We get about six murders a day in the city," Abrams added. "Something like twenty felonies. I'm so far behind in all my cases, I can't ever catch up...."

He blew a whistle, and the men appeared and walked quietly to the waiting cars. Roy and Abrams were last. The big cop was rubbing his bald head as he talked.

"...never catch up if I life to be a million years old. Nobody wants to pay for a full-strength police force, so what do people expect?

Now that Roy had been defeated, Abrams was graciously talking as if to a friend or colleague. As they left the park, he asked if Roy wanted a lift. Roy started to shake his head, then nodded. In less than 5 minutes, the car was on Hallidon Street in front of the tenement in which Hector Gómez lived. Although the boy had recently absorbed a bad beating, he didn't spend much time at home.

Abrams wished Roy luck, told him to call in if he got on to anything, and at his signal the car sped away. Roy was on his own. He threw back his shoulders and walked up to the right apartment. Hector's mother answered the door. A smell of spicy foods came at him just as last time when the door opened.

In Spanish, Roy asked where to find Hector.

"I don't know. I have eight kids and I can't follow them all."

"It's important that I get to him quickly, Mrs. Gómez." He racked his brain for an excuse. None came to him so he said nothing.

"I've got eight children. My husband, he's a night watchman. We can't always...."

Her mind couldn't seem to make the connection to what was wanted. She circled around the subject, making excuses for Hector, telling about his acts of kindness.

From the kitchen came various youthful cries in Spanish. The persistent wail, *"¡Mamacita!"* caused Mrs. Gómez to say, "Be right back." The door swung shut. Mrs. Gómez's voice rose as she settled a dispute among several children.

Sounds could be heard from other apartments, too, as almost every door in the building was kept open on account of the heat.

Roy was about to charge into the house when Mrs. Gómez returned, wiping her hands. Back of her, a girl child was squalling very loudly.

"Kids don't behave, you give 'em the back of the hand," Mrs. Gómez said belligerently. "Now about Hector." She blinked. "Is he in trouble/"

"Of course not." Roy tried to sound surprised.

"He's a good boy, but I've got eight children...oh yes. Hector said something about a meeting tonight at the club."

Roy shrugged. A dead end, after all.

"Hector didn't say anything else, I suppose. You didn't hear him talk to anybody...?"

"I got eight kids," she began as Roy turned from her and left. Her cry, *"¡Madre de Dios!"* was loud as she raced back into the kitchen, probably to see what new outrage had been done there.

Roy paused only briefly, then he nodded to himself and began running toward the clubhouse.

It was a four block run and he knew better than to look for a cab in this neighborhood. There was no time, either, to call Abrams.

The possibility that the clubhouse might actually be used for this rumble had suddenly become a vivid one. The boys would want close quarters and in this section most of the people thought of policemen as the enemy. Or they would feel as Abrams did— let them all kill each other. One cop walking the beat might call for help which would be sure to arrive when the mess was over and done with.

As for being caught, the boys, like most amateur criminals, simply didn't think of it. Or they might feel that capture by the police would a neighborhood honor. Such facts of life had been hard for Roy to get used to, but nowadays he accepted them as another proof that he had learned more from gangs than they had learned from him.

The clubhouse was quiet, but a light was on. Dead end? Roy stood across the street till he caught his breath, then walked toward the shanty. From inside it, somebody coughed.

It was possible that a boy and girl were loving it up, but not at this time. If one gang member was in the place, all the boys in two gangs were there as well.

To check it, he walked around the building. He moved quickly and as much as possible stayed out of the range of the one window. Twelve chairs were stacked in the rear of the club-house, every two chairs seat-to-set so that one stood with legs on the ground while its mate was up-ended with legs in the air.

Roy's watch showed a minute before 7:30. He glanced at the dirty houses all around, some not occupied and all waiting to be condemned. Avoiding the window for a second time, he knocked in code on the door.

The sudden murmurs alone nearly pushed him back. H reached for the rusty doorknob. The door held. Probably the one table was being used as a barricade.

He waited, on the chance that somebody would pull aside the table and let him in.

"Who—who's it?"

"Roy."

Somebody else said reproachfully, "I told you we should never have picked this place."

Another kid called out, "D.D.T. Drop Dead Twice."

"Let me in, I want to tell you something. This whole business is a mistake and I can prove it."

"The hell with him," Duke Hardin snarled. "If he wants to call the cops, let him. We can get this over with, first."

Duke's voice was high-keyed and less than a pitch from frenzy.

"I won't call the cops." Sweat poured down Roy's face. "I just want a minute, one lousy minute. You can't give me that much?"

Silence. Roy drew back and threw his body against the door. The table gave an inch, enough for him to see two boys lined up against a wall. One held a zip-gun. The other, Hector Gómez, still swathed in bandages, held a bullwhip coiled in a hand.

"Damn idiots," Roy called to as the door was pushed back into a closed position.

A girl's voice said, "Half-past seven." Something crashed to the floor, probably a glass. It must have been the signal to start.

The noises were so loud and so expressive that Roy was frozen briefly by the knowledge of failure; it had started, whatever else might be done now. Water was pouring through the hole in the dike.

With a chair in hand he managed to smash the window glass. It took three swipes because he missed twice, and then he had to clear debris with a tip of the chair. As he worked he could look in.

One boy was down and another boy stomped him. Kevin, leader of the Wizards, had lost his weapon and was crawling for it across the floor.

And watching with wide eyes and with spittle forming at the sides of her mouth, was Crystal.

Of the other girl who was supposed to be present, there was no sign. Roy learned later that a family function had kept her away.

Careful of his hands, he bounded over the sill into the room. Once inside, his ears cruelly assaulted by the din of shouting and whip-cracking, he made his move.

He turned on the nearest boy, his fist crashing into soft stomach. A length of tire-iron snaked out on the floor and Roy kicked it aside.

Another boy confronted him with a coiled bullwhip. It flicked out at Roy and touched his shoulder. A wet soreness appeared in its wake. He caught himself, if only briefly, wishing for the length of tire iron or a zip-gun.

His only weapon was speed, and as the boy drew back the whip and it hissed in the air, Roy ran straight at him. A clean one-two sent the boy down. He reached for the whip and cracked it against the floor.

Three times he did it. Boys around him paused to look and, once pasued, stayed with eyes open as the whip was cracked against the wooden floor.

Only Duke Hardin, cuts running from his face, shouted, "Get the hell out! Who needs you, you goddam snoop!"

The best possible timing was necessary. Roy judged himself ready.

He glanced at Hector Gómez. "Stop those two!"

One boy was on the floor reaching for the legs of his antagonist, the latter flailing with tire-chairs. As Hector hesitated, Roy flicked his whip toward the hands of the boy with the tire-chains. The chains rattled. The boy on the floor gave a thankful sigh. It was Kevin. His face was bloody and redness seeped through his clothes.

"I can't get up right now."

It was impossible to give first aid at this time. Foy Roy to try it could send the rest of them against each other all over again. Right now they were only staring at new-made welts on each other and at blood against the wooden walls.

Somebody called out sarcastically, "Squarehead, you look like a block with a hole in it."

Squarehead Gerrard grinned. Another boy began to wipe dirt from his clothes.

And Crystal, head turning from side to side, asked loudly, "Why don't you go ahead? What's the matter with you, letting this damn snoop stop you? You said you were going to get it over with once and for all."

Duke Hardin nodded. "The broad's right. He's just another cop and we need him like holes in the head."

Roy wiped sweat form the area around his lips. "You finished for now, Duke?"

"For now. If you want to make your pitch, I'm going to give you onoe minute. No more, or less. If you're not finished by the end of it, I go right to work on this creep here."

And he thumbed at one of the Wizards, who cursed him.

"All right, one minute." The words Roy had planned were hollow against his tongue. "If you want a rumble...."

Duke Hardin turned to one of his men. "Got your watch, Harry? Okay, then time him. One minute."

"...you can have it. Nobody in the world cares if you beat and kill each other, nobody."

Was it true? At the moment he wasn't sure, but he was frightened that he sounded so convincing.

"At least have your rumble for good reasons. Don't go off wild because you've all been told one lie after another."

"The beatings," Hector Gómez said quickly.

"Somebody could get four guys from another part of the city and rig up a deal with them. If it was a woman who did it, she could pay the four guys in just about the way you'd figure a woman to pay up."

Duke Hardin said sharply, "My men had nothing to do with two Wizards getting polished off."

The shouts and denials, the angry fist-raising, had to be stopped.

"All right, let's go on from that to the next thing. Crystal claims...."

As if startled by the sound of her name, the blonde girl said sharply, "Bull-oney!"

She had forgotten herself for once, her veneer of grace entirely gone. She snarled and spat and shook both fists in anger.

Roy let the gangs watch her for only a few seconds, then turned away from her and asked gently, "*She* wouldn't tell a lie, would she?"

He drew a deep breath. His shoulder was paining keenly, as if the bullwhip's tail was buried inside it.

"Crystal says she was burned by a cigarette, and that Duke Hardin did it. If I can prove that's a life, it ought to convince you how useless this rumble is."

Kevin said through his teeth, "Prove it." He brought up his legs under his stomach and palms to the floor at first, slowly got to his feet.

"Crystal, show 'em that the scar didn't exist in the first place, that you drew it on with dirt."

The girl spat at him. Roy could do nothing else to keep his respect with the gang; he backhanded her. Crystal fell against a wall and straightened herself with difficulty.

"Well, Crystal? Are you going to show them?"

The silence back of him was so thick it might have been treacherous Duke Hardin or Kevin, seeing the girl hit, might have stepped in to start a fight with him.

It had to be done quickly. Roy drew a section of her blouse between his hands and ripped it partway. She was wearing nothing under it and for a moment it was possible to see that the skin of her belly was smooth and even. Roy quickly set the torn blouse over it.

"You damn, you goddam...," she began.

"Shut up!" Again it had to be done. Another backhand smack across her right cheek. "I don't want to hear another word out of you about anything. Is that clear?"

Kevin told Crystal, "We're finished." And he added to Duke Hardin, "You want her, Duke, you can have her with my compliments."

And Duke Hardin, seeing the mood of both gangs, had to say, "Who needs her! A troublemaker!"

To take somebody's cast-off girl would have caused duke to lose face with both gangs.

The sound of a police siren, then another, froze them all. Roy was the first to speak.

"We can't get away. Two of you, one from each gang, get in the center of the room and start hitting each other."

Duke Hardin, who had finally recovered from his daze of the last few minutes, turned and pointed to one of his boys. Kevin nodded at Squarehead Gerrard. The two who'd been chosen walked groggily to the center of the room.

"Hit with your fists," Roy said wearily, although neither boy had pulled a weapon. "And I want a clean fight."

Kevin asked, "What about the artillery?"

It was the first time Roy had ever been asked for advice by a boy in either gang.

"There's no time to ditch it, so keep it on you." And to the room at large, "You men cheer 'em while they scrap. I'll talk to the cops."

It was Hector Gómez who asked the others, "Do you think we can trust him?"

"Our only chance now." Duke Hardin shook his head as if to clear it. "We were silly to pick this rat-hole in the first place. Get moving, now. Do what he says. Get on the stick, you men!"

The fighters moved back and forth. Roy was glad to see that Squarehead, the lying stool pigeon, was getting much the worst of the fight. The wrong attitude for Roy to take, but it didn't bother him.

He had no notions whether it was right or wrong to be helping the gangs to get out from under the consequences. Perhaps he was trying to make up for his own savage feelings of a few minutes ago, when he had told them just what they would have heard from Sergeant Abrams.

The sirens had stopped, and heavy feet could be heard approaching the clubhouse, then the sound of a battering ram of men against the door. Roy approached and pulled aside the table, then opened the door himself.

"What do you want here?"

The cops drew back in confusion, but it was Abrams who walked up to the door.

"I'm pulling in this bunch of hoods," he growled. "Every last one of 'em."

The fighting in the center of the room stopped at Roy's shout. He turned to face Abrams.

"How about telling me what the charge is?"

"Disorderly conduct. Fighting. Possession of deadly weapons. Two neighbors called up and yowled to high hell."

"It's not disorderly," Roy countered. "I thought that the boys were planning a big-scale fight, and I told that to you. I was wrong. They appointed one boy from each gang to fight for them. I've been asked to referee it,"

Abrams drew a hard breath. "For my part, they can all kill themselves." (Roy winced.) "There's still the little matter of possession of deadly weapons."

And he added, more loudly. "I want all you punks to line up against the wall. A good shakedown will work wonders."

"There isn't going to be any," Roy said calmly. "I'm vouching for all of them."

"*You're* the one," Abrams was livid, "who kept saying—"

"I'm responsible for them, tonight. A search wouldn't be lawful, unless you've got a warrant. A good lawyer could make mincemeat out of you in court and I'm just feeling mean enough to pay a good lawyer out of my own pocket. Now get moving."

Abrams suddenly paused. "A nice grandstand play," he said quietly. "It won't get you anyplace, not with punks."

The big cop turned on a heel, military fashion, and walked to his car. The other cops followed. Roy closed the door and rested up against it.

Kevin said, "Let's break it for tonight. *He* stuck his neck out for us."

Roy asked about Kevin's hands, which were in good shape, and then asked whether the peace treaty was on, now. Duke and Kevin nodded. When he had arranged a ride home for Crystal, he walked part of the way to his own car with Duke Hardin.

As no one was in earshot, Roy said, "I guess you almost aggravated the Wizards into a full-scale rumble, after all."

"Sure," Duke nodded. "I wanted it to look like my gang was egged on to a rumble we didn't want. Crystal's a teaser and she deserved it when I burned her. How come it didn't show back there?"

Roy smiled. "I arranged with City Hospital to fix up her skin with cosmetics, for a while, and scared her into keeping quiet. She'll need surgery later."

"That's rough on her," Duke said soberly. "I guess I owe you something, Roy for fixing it all with the cops. I'll try to work things your way from now on. I can't say better than that. I'll try."

Of course there could be a rumble tomorrow night all over again and the boys would head for jail. Or they'd have some confidence in him now, Kevin, Duke and the rest, and a few of them might turn into decent citizens.

But at the very least, and mainly by telling lies in a good cause, he had kept the flood from breaking down the dikes tonight and kept the boys from going to hell in the last 24 hours. On this job, he couldn't expect anything more.

TOO MUCH LAW

"I can't imagine that you'll have any real trouble, young fellow," said the chairman of the Business Improvement Council with a not-too-patronizing smile. "After all, you won't really be breaking any law."

Duane York tried not to look skeptical. The job interview had been taking place in the office of the Stars and Stripes Restaurant, a stuffy area that wasn't comfortable for the fresh-air enthusiast in him.

"Won't the police resent what I'll be doing?"

"Absolutely not." Mr. Leonidas Xenoulis looked around his domain and smiled. "The police lieutenant has taken a meeting with the Council members—talks over the lunch table, with the best *baklava* and the strongest coffee made, I can tell you—and firm agreement has been reached. The police will not, *won't* interfere with this project."

"Does the beat cop know about it as well as the top brass?"

"Only a meter maid or two will be involved on the street level."

"You can't always depend on police at any level," Duane remarked temperately from the depths of his own experience.

He was thinking about a past episode he wasn't going to bring up. Not too long ago, as a kid back in Weatherford, when some bastard tried to mug him on the street while he was jogging. Duane had turned and struck back fiercely. A passing cop, knowing the criminal, urged Duane to keep at it. When Duane stopped himself, very soon afterwards, the frustrated cop arrested each man for assault. Duane had never been in any other trouble, and he was freed of that mess quick enough, but he did have an arrest record in his native Texas town. He had cut out of there as soon as possible....

"You'll be acting for the Business Improvement Council," Mr. Xenoulis pointed out firmly. "We represent two hundred and fifty law-abiding mom-and-pop store owners in an eight block stretch of Blanford, and there are politicians who won't want us to lose our businesses to the Blan-Son shopping mall and superstores, as you must know. Our representatives in the City Council will go head-to-head with the police if neces- sary, which it won't be unless there's some unforeseen disas— surprise."

And while they're doing that, I hope I won't be under arrest again.

"If you have even the slightest trouble, Duane, I'll deal with it personally." Xenoulis surged to his feet, smiling. The inter- view was over, and its results met with his satisfaction. "You start work at ten-thirty tomorrow morning."

Duane walked out of the restaurant into one steamy July afternoon. A chunky looking woman at the curb was writing out a ticket and he made a point of passing by only a few feet from the parking meter. There was still a minute to go before the one hour's time expired. No doubt if the driver came running out before hand, the ticket would be torn up. The meter maid had started early, though, and it didn't make Duane feel optimistic about this new job of his.

He returned to the restaurant some fifteen minutes early on the next day, sure that he'd have to spend time filling out forms about himself. Along with name and address, age and social security number with other information, he wrote that he was on the short list for a job as ambulance driver at Blanford General Hospital. That done, he signed out for forty quarters, his day's quota. He was outside, by ten.

The chunky meter maid was stalking that row of cars at the nearest curb when Duane approached, smiling his best smile as he introduced himself and waited to hear her name.

She didn't pause on her way to those cars, and actually looked angry. "I heard that the storekeepers were going to hire somebody to bend the law by putting coins in the meters along the street." Her voice was as light in tone as her body was heavy. At one time she might have taken singing lessons. "If you get to a meter and I'm a block away, I suppose I can't stop you from keeping other cars out of the area. But you have to get there first."

He turned, hoping to walk before her in the direction he expected her to take, but she promptly crossed the street. He put a quarter into one meter and left a leaflet on the windshield to explain the service that the local business people were performing for their customers. The meter maid, who had previously given her name as Ramona Beale, looked daggers at him but could do nothing. Worse yet, from her point of view, she hadn't recently found a car to ticket.

Just before Duane's lunch break, a flame-red Toyota parked near the end of the meter's expiring hour. The driver, seeing what Duane was up to, got out and walked off without putting in a quarter of his own. Duane took some pleasure in leaving that meter alone so that Ramona Beale, when she came back, would write the ticket.

He happened to be one of those snobs who was firmly convinced that the best food was served in diners, and discovered one a block away. The counterman looked like Duane's late father, and he almost expected to hear the man say smugly that the big bands would be coming back very soon now, like his father had often done. As one result, he didn't think the food was better than fair.

He saw no sign of Ramona Beale when he left the diner. A nearby car's meter had two minutes to run. There was no leaflet on the window nor was there a telltale white chalk mark on the front tire to indicate he had previously put in a quarter so that the driver wasn't entitled to more help. He reached into a pocket for a coin. Before he could raise it to the meter slot, it had been pushed out of his hand from behind. The sturdy Ramon Beale had padded up back of him and was just about finished with one of her tickets written in advance.

"Wait a minute," he started, willing to talk it over.

"I was here before you," she insisted, lying in that graceful trained civilized voice. "Stay out of my face now and forever if you know what's good for you."

Ramona Beale had declared war. Duane York was more than willing to take up the challenge.

Leonidas Xenoulis cursed under his breath when Duane reported what had taken place. The restaurant owner and chairman of the Business Improvement Council kept his word about acting for Duane in case of trouble. He phoned Police Lieutenant Lloyd Sutherland for a meeting as soon as convenient. While waiting he also contacted Miss Constance Vitrenko, the haughty but kind Russian refugee who managed the Glorious You Beauty Salon as well as being Xenoulis's right hand at the Council.

Sutherland, a ramrod-straight man with icy eyes, ordered a reluctant Ramona Beale into the restaurant office and literally laid down the law. "Beale, you are free to issue tickets when they are deserved, but not until then. Nor are tickets to be written in advance of meter expiration."

"But the state law allows—"

"The department is fully cooperating with the local association in order to keep as much business as possible in the area and not send it to the Blan-Son Mall. That had better be clear."

"Will you have me transferred for having done my job, Lieutenant?"

"Just go back to work, Beale, and don't give anybody a hard time unless he or she has been parked too long."

Duane, who had listened gravely, made a point of smiling in a friendly way as she started out. Ramona Beale turned back long enough to look poison at him in return.

Duane couldn't help getting the impression over the next days that Ramona Beale was spending a lot more time than before on these particular downtown streets. She obeyed the orders she had been given from Sutherland, but must have been hoping to issue even more expiration tickets than in the past. She plodded grimly down the streets, not saying a work to Duane when they were near each other or behaving as if he existed at all.

Toward the end of the second week's work he saw her directly across the street. She looked away when he nodded at her.

Wouldn't it be sensible to cross, now that Lieutenant Sutherland had made it clear what was right, and say to her the whole idea of continuing in some kind of a competition was just so much kid stuff? He'd smile and offer to take her for coffee when both of them were finished working. They could talk together and treat each other like humans. They might never turn into good buddies because she seemed to have no sense of what was important and what was ridiculous, but the work would be easier for both of them.

He had a powerful feeling, though, that she'd look through him if he tried to change things, and turn away without a word.

His eyesight wasn't as good as usual on account of the stabbing summer rain which had been going on for the last couple of hours. He had a hard time making out that the nearest car was a black Corvette '92, and a harder time picking out the driver behind the wheel. He rapped lightly on the window, and didn't see that the driver looked resentful until the glass had been let down.

"Excuse me, sir, but your meter will be running out eight minutes from now, exactly. If you plan to stay around and do more shopping, you'll have to put a quarter in."

"We haven't started shopping," the driver said, and because the umbrella give Duane the chance to look inside the car it was clear that three men were there.

One of the others was arguing bitterly with a third, and the man in the driver's seat joined the argument against number three, as Duane thought of that passenger. He pulled away, not wanting to make out a word of the bitter discussion which had nothing to do with him. An occasional barked-out word proved that the men were speaking English, but no more than that on account of the rain hammering against the car roof.

As Duane stepped back and turned, car doors closed heavily back of him. He glanced around and realized he hadn't heard those same doors open seconds before. It struck him as odd that none of the men carried an umbrella or was wearing raincoat and rubbers. They must have wanted to give themselves the most freedom possible for carrying whatever they were going to pick up. The three of them, two of whom hated the third, walked side by side in solidarity now, their steps almost in military unison.

Duane might not have looked around a little later if he hadn't been kept busy on the same block. A glance at the emptied car convinced him that business courtesy called for him to put in one quarter.

Ramona Beale may have been striding toward the machine from the other side and even glaring down at the meter, but her hand didn't move toward the ticket and she didn't pull it out to start writing. She was like a tiger defanged.

Duane put in a quarter and firmly drew a white chalk on part of the front wheel. He didn't know whether to talk politely or at least smile, but settled for inclining his head.

No response, of course.

He was four blocks down by the time those three men hurried out of the Blanford First National Bank. They had driven away by the time the bank siren started keening.

Details of the crime were known to just about every passerby as the police were arriving to investigate. Duane had rushed to the bank to tell what he knew and maybe help identify the driver at least, pausing only to get the latest word from Constance Vitrenko, along with her customers in different states of being beautified at the Glorious You Beauty Salon.

It seemed that the men had rushed in at an off-hour, hats over much of their faces. Each man took a sack out of a jacket pocket and ordered it filled. The job was done quietly, no customer or guard being disturbed while the newcomers made their withdrawal.

Duane told a uniformed officer in front of the bank that he had some information to offer, and was admitted to the manager's office, a musky smelling cubicle. Here he found Lieutenant Lloyd Sutherland using the manager's desk while rummaging through some of his own papers. Sutherland glanced at Duane out of those icy eyes and nodded sparely.

"If you hadn't come in, York, we'd have had you shoveled in. Now you're here, you can talk."

Duane began, halting himself when Ramona Beale surged into the small room like the *Starship Enterprise* roaring into a star field in the galaxy. She made the room smaller by her outsize presence. Duane resumed his account, talking more slowly about the two men who had argued venomously with the third—he couldn't know why—but all of whom walked with firm precision when they got out of the car.

"Anything more?" Sutherland was making it clear that Ramona Beale was supposed to listen in on his statement.

It turned out to be the prelude to as odd a q-and-a session as any police officer could ever have conducted. After almost every sentence, Sutherland would turn to Ramona Beale and ask silently for the meter maid to confirm, if possible, what the civilian had just said.

At one point Duane called the man in the driver's seat "a pasty-faced dude with silver-rimmed glasses."

"Maybe we'll send you downtown, York, to snuggle up with the image computer and work out a description that can lead to identification." Sutherland nodded, as if agreeing with himself, but the item wasn't number one on his agenda.

Duane went on with his statement. The lieutenant glanced at the silent meter maid less often, now.

At one point, most likely to retain Sutherland's attention, she said accusingly, "*He* put a quarter in that meter."

"It's my job," Duane responded, looking only at Sutherland.

Ramona Beale said coldly, "I could have written out a ticket and we might have the driver's name."

Duane hid the anger he felt. "You'd have a name, but very likely the wrong one."

"We'd certainly have a license number and when the car was found it could be gone over for fingerprints." She was trying to hold Sutherland's cold eyes with her own. "This idiotic, this moronic idea of putting quarters in parking meters to help negligent drivers has made it possible for those men to get away with a bank robbery."

Sutherland said nothing, but it was clear that he agreed.

Duane finally appreciated what a miserable spot he found himself in. This whole business could keep him from holding on to one outdoors job until he landed steady work as an ambulance driver. His livelihood, in the immediate future, was up for grabs.

He didn't get the least satisfaction out of his time spent with the image computer and its handler, or whatever that department member was called. He couldn't offer enough of a description of the Corvette's driver so that a set of features might arranged to make Duane feel the face was familiar. He had ended up wasting two hours in a big draught-pocked room when he ought to have been on the street and working.

He was invited to an emergency meeting of the Business Improvement Council, probably so he could get fired in every member's sight. Before going, he turned in what was left of his day's supply of quarters and walked briskly under puffy skies to the meeting site in the back of Mr. Harry Weinberg's hardware store. Nobody greeted him except Miss Vitrenko with one of her haughty looks and, when he came in, the chairman, Mr. Leonidas Xenoulis.

"The lieutenant has told me that he is thinking seriously about whether to extend the permission he gave us to liberate our car owner patrons from the tyranny of curbside meters," Mr. Xenoulis said at the start of the proceedings, almost as if he was reading from a classic novel. "You all know what that will mean to every one of us."

"Bankruptsville," said the delicatessen store owner, whose

name Duane had never got straight. "My customers and everybody else's will be going straight to the Blan-Son Mall and taking their own sweet time buying more and more. That's what it means, Lenny."

Miss Vitrenko wasn't the only storeowner who shuddered in response, Duane felt sure, but he happened to be looking at her from the back and he noticed her response most clearly. He expected her or one of the others to suddenly turn and say he'd better consider himself out of work again, but nothing happened.

The owner of the local video store asked sensibly, "Can we go to City Hall and ask the Mayor directly to help us?"

Chairman Xenoulis made no secret of his feeling that a politician wouldn't be inclined to overrule the police officer in the field, and that the organization's friends on the City Council would be pitting themselves against a brick wall, in this case Sutherland.

Convinced that the last hope had been proved useless, Duane stood up to ease his way toward the door. Before he could get there a quick vote had been taken in favor of making an application to the Mayor in case of need but meanwhile carrying on as before. Duane paused, not sure if he ought to leave after all.

Xenoulis noticed him, of course. "It's understood that you'll stay on the job until further notice, Duane York. If Sutherland terminates the arrangement unilaterally, you'll go along with him until the Council's application is answered and the matter is settled." Inflating himself, he added, "I never fire my people without ample notice."

No one bridled at his use of "my people" in referring to somebody hired for the Business Improvement Council.

The mid-afternoon weather helped perk him up, with rain-washed air suddenly smelling like some expensive after-shave lotion. He had got done with the first go around of inspecting the meters when he saw Ramona Beale again. Not even the sight of the stock meter maid lowered his spirits.

This time she walked in his direction. No car was nearby, so he didn't have the slightest idea why she should be approaching.

"Are you still on the job?" What she wanted was to needle him.

Instead of a glare or an insult, he pointed firmly at the special armband he always wore at work.

"The lieutenant will tell that restaurant man the arrangement is cancelled," she said in the speaking voice that always surprised him in pitch because it reminded him of an opera singer. "The perps haven't been found, there's no sign they ever will be, and this set-up made it possible for them to get away."

"The Mayor and City Council might feel different."

"When was the last time those wimps overruled the department? Sutherland will pass the word before the day is out."

"Nobody has told me anything yet."

"You might have to be arrested first for interfering with a police representative on duty," she said almost gleefully. "I'm empowered to make arrests, you know. Might as well get out while the getting is good."

"Until I hear something official, I've got a job to do."

She talked to his moving back, easily making every word clear. "If you expect a city job after getting in the law's way, forget it."

He didn't stop walking, but made a pair of fists and kept them tight for most of this block. To calm himself as he went at the job, he played with the notion of finding the perpetrators himself so there'd be no reason to drop this arrangement and he could keep bothering that arrogant meter maid by his continuing presence on the job. Images of Ramona Beale gnashing her teeth gave him a few pleasant moments of fantasy and kept him from stewing even more.

If the case was quickly solved, the Business Improvement Council might persuade a mayor who'd be up for re-election in three short years to order Sutherland to do what the store owners needed so desperately. Not likely, but possible. Duane took a late lunch at the Stars and Stripes in hopes of asking Xenoulis about any news, but didn't see the owner. The sound of news on his pocket radio disturbed two men in the smoking section, so he had to turn it off. A copy of the morning paper offered no important news, but gave him a chance to find out he had lost at the lottery once again. No way was he playing in luck.

A nasty surprise came at him when he was on the job again. Ramona Beale, instead of prowling among cars, was standing still and looking out at the gutter. She was smiling, which would have unsettled him at any time.

An unmarked car with a uniformed police driver stopped almost in front of Duane. Lieutenant Sutherland was looking out at him from the back, having managed somehow to sit stiffly in a car seat.

"Better pack it in, fella," Sutherland said, almost polite to an enemy who had been beaten. "I've talked to the mayor's office and they want you out of here and the whole arrangement dropped down the tubes."

"Will that be permanent?"

"There's no choice. If the media finds out what the department let happen here a few hours ago, City Hall and everybody connected with law enforcement in this administration will be in deep yogurt as it goes on. Believe that."

"I'll turn in my quarters again, and this," he pointed to the armband and tried to ignore Ramona Beale's widening grin.

Sutherland walked into the restaurant, wanting to explain the circumstances in a quick talk with Xenoulis. Duane decided against putting anything more on the restaurant owner's agenda, and handed over everything to a regretful Constance Vitrenko. She promised that whatever salary he was owed would be sent out before the week was over, and surprised him with an affectionate hug and a moist kiss on the line of his chin.

Ramona Beale hadn't moved when he came out, wanting to see him slink off like a dog with its tail between its legs. Sutherland, having left the restaurant just a minute before, looked sour at the sight of a department member gloating over somebody else's rotten luck.

Making up for it in part, he asked Duane, "Is your car in the neighborhood?"

"I usually walk to work and back."

"A glutton for walking in the street? Get in if you want, and I'll take you home."

Duane hated to be in a car that somebody else was driving, but he didn't want to seem like a sorehead. He climbed in. Sutherland turned to Ramona Beale, who had watched disapprovingly.

"You're about finished for the day, aren't you? If I can take York home, I can take you to your car. Get in front."

They proceeded quietly, Duane relieving some tension by looking out at a billboard for the 24-Hour Baln-Son Mall, which was likely to put most the Blanford stores out of business. He suddenly leaned forward.

"Have you looked for the car at the Mall parking lot?"

Ramona Beale, offended by any suggestion from Duane, snapped, "He wants to find a car in an open-air facility that parks hundreds of cars at the same time and has a theft every ten minutes in spite of precautions. That's make a cat laugh!"

Sutherland said judiciously, "the bank hold-up cost Mr. York his job. No wonder he wants to make one last try."

Ramona Beale kept her place when they halted at Garden and Drew Streets, where her pink Chevy was parked. "I'd like to hear what he says when he doesn't see any evidence at the Mall, Lieutenant. If you go with him I think I ought to be along, anyhow. You might need help with him, you know."

And she flexed her fingers, looking forward to an opportunity for putting Duane under physical restraint.

The driver was making good time when Duane asked thoughtfully, "Is there anything new on the case that hasn't been on radio or TV?"

"Not really. Descriptions of the men have been useless, including yours. There hasn't been time enough to track the money or get anything out of our usual stoolies."

Ramona Beale was shaking her head, dismayed at hearing a police official talk freely to a civilian.

"As for the Corvette '92 that they used, we've had highway patrols on the outskirts of town—like those men at the next fork in this road. Useless, so far."

Ramona Beale, her one-track mind remaining on the subject of car theft, said, "It would only be driven out here because the bank robbers wanted somebody to steal the damn thing after it was left a long time and take it off their hands."

Sutherland, considering, said, "The sacks with loot must've been dropped off first, of course. For Mr. York's sake, though, and admitting you could be right, we'll give a quick look."

"How could we identify the right car among dozens like it?" Ramona Beale protested as they pulled into that always-crowded parking lot of the twenty-four-hour Mall.

Duane snapped, "If it's there, I'll pick it out."

"He'll divine the truth with a crystal ball!"

"No, with a flashlight."

"Lieutenant if he can find the right car in this—this jungle, I'll ask for transfer to another beat."

"Hold her to that, Lieutenant," Duane said, getting to his feet. "It's important for my blood pressure."

Glad to be in the open air, he briefly inspected parked cars while evading the bag boys who carried boxes of merchandise out of the bustling supermarket and over to different cars. At the sight of any Corvette he snapped on the flashlight he had borrowed from Sutherland over Ramona Beale's drawn-in breaths of disapproval. Every time he turned away, frustrated, he was aware of a heartily operatic laugh from the meter maid.

So many '92's on one parking lot!

He remained in place, though, after using his flashlight on the ninth car three rows across.

"Your men might very likely find useful fingerprint inside and you can make at least one quick arrest," he said without showing his relief.

"Oh, sure," Ramona Beale said thinly. "Now Mr. Sherlock Holmes is going to expose the department to a lawsuit from some innocent driver."

Sutherland probed cautiously, "How can you be sure this is the right car?"

About to answer that question directly, Duane stopped himself, sniffing. "Come here, both of you!"

Ramona Beale stayed in place at first, but moved forward at the sight of Sutherland's sudden shocked wince. Like the lieutenant, she looked stricken.

"That decay has to of once-living flesh," Duane said. "Don't bet it isn't the man that those other two were arguing so bitterly with."

Ramona Beale was silent.

"No wonder a car thief wouldn't want to go near this daisy," the lieutenant said. "Beale, stay here until I come back with a morgue wagon."

Ramona Beale nodded weakly....

Sutherland met Duane on his rounds just a week after two arrests had been made in the case. "How did you know enough to put your hand on the right car, York?"

Duane smiled. "When I'm on the job, I mark every car I put a quarter into the meter for, making sure I won't help the same driver twice in a row. That's a matter of policy. On that car, the chalk mark was right where I'd put it."

"How come the mark lasted so long?"

"I guess I made it extra hard because Miss Beale had been pestering me and I couldn't talk back," Duane considered. "I suppose that even Ramona Beale can be helpful—but not unless she wants to be, I'll tell you that much!"

A SNARE AND
A DELUSION

Olivia Hartrig had expected that her new assistant would be waiting on her arrival, but the apartment seemed empty except for her. She was starting past the narrow but spotless foyer when she heard a key moving softly in the outside door lock.

She waited in place, glancing at herself in the half-sized mirror where she faced an assured blonde in her early thirties, hair done stylishly, her body covered in clothes as expensive as they were fashionable. An impressive looker, she told herself approvingly.

She didn't look around until a man's footsteps sounded in the hall at last. At the irritation that must have been reflected in her sharp features, he didn't stop directly in front of her, but kept a distance.

She had to raise her voice slightly but perceptibly. "You were sent over from London to assist me." The photograph she'd been shown was an exceptionally good likeness.

"I'm Roland Mercer, yes."

"I had been sure you would be waiting." Olivia gave the impression of making a mental note for some later report, probably in triplicate. She was the perfect female executive (as the poem ought to have said), shrewdly planned, to warn, to nettle and demand.

Roland Mercer shrugged at the suggestion of negligence on his part.

The violet eyes, which were Olivia' best feature, were glittering angrily. "I know this isn't the British Secret Service, Roland, where you were employed for a long time. We, at Global Electronics, do happen to think, however, that our work is important, too."

Global Electronics—Shaping a Different World. That was the company's slogan, used on its stationery, on newspaper and TV ads, in muffled commercials on the Internet. Almost impossible to think of the firm name without remembering that, and sometimes humming the particularly obnoxious music that went with it on the boob tube.

Mercer didn't apologize in words or manner. A pulse rippled briefly in his papery skin stretched tautly over thin cheeks and sharp bones. His silence, his immobility, would have been offensive to any supervisor.

"Please remember that we take ourselves seriously at Global Electronics...." She heard herself talking like an insecure teacher without tenure and in front of a class, but couldn't stop. "I can certainly understand why you're being so difficult, Roland. It bothers you to be assisting a mere as you must think it, woman."

"I have worked with women supervisors in the past."

He might as well have said that the women to whom he referred had been more highly experienced. In his opinion, of course.

"And it certainly bothers you to be dealing with these foreigners on any peaceful basis. I know something about your work for MI-5 in British Intelligence before you joined Global over there, when you often had to use violence against enemies."

He nodded, as if to say in cautious silence that he could adapt himself to the post-Cold War world in which espionage involved no military actions. Was it possible that Olivia Hartrig had misjudged his capacity for doing espionage work under entirely different conditions?

"I have to make sure that you know what the job will be." And, she thought to establish again that she was his Control, to think in terms of that rancid out-of-date vocabulary of terror he must know well. "You had better tell me what you know about the deal that we're going to finish tonight. I have to make sure you've been put in the picture, Roland. I'm the one who'll be responsible to the front office if anything goes wrong."

"What I have been told is that you are to conclude a transaction with a certain person a little later on in this apartment."

"You were certainly told more than that."

"If the other person's English is at all shaky, I am to translate," he said after a moment.

"And you were told the woman's name, her position at her work, and the nature of the job to be performed secretly for Global Electronics."

Mercer took note that her look hadn't wavered and said, "She is Niu Mo-Lan, a minor official in the current Chinese trade mission to the U.S. She is to sell you a number of computer printouts which give in detail the lowest figure that China will accept to permit Global to do business on the Mainland."

Better to offer a sickly carrot now that he had practically run for the stick.

"With your previous achievements, Roland, I'm sure you can also work in a situation that puts financial interests foremost among a nation and a firm."

"Thank you for your confidence in me." Was there something he kept from saying? "I can assure you that I want to become proficient in the current type of espionage, industrial espionage. I want to help shape a different world, as the firm's slogan says."

It was best to give him the benefit of the doubt after what she considered a respectful apology, to insure herself having a loyal subordinate.

"Look here, Roland, it's unfortunate that you got started on the wrong foot with me. Since you'll be under me a little while longer, at least, it's best for the mission—I suppose I can call it that—if you hit it off with me."

Her hand was thrust out as a symbol of new beginnings. Was there the shortest of pauses before his hand clasped hers?

She indicated the next item on their agenda, proving her rank. "We'll look through the apartment now, Roland."

Without a word of acknowledgment, he turned and softly walked ahead of her into the perfectly designed room.

"Leave it to Global," she exulted, "not to spare expense and give its executives first-class accommodations when they're needed."

He didn't pay attention to what she herself suddenly thought of as bootless talk, but looked form one item of furniture to another, almost as if he was counting.

"There's a recliner and a three-seater sofa," he murmured, then raised his voice for her benefit. "I hope that you'll seat yourself on the recliner and leave the sofa for our guest."

"What difference does it make?"

His explanation was smoothness itself. "I have to sit, too, and if I'm at an end of the sofa, it won't look as if we're two against one."

"I can't see that it matters at all."

"Nevertheless, Olivia, I ask that you follow my...ah, suggestion."

He should have been more tactful and made his brainless suggestion hopefully.

"Roland, one of the rules for getting on in private industry is that if your idea is turned down, you must realize that it is not considered usable."

"I ask you to reconsider this one."

"Since you feel so strongly about it, Roland, I'll make my final decision when the time comes." She felt a little like a mother confronting the baseless worries of her child. There was a positive pleasure, though, in making it clear that she was the one in the saddle.

After another look at his motionless features, she took the sofa a made a point of leaning back briefly. "It's really very comfortable."

Almost eagerly she found herself waiting for her eccentric British subordinate to offer one more reflection about how he wanted her to behave, so she could feel provoked into another show of her authority.

Before she could ask irritably what he was mooning about, the telephone shrieked.

"Answer that, Roland."

He was looking around for the phone as she reached over and, after a scalding look in the unflappable Brit's direction, picked it up.

"I wished to be sure that you were at the place," the melodious voice spoke quietly but clearly after the briefest of mutual greetings, a bright woman to whom English was a second or third language.

"I am here, Niu Mo-Lan. You have the address?"

"Certainly. Fifteen minutes at the most, and I join you."

Mercer must have heard those carrying tones. He rubbed his hands together in anticipation and looked around to refresh his memory as far as the furniture layout was concerned, it seemed. Olivia Hartrig had the disconcerting notion that she was completely out of her subordinate's thoughts, as if she wasn't directing him.

Annoyed by his behavior, she put down the phone angrily and snapped, "Ms. Niu speaks Engish pretty well, as you hear, so I don't need you after all, and your trip from England to help me—why the firm would transfer you at all, I will never know—has been a complete waste."

His face darkened, and he spread his feet a little wider apart as if to dig himself in.

"You can leave now."

He didn't stir, but pursed his lips as if nothing she said had registered with him.

She wasn't going to take part in a childish contest of exchanging stares. She was starting to repeat her last order with a more imposing choice of words when the building intercom buzzed with a sound like a dentist's drill.

Another chance to show her authority had come up. "Take that message before you leave, Roland."

His eyes seemed to sting her lips. Rather than snap at him when there was business to be done, she hurried into the kitchen herself to answer the summons.

The doorman's voice was clear as she picked up. "A Mrs. Noo is here to see you."

Olivia wasn't surprised that the woman had wrongly gauged travel time in a city strange to her. Trying to sound casual, she said, you can stay long enough to put up coffee for Ms. Niu and myself, Roland, there's a good boy! I'm sure that suitable arrangements have been put down in the kitchen."

He hadn't moved.

Even before she made out the adverse report on him, it was necessary to set the Brit down in place.

"If you refuse a direct order, I'll call downstairs and ask the doorman to send a police officer here right away to throw you out of this apartment. Do I make myself clear?"

This time he nodded. Slowly, but it was a nod.

The suggestion of a smile crossed Olivia Hartrig's lips as he walked into the kitchen. Wasn't this a sure sign of her triumph? The former Cold War operative from British Intelligence had learned at long last the his new job at Globe Electronics (Shaping A Different World) called for him to take even the most trivial order that a superior chose to give. It was one added victory in a position where she'd already had many.

The outside door sounded almost as soon as he was out of sight. Olivia took a deep breath to order him to answer the door; any time there was an underling handy, she wouldn't be found doing scut work.

It seemed that almost as soon as the chimes sounded, Mercer turned the tap water to full strength.

She decided against keeping the Niu woman waiting and walked out to the hallway. Mentally she was turning over phrases for the report she would be writing on Mercer, a report that would sting the eyes of anybody who read it, a report fit for no vehicle except asbestos paper.

She opened the door on the heavy moon-faced Niu Mo-Lan, taking her coat as she spoke cordial nothings which won appropriate responses.

"My assistant," she added a little more loudly, leading the way into the living room, "is preparing coffee for us."

The Chinese guest sank gratefully into one of the comfortable sofa seats. Olivia, in return, did exactly what Mercer, now taking his own damn time about bringing in the coffee, had asked her not to; she sat down beside Niu Mo-Lan in the next sofa seat.

They smiled and kept talking polite nonsense about the pleasures of visiting such an awesome city, the intelligence of some taxi drivers, the number of well-dressed women and men.

In the course of talking, Olivia, with practiced casualness, opened her handbag to show an envelope with a good-sized check made out care of a number account at a Swiss bank. The woman would be leaving with her pay, and probably not be seen again by those who knew her.

Not to be outdone, and with her own smile in place, Niu Mo-Lan opened her handbag and showed a thicker envelope with sheets of computer printout inside, her part of the bargain with Global Electronics.

"Why don't we get the business done now?" Olivia suggested calmly, having become impatient with banalities. "We've brought the material, as agreed."

Niu Mo-Lan started to smile again, but didn't finish. Her lips froze. She was looking across the room in sudden fear that narrowed her eyes and clenched her hands.

Roland Mercer had suddenly opened the kitchen door and surged into the room. He held a gleaming pistol pointed directly at the pudding-faced woman.

"Put that down!" Olivia said immediately, her voice just short of shrillness. "Put it down immediately! That's an order from your superior. Do you hear?"

As usual between them, she seemed only to give a clear direction for him to do exactly the opposite. He fired, the pistol making a noise no louder than the opening of a soft drink can, the bullet missing Olivia by inches. Niu Mo-Lan widened her lips to scream, but no sound came. She dropped to the carpeted floor, dead.

Before Olivia could speak, he said, "I'll plant her where she won't be found for years."

Olivia spoke with venomous quiet. "Is this what you do to impress the top brass at Global, to prove how useful you can be?"

"No."

"I can show you immediately how useful and important you are to my firm." She reached for the telephone and punched the button for the operator. "I want the pol...."

"Put that down." The pointed pistol was enough to insure his success in having the phone replaced.

"Even if you could get the police force here in time, I'd be freed and you'd lose your job and never get another."

"Nonsense! Nobody ordered you to do...this!"

"It was clearly understood when I was instructed to make certain she doesn't give the firm any trouble.: His unnaturally shiny eyes gleamed. "As an amateur in the spy game, she could be tracked down immediately by professionals and made to tell exactly what she had done. As a result, Global Electronics would be forbidden to operate in China."

"What are you saying?"

"I'll make myself even more clear," he offered, taking out the thick envelope from the dead woman's handbag and extending it. "International business, as conducted by Global Electronics at least, is nothing but the cut-throat Cold War under different auspices and with changed goals. My task is to deal with extreme situations like this one."

"Lies, all lies! Liar, liar, li...."

Mercer shut her up without touching her or going near her or even looking at her.

"Global Electronics," Roland Mercer mused out lo9ud, with bitter but unmistakable sincerity, glancing down at the body of the woman he had murdered in the course of his employment. "Shaping A...." pause "...Different World."

Hearing her beloved firm's slogan from this man in these

circumstances, the loyal executive threw back her head and screamed without end.

PERIL IN PARADISE

"My figures show that each and every commercial enterprise on the island has had another miserable year," the dark-haired stranger began, surging to his feet at the October town meeting. "Tourism is the only money maker on Kinscote Island, and profit margins have been dropping steadily down to the cellar. What's more, you all know it."

A burly local man with a bull voice interrupted promptly. "We can get extra people to come out here, mister whoever-you-are."

"Why should anybody come out?" the determined gadfly snapped, looking at one of several sheets in a hard hand. "No one wants to rent rooms in decaying boarding houses or falling-apart hotels. Why do you think so many prospective summer residents are going in for houses or time shares in Nantucket or P-town or even out at East Hampton? That explains the big drop in Kinscote's over-all income."

His opponent stood up in turn, belligerently, "And I say we do more advertising and get more day visitors; then raise prices so we can make up the money on higher turnovers."

"And you think visitors will pay even more money for postal cards with fuzzy pictures, t-shirts that have got idiot slogans and ocean blue baseball caps with big K's all over?"

"One-day visitors buy plenty of food, too, and that's sure to hike profits."

"Oh, you'll sell fish-and-chips and clam chowder and hot dogs at higher prices and more of them if there are more people, but one-day visitors are famous for not caring where they drop their garbage. Kinscote's streets are already filthy heaps of plastic containers and cans. The more people, the more garbage. Any fresh profits will be chewed up in having to hire extra sanitation workers and pest control experts to get rid of roaches and rats. You end up losing money unless you do what's absolutely necessary."

After an outbreak of discussion caused the harried chairman to call for order, somebody put in, "All right, we've had a few bad seasons. How do you think we can do better?"

"By taking a tip from Nantucket and P-town and even the Hamptons, and changing Kinscote so that it's less like Coney Island and more like a small town of the sort that everybody thinks he or she remembers from childhood, when everything seemed better. I remember things that way, and others do, too."

The burly man bristled at murmurs of agreement with the stranger and snapped, "Somebody as pushy as you, mister, ought to damn well watch his back all the timie."

The good-looking woman sitting next to him, her wedding ring flashing as she put a hand to his arm, whispered urgently and gasped when she was brushed away.

The dark-haired stranger's eyes had snapped at the rudeness, but he was quiet and sat down in the teeth of a frozen silence.

Kim Nichols was hurrying across the High School gym even as the Town Meeting staggered to a typically inconclusive finish. Her momentary quest turned out to be useless, the handsome intruder having put a flea in everybody's ear and then taken himself off. Somebody knew who he was, though.

"His name is Weldon Jory," she was able to tell the purse-lipped editor at the Kinscote Herald, blunting criticism for not having obtained an interview at the scene of the uproar. "I'll know very soon if he's staying on the island."

Weldon Jory, it turned out, had taken an office in the Devlin Building downtown on Jurney Street. An eager Kim, reaching the freshly opened door at noon, found her way to the inner office being blocked.

"I'm Mr. Jory's second-in-command," Chris Yarett said after introducing himself. The young man looked deceptively as if he could have been knocked over by a couple of broom straws.

"Can I help you?"

Disdaining violence, Kim settled for a brief explanation followed by an interoffice call. It was enough to insure her being admitted to the Presence.

Weldon Jory stood up mechanically to greet the visitor, but his pale eyes warmed in appreciation of the sunny blonde whose appearance lighted the meagerly furnished office. Kim, for her part, noticed immediately that no pictures of family adorned Weldon Jory's desk, and smiled with rue at herself for having given his marital status almost her second thought.

"I can offer you a general idea of what my plans are," Jory said after a moment in a voice that could be deliciously soothing when he wasn't trying to sway some undecided crowd.

She wasn't sure what made her say, "I hope you're going to be tactful about shaking up the islanders."

"I'll try to be, but the meeting made it clear that not everybody is coming from the same place I am."

"That was Felix Vance who put up the main argument against you. He owns Pride of Kinscote, the only licensed excursion boat to the island. He's bound to feel strongly against anybody who might cut down the volume of one-day visitors. He can turn into a rough customer. I'm sure he meant what he said about you watching your back."

Of course the confident Jory had already worked out one answer, at least, to that particular objection. "If you offer anybody in business a chance to make more money honestly in the long run, I don't think you'll hear sustained complaints."

An exception to Weldon Jory's rough-hewn proverb appeared thunderously at the inner office door almost on cue. This overweight bearded year-rounder, trailed by a strongly protesting Chris Yarett, was waving a sheet of stiff paper that seemed to have mortally wounded him. Bellowing about the wickedness of outlanders, he hurtled himself into the room.

"You...you're the new owner of Lombard's!"

"That's right. I did buy the Lombard Real Estate Company." Jory was shrewd enough to lower his voice when somebody else shouted in a one-on-one confrontation, another good point in his favor. "And you've just heard from Lombard's."

"What do you mean telling me my lease won't be renewed? I've been a good law-abiding tenant for twenty-two years, and Felix Vance says he'll help me pay for taking you to court."

"You and Vance will lose." Jory gave no more than a swift look at the paper being waved around in the vicinity of his eyes. "You're Jamie Lessing, yes, from the Beta Way store on C Street, and your lease won't be renewed on the previous terms."

"It's blackmail!" Lessing's oversized nostrils writhed in a spasm of fury. "I can't afford more than I'm already paying, business being the way it's been for the last couple of seasons."

"No added payment will be charged if you agree to my terms, Jamie. What I want is for you to drop the line of souvenir garbage you've been peddling for twenty-two years."

"Drop it and put in what?"

"You'll be selling upscale souvenirs instead. Needlepoint or native-woven rugs, something along that line. Fewer sales, I know, but the profits on each item will be a lot higher, improving your overall gross and profit."

"If people buy that stuff, maybe."

"Upscale visitors will buy, next season."

"Not from me." Felix Vance's friend shook his head firmly. "Even if I thought there was a chance of this looney-tune idea taking off, after the last few seasons I can't get the money to upgrade my store layout and to redecorate, too."

"You've been a long-term tenant, so if there's security, I'll see to it that you get an interest-free loan from Lombard Realty." Weldon Jory ventured an understanding smile. "I know it isn't the easiest decision in the world, but I'd suggest you go home and talk it over with your wife and family, then let me know what all of you decide on, together."

Lessing nodded sadly. "Sounds sensible." In silence he

trudged to the door and closed it behind him. Softly.

"He may not see the potential until next season is half-over, but when May comes around he'll be in the tent with me."

"How can you be sure?"

"Because he's married," the experienced real estate developer answered with a sly smile. "Tell a wife about upgrading and redecorating, then stand out of her way because you can't keep her from getting on with it."

He had manipulated two other people, man and wife. Kim was tempted to think of him as polite but ruthless, the Velvet Dictator.

Over a light lunch in the spacious restaurant where the interview was eventually finished, he swore solemnly that Kinscote would soon enough resemble the safe and clean town of his childhood—and hers, too, he was sure. Trying to pin him down to details was work wasted.

During the next weeks, though, she became aware that the smiling autocrat had meant every word. For a start, in spite of the brisk fall weather, downtown cobblestones were being repaired and replaced for the first time in memory. One guess as to who had gone to the mayor's office and raised high hell with at least two intimidated friends of Felix Vance.

Many of the more than middle-aged two-story houses, especially those near the downtown district, were being repainted even though a quantity of paint had been stolen and some of it spilled late at night. Jory told Kim during one of their now-infrequent talks—he wasn't seen in town very often any more—that he was going 'halfies,' as he put it, with the home owners.

Kim didn't know anything about later changes until a breaking news story took her reluctant steps to the decrepit John Dillard House on L Street. The Dillard was the only really scabby hotel on the island, where rats and roaches were said to have raised entire families. Kim always tried to take as few breaths as humanly possible in the grimy premises.

She was hardly surprised to find many repair people, painters and plasterers among them, swarming over the place. The day clerk, who had discovered the vandalizing of several rooms and the Jory Go Home graffiti on a number of paint-drenched walls, forebore making his usual abashed apology for the condition of the place and nodded proudly instead.

She couldn't help asking, "Do you think Felix Vance arranged for all the damage?"

"Wouldn't say so if I knew for a fact," said the spidery Mr. Britt, who liked to tell children he had been a fixture at the Dillard since the British occupation in the Revolutionary War. "But it did pretty much bother Felix to know that Mr. Jory has bought an interest in every hotel on the island. Each one is gonna be prettied up. There'll be a sauna on the top floor, computers for kids or grownups, faxes, and whatever else is current."

And he never told me! What reporter wouldn't be furious at a self-declared leader who didn't give the press word one about his next move? Adroit and clever as he was, the rarely-seen Jory did his leading without thoughts of the needs or feelings of any who were led. You'll be better off, so you're being helped by my ruthlessness.

As for the feelings of a vicious Felix Vance, outwitted in every way, Kim wouldn't let herself think about them.

She was leaving her new car across from the Calico Cat restaurant on H Street and Jurney when she became aware of loud complaints on the sunny street. She recognized the Sturdy owner of *Pride of Kinscote*, the only excursion ship licensed to bring visitors to the island. Not seeing Jory in turn, she supposed that a marital argument was under way. It turned out to be true. Mrs. Vance, her well-shaped lips drawn down, had obviously given up trying to keep her husband quiet.

Weldon Jory strode down H Street, ahead of a rattled deputy. Vance, stopping him, had p;lainly become angered by Jory having set up private guards at points where long overdue repairs were being made.

Jory spoke scornfully and dismissively.

Vance was shaking his huge fists by the time Jory turned and he was led away, Mrs. Vance walking shakily behind him and twisting a kerchief in her graceful hands. Vance's shouts faded into a series of fanged mutters....

"That poor woman," Jory said reflectively when Kim was sitting opposite him for lunch, to which he had surprisingly invited her. It was probably the only sympathy he had shown for anybody on the island whose residents he was going to help on his terms only.

With the soup course, Jory was handed a four-page newspaper freshly turned out by desktop publishing and trumpeting that the newly hired guards were an example of American gestapo tactics, and that Kinscote would soon be turned into a Nazi-style concentration camp with the infamous Weldon Jory in charge of everybody's life.

Kim's senses were immersed in the thickest creamiest chowder ever conceived, but she noticed other patrons reading the same scurrilous paper and looking speculatively over at Weldon as if the print gave credibility to the most bizarre accusation.

She said, "You've made yourself at least one really nasty enemy who'll try anything to get rid of you."

"When the year-rounders see how much better their lives are going to be and how much more money they'll all be making," Weldon said confidently, "they'll change their minds quick."

But who knew what might happen till then?

The accident, if it was one, took place in front of the restaurant. Weldon's attention was on her at the time. He happened to be performing the gentleman's traditional service as a buffer between the lady he escorted and the gutter. One second he was talking while he accommodated his usual ground-eating pace to Kim's slower steps, and then he was on the ground.

She called out, but the bicyclist who had knocked Weldon down kept riding off furiously. No deputy was in sight this time. Worse yet, two strangers had to help Weldon to his feet, and one of them stayed to let Weldon lean against him.

Kim insisted pluckily on driving him to the nearest doctor, who she happened to know would be in his office. No other patient occupied the waiting room, a godsend to her inflamed nerves.

"We'll take a few x-rays," Dr. Elias Onderdonk promised after a careful preliminary examination, "but I don't think we'll find anything seriously wrong."

By the time Dr. Onderdonk had satisfied himself, Sheriff Zack Terhune had joined Kim in the sunny waiting room, having been summoned to the scene. Terhune's calmness made it certain that there was nothing of interest to pass on. He spoke about how hard the *Herald* had campaigned to get the island Council to pass an ordinance against bikers, not having to add that the *Herald*'s crusade had been unsuccessful.

"I don't see any way to zap this hooligan," he added soberly as a tight-lipped Weldon was helped into the waiting room to join them and offered black coffee. "Nobody could identify the bicycle. As for the rider, he was wearing a metal hat and wraparounds. Nobody could see him to identify anybody, so he gets away clear. He rides, as you might say."

"Do you have any idea if it could have been done on purpose?" Kim asked over Weldon's irritated denial of the very possibility. "Could somebody have paid a cyclist to hurt Mr. Jory by way of warning him to get out of Kinscote?"

"How can I tell you for certain, Kim? Me, I would say that maybe it's Felix Vance, who'll try plenty to stop the one man doing so much for the island. Behaving like a nut case."

"How far do you think he might go to get his way?"

"Felix is bull-headed, but all he usually does is yell and fight." The sheriff shrugged. "Sandra tries to stop him."

The doctor shrugged and became quiet.

"I don't like the dock area because there weren't any docks in my home town," Jory said surprisingly on a February afternoon. Kim hadn't seen him for a while, but joined him on the way to inspect a section that was being rebuilt. She hoped for a news story in this week's paper. "I come from Andamar, in Wyoming, which has turned into a computer haven, believe it or not, into cyber valley. Otherwise I might've used this much of my money to—never mind that."

He didn't need to say that he'd have rebuilt his home town to reflect his memories, as he was doing with Kinscote. Kim, startled by the revelation, didn't trust herself to respond.

She had seen him argue that a confectionery store had to be placed on a corner of Paget Street, a name he had insisted on using. No doubt there'd been a store just like it on Paget Street in his home town, in Andamar, where he had probably taken his first girlfriend. He was moved by the sight.

Which was why he heard Felix Vance's bull-like voice before she did. Vance was strongly insisting to a number of workers that the changes ordered by Weldon Jory would turn Kinscote into an island of scared people not able to say what they really thought of "the new order," as Vance maliciously called the changes.

"I damn well meant every word I just said," Vance snapped at Weldon Jory nervily surging into the workers' midst.

"What you're saying against me is a bunch of lies." Jory's voice seemed to fill the charged air. "The final proof will come halfway through next season when the different system of work will bring every resident more money than ever. That's the truth, Vance, and truth counts. Truth matters."

The last two words echoed. Vance made fists, but a guard came closer and he stalked off toward an old bicycle that rested on decayed pilings. The sight reminded Kim of the incident that might've cost Jory some severe wounds.

Correctly interpreting her expression, Jory said confidently, "Give Vance enough time and he'll turn into a happy camper after all, Kim. There'll be no real trouble from that direction— or any other, if you want to know."

In this self-confident mood, there was no point in suggesting again that he hire a special guard for his own skin's sake.

"I'm afraid Mr. Jory can't see you today," Chris Yarett said over the phone to Kim at her *Herald* office.

She heard the tension in his voice. "Tell me why not, Chris, and save both of us some time."

"Mr. Jory is with the sheriff. Somebody fired a gun near him and the bullet came pretty close."

"There's nothing we can do." Sheriff Zachary Terhune, on the edge of a visitor's chair in Jory's freshly furnished office, briefly twisted his body as if to show he shared the builder's discomfort. "The shot was fired from a window at Cheney's, and there are so many bowlers on an off-season night that nobody saw anything unusual. As for finding the gun, if a miracle doesn't happen you can forget about that."

Kim put in bitterly, "Leave it to Felix Vance to wait for improvements to be almost finished before he comes closest to—to doing what he seems to want."

Weldon said thoughtfully, "So many things have happened that you must all be right and Vance is really literally gunning for me. Something has to be done about him, I'm sorry to say."

He sat back in deep thought, eyes half-open, hands folded, lower lip between his teeth. He paid no attention whatever to the quiet but impassioned talk that swirled around him.

Chris Yarett, without asking Jory, hired a bodyguard from a detective firm that Jory often used. Ben March turned out not to be especially big or powerful looking, but he was a sturdy well-knit man who kept close to Jory without ever irritating him.

The pre-season Town Meeting was getting under way, the only item on the agenda being a vote of thanks to Weldon Jory for his unremitting efforts to improve Kinscote. The Mayor and his cohorts didn't mention that the year-round residents, as well as Jory, stood to make a pretty penny from the hard work. It was just as well that no one else knew about Jory's trying to rebuild his home town as he remembered it, through rose-colored glasses.

Jory was the object of various barbed looks from dissidents. He ought to have taken the opportunity to press some flesh and come across as a democratic fellow who was just like everybody else when you got to know him, instead of a benevolent Maximum Leader.

He was on his way out, the bodyguard behind him with Chris

Yarett, when Kim realized that the meeting had been orderly, with no protesting. A look around showed her that Felix and Sandra Vance hadn't come around. Kim was too glad about that to feel any disquiet. Maybe Vance had grown to accept the changes and wanted to profit from them now, just like everybody else.

Felix Vance's burly dead body was found early on a sun-dappled April morning. It seemed to have fallen into a narrow but deep hole on the northeast corner of the newly named Friendship Street.

A taut-tempered Dr. Onderdonk told Kim over her cell phone shortly afterwards that the death had taken place early last night. "He broke his neck against a thick pipe along the length of the hole. No sign of foul play. Personally, I only hope Weldon Jory has got a tight alibi."

Word of the death got around very soon by radio and internet, the local versions of bush telegraph. Jory, speaking at a trade association meeting, was defiantly booed. After he left, having cut his speech short, a trio of children threw rocks at him on the street.

Dr. Onderdon's nurse told Kim wearily that Mr. Jory had been graced by a rock and was with 'doctor.' Kim walked past Jory's sullen and now-useless bodyguard and into the office. Jory was lying on a fudge-colored couch and pressing a wet bandage to his forehead.

The door opened to let in the newly spruced-up peace officer, Zachary Turner, who now wore a five-pointed tin star like a Western sheriff. Turner had been sternly instructed to do just that at a talk just before the Town Meeting, which was at about the time Vance had departed this life. Weldon Jory had been in sight of a large number of Kinscote citizens.

Interviewed in front of a store on Commercial Street, Sandra Vance, the widow, insisted that nobody had ever disliked Felix for long. Asked about Jory's attitude toward her late husband, Mrs. Vance denied that there'd been any antagonism. Even the local interviewers sounded skeptical.

A circular that had been desktop published called on Kinscote to turn its back on a murderer who had somehow pulled wool over their peace officer's eyes and was a tricky tin-pot dictator.

Turner told Kim that Weldon Jory had to be detained a while for his own safety's sake, innocent though he was. Accompanied by a surly *Herald* cameraman, she walked behind the natty Turner to Jory's hotel. They found out that Weldon Jory had left the island by helicopter, evading restraint in the town whose revitalizing he had closely supervised, the town he had certainly saved.

Bright and early on the shiny morning of May first, the official start of the tourist season, Mayor George Wallington welcomed the arrival of the only ship licensed to bring visitors, *Pride of Kinscote*. The neat little island was spotless, with gleaming cobblestones and newly erected lamps that could light the squeaky-clean paths.

Chris Yarett, Jory's assistant and who was representing him, gave an icy smile that reminded Kim of Jory himself. "Just the way Weldon wanted things. What a shame he can't be here!"

Kim smiled and accepted his excuses for bumping into her, then suddenly turned to her cameraman and said, "Tell the office I'll be back a little later. Something important may have come up."

Sandra Vance, the widow, had moved into a large apartment just above the confectionery "shoppe," of all 9places. She gestured Kim in after only a second's pause, a woman in no mood for a reporter's visit but a woman without great reserves of willpower. Otherwise she wouldn't have stayed married to the overbearing Felix Vance, whose death had taken away the core of resistance to the profitable changes in town. She was dry-eyed and incurious about the reasons for this visit.

"Somebody had to get very close to your husband in order to push him into that hole," Kim started bluntly. "You were often next to him, touching him in hopes of restraining him, and he wouldn't have been suspicious of you,"

"Do you think I killed him?" The meek-seeming Mrs. Vance

asked another question. "Can you prove it?"

"I will if you make it necessary." Kim rose to the challenge. "I hope I won't have to root around in your past life and your late husband's to prove you caused him to break his neck."

"I can't stop you." Sandra Vance got to her feet, indicating wordlessly that she wanted to see no more of Kim. "And you'll have to prove what caused me to do it all of a sudden after a number of years being married to him."

Absolutely right, but Kim decided against saying so.

Her editor said firmly that no proof was available and with the busy season under way no reporter could be spared to do any digging. The two-person writing staff had to be on tap constantly to track down and write human interest stories about visitors to Kinscote.

Zachary Turner pointed out to her that there was no indication of murder and that even trying to get information would bring the island's Trade Association in all its majesty down on his neck for doing something that might be bad for the money-spinning tourist business.

She ran into Turner that night at the band concert, an innovation which Weldon Jory had instructed others to put into effect. Turner was buying snow-like taffy and neutered fruit juices for his wife and three daughters.

"Looks like Weldon Jory was right about this town's future," he beamed after they had talked about the other matter. "From a distance he still wants everything his way, but he's been right all down the line."

Back at her office, the concert having blessedly finished with a thunderous version of *Stars and Stripes Forever*, she wrote up her account of the night's event. Tiredly, she left for a walk along the dock, which she always found soothing, but which Weldon Jory disliked because there'd been no dock in his home town.

A privately-owned yacht had come to rest. Water was reflecting the moon by cutting it into thousands of slivers when a door opened on the yacht and a man descended the gangplank which had been eased into place. His aggressive walk and firm posture made it clear that Weldon Jory had come back to see his experiment, his attempt at rebuilding his home town in a different place, and how it was working out.

At one point along the way he stopped and firmly altered the position of a hand-painted sign. Then he shrugged, knowing he could do nothing more about it. His own so-called tin-pot dictator ways had pushed him out of the home he had desperately wanted, probably for his own leisure, his own retirement.

The confectionery store, the business he had insisted on putting in place on Paget Street, was closed. Jory had demanded that all stores close early as they would do in the small town he had insistently reproduced here.

He strode into the nearest building as Kim watched. She heard him pounding up the stairs. Coming down more slowly, he carried a suitcase. Walking slightly back of him, as she had always done with her late husband, was Sandra Vance.

At the dock Jory looked around again, probably the last look he'd ever have. Sandra smiled, knowing that he had kept a promise passionately made to her. She had been maneuvered by a master-manipulator into committing the murder of his enemy and now she was leaving with her lover, with the motive for the murder.

KNIGHT'S MOVE

The phone was ringing as Wade walked into his house with the day's paper under an arm. He picked up his stride on the way to answer it, ignoring a twinge of sciatica that had probably been brought on by twenty years of nighttime stakeouts up and down Manhattan. Knowing that his chosen occupation during those active years had caused minor pains made it easier to accept them.

"Am I speaking to Detective Wade Coffey?" a male stranger asked in a depressingly high tenor voice.

"I'm retired." This time he didn't add "after twenty years" to excuse himself for not working now, today.

"Oh, I see. We don't know each other, sir. I started practicing criminal law only a few months ago."

Lucky David Kaplan, which was the name Wade was given, sweating at criminal law in crime-clotted Big Appleville. Wade had thrown down his papers all of six years back, thanks to Veronica's firm insistence that it ws time he got something out of life, and he lived comfortably now. He'd earned that privilege, earned it and then some.

"What can I do for you, counselor?"

"A client of mine wants me to ask you to visit her in detention."

"I just told you that I'm retired."

"Before you decide what to do, just let me give you my client's name...."

Wade was sitting grimly in the least comfortable chair when

Veronica came into the house and eased three festively wrapped packages onto the hall table. She was a cheery woman, bird-like and perky, who found herself startled at having to call her distracted husband's name three times before he looked up.

"It's a debt, all right," he muttered hoarsely, not going into details about what bothered him. His lips were dry. "I didn't get that debt on purpose, God knows, but there's nothing else I can do now except go."

The detention facility, no more than a whisker away from rainy Foley Square in Lower Manhattan, had changed in one way only: the current guards didn't know him. Six years of retirement had turned Wade Coffey into just a visitor who wouldn't have to remember anything about the place from the moment he left it.

Sabrina Kelvey was escorted into the visiting room after Wade had spent five minutes sitting on his side of the fine mesh screen. Over the distraction caused by a woman two chairs away and sobbing bitterly, he and the girl examined each other. Sabrina Kelvey's slate gray eyes looked stubborn, and her slim hands were folded tightly on her side of the table as if to keep herself from clawing her way out. This girl, whom he hadn't seen in years and who was no older than his always-placid daughter, would control herself until it became necessary to do battle for what she needed, what she deserved, what she wanted. A cautious fighter, this girl. No scalded virginity here.

"I asked you to come because you did some nice things for me when I was younger, and I suppose you felt I had some favors coming."

Did she see him wince? Probably. Not too much would get past her. "How do you know I helped you?"

"My foster-father told me. He was a bully, and once when he saw I was happy in summer camp he wanted to make me miserable. He looked right at me and said that the money to send me away for summer had come from the man who killed my father."

She put only the slightest emphasis on those last words. A

tactful fighter, this girl, as he'd guessed.

Wade sat quietly, his silence admitting the truth. Years ago, during a shootout after one failed drug bust, his wild bullets landed in the throat of a bystander. Lyle Kelvey, the victim, had a motherless child. No relatives wanted little Sabrina, so Wade arranged a foster home for her and sent extra money when he could spare it. Eventually, Sabrina ran away—easy to understand why, now—and he hadn't known more about her until the contact with that young lawyer, Kaplan, this morning.

"You haven't heard anything about me in years, mostly because I never needed anything that I didn't earn for myself." Sabrina Kelvey's voice faded. "Now I have to ask you for something. It isn't easier for me to do than for you to hear"

But the fighter had thought of how the other person might feel. Full of surprises, Sabrina Kelvey was.

"I'm sure you can use help to get you out of here, but your lawyer has the connections to hire private detectives who can run around and get any information he might need."

"I can't afford those extra expenses. I've had the same office-managing job for years, but now I'm a temp at the same job on half my previous salary and no pension or health plan."

"You'll have to borrow what you need. I can give you some money, but not enough. I hate to think of somebody else who depends on me financially and I can't stick me and my wife on welfare, much as I'd like to help."

"Could you investigate, yes, that's the word, investigate, and find ot who really did this thing that got me where I am now?"

"I'm retired and nobody on the force would talk to me about whatever the matter involves. A look into this on my own, and I might get in trouble clear up to the neck."

"If you can prove I'm innocent, you'll be giving me back my life."

And she didn't have to add that he owed it to her; the death of her father, the death of a bystander as caused by former Detective Wade Coffey made him a debtor. That miserable deed done without intending it so many years ago made him vulnerable, made him a genie who was forced to act whenever he was summoned. He could only thrash around in an iron net and then do what she wanted. He had brought it on himself, he deserved this penance.

"You haven't told me what y—what we're up against. What do the force and D.A.'s office think you did?"

"They think I killed a man."

He sighed inwardly. "You'd better tell me everything you know."

"Oh yes, Mr. Coffey, I heard from Sabrina Kelvey shortly before she committed the murder," Marlin Pollard said.

"He heard from her," Mrs. Pollard put in needlessly, as if her husband hadn't spoken.

Wade found himself on this soggy spring day in the emphatically middle-class Brooklyn Heights address that Sabrina had given him, planting himself on Mr. and Mrs. Pollard's hefty sofa to ask his few skimpy questions.

Pollard, a think small man, said edgily. "Sabrina Kelvey phones the office early that evening. I was there till nine, getting material ready for next day's Board meeting."

"That creature phoned and interrupted Marlin," Mrs. Pollard put in, as if her husband's words weren't clear.

"She wanted to know if Mr. Napier was in town and I insisted I couldn't talk about his whereabouts. She was angry, of course, but didn't hint as much in so many words."

"Marlin told her nothing, just as he'd been ordered," Mrs. Pollard summed up needlessly. The late Quentin Napier might have been her spouse's C.E.O. at Napier Enterprises, but Ottilie Pollard was his boss in other parts of his life.

"At about half-past eight, Sabrina Kelvey thanked me through gritted teeth, I suppose, and waited till I broke the connection. By ten o'clock that same night, Mr. Napier was dead." The secretary paused, thinking hard. "I knew her voice because she had called over the last months to speak with Mr. Napier. When he was able to talk on the phone without one of his coughing spells, he always took her calls no matter who he had to interrupt, if he was available."

"Do you think there was anything personal going on between them?"

"I doubt it. Mr. Pollard was very tired a lot of the time, and I don't think he'd have had the energy."

Wade was nodding to himself when he finally got away from the Pollards. He knew why Sabrina Kelvey had suggested his first interview be with Marlin Pollard. The man, guessing that Sabrina and his employer were doing some business about which he knew nothing, was no more sympathetic to her than the D.A.'s office. He couldn't offer the slightest evidence against her. Negative proof was no proof at all, of course, but it spurred Wade on as she certainly hoped it would.

The upper Madison Avenue area, before Ninety-Sixth Street, was a stamping ground for the rich, who lived in quarters that looked modest from the outside. A typical town house had been the local home to Quentin Napier. The tense housemaid swore that Mrs. Napier wasn't in residence. Two twenty dollar bills pried another address from her. It occurred to a momentarily bemused Wade that America's years of recession had actually doubled the going price for information from a servant over what it had been during his time on the force.

Mrs. Edith Napier was visiting with a friend no more than eight blocks away. Wade's official detective manner eased him into a large room in the other house, a room that spoke quietly of money the same way that his and Veronica's house spoke of middle-class contentment.

Mrs. Napier herself was a redhead on the right side of forty, with the attractiveness that good posture allied to wealth lend to only average features. Her tastefully dark clothes were expensive, and her soft voice was well-trained after many costly lessons.

"I don't know that I'm surprised by what happened," she told him, distracted by condolences, her thoughts far from this rumbling visitor. "Quent was an unusual man, a good man in most ways, but not—well, not with a conscience in the sense that others have."

"You mean an account of his having anything to do with Sabrina Kelvey?"

"I'm not exactly sure what I do mean," she admitted, her voice responsive while her mind searched the past. "Quentin felt that he was above the petty restrictions hampering other people. He was a success in business, and nothing else is more highly prized in this society, so the laws of normal behavior shouldn't really apply to Quentin Napier. That's how he put it."

"Did he ever give you an instance of laws that wouldn't apply to him?"

"Quite a few, but one that I remember was his saying that if he was resting at home—he got tired very easily in recent months—and it became necessary to kill a criminal intruder, he wouldn't hesitate or have any regrets and that the law wasn't going to touch him for murder."

"The guy didn't kill anybody though." Blank-faced, Wade looked up. "Weren't you home that night?"

She had been with friends, helping to plan a charity dance. "There wasn't anybody home to see that murderess arrive, nobody to hear her arguing with Quent as she must have, and no one to hear a—a pistol shot."

"Sabrina Kelvey must have been born lucky," Wade said, straight-faced, and didn't hear a contradiction.

There wasn't much time left to the moist spring afternoon, and he and Veronica spent it in the maternity wing of Mount Sinai Hospital with Robyn and his three-day-old grandson, who looked from the neck up like a fresh orange.

On the way back he left a cheery Veronica off at their home and drove out to that Greenwich Village street where the phone book had shown that Sabrina Kelvey lived. He had put off a visit to that building, where Sabrina claimed to have been in her apartment the night of the murder. It would bother him to see a shabby place where she stayed because she didn't have a father's help and Wade knew whose fault that was. He wasn't encouraged to find the building located between a pair of scruffy art galleries, and smell marijuana smoke on the street.

A preoccupied little man came out in response to Wade's ring at the janitor's buzzer, most likely a solitary drunk in whatever spare time his job left him.

"No, I don't know much about Miss Kelvey," the janitor answered slowly in response to Wade's well-honed brusquely official manner. "She's quiet, minds her own business, doesn't bother a hard-working guy if she doesn't have to."

"While you were working your fingers to the bone late last Friday night, did you happen to see her?"

"No way, man!"

"Does Miss Kelvey have any special friends here? I know you're always too busy to have any idea, but I'll talk to some people. What floor does she live on?"

The janitor led the way shakily up four flights of narrow stairs. Three neighbors on Sabrina's level who knew her exchanged greetings but had nothing to say about what had taken place. The door of the one remaining apartment opened on a young guy eccentrically dressed in a topcoat over pants, a ragged sweater, saddle shoes, and the combination peaked by a Dutch boy cap.

"I heard Miss Kelvey's name mentioned," he said, looking Wade up and down in turn. "You another detective? Might as well come in. I never talked to a detective before."

The janitor interrupted, sounding surprised. "I didn't know you was back."

"Don't worry, I won't call you for anything." He waved the janitor off and let Wade go ahead into the three-room apartment with a made-up double bed and a living room sofa.

"Nobody told me anyone else lived here," Wade began, annoyed.

"My name is Dunne, Hannibal Dunne, and I've been sharing for a year. The landlord doesn't know and my name's not on the lease. I have to *shtup* the janitor with extra mooney so he'll keep his mouth shut about me."

Wade must have looked his next question.

"We combine rents to save money, in case you can't guess. Sab had taken a bad hit at work and I'm an artist whose current contacts are worth less than zits. Every once in a while, if we're both in the mood, we might mix it up together in bed, but I've been making it for a while now with a girl in Brooklyn Heights and staying over when she can let me. I just got home from her place and I was on my way to pick up some sour cream."

Hannibal Dunne's elastic features showed surprise and dismay when he was told about the murder, like an actor in some old-time movie with every feeling on his face. Police had not seen him, and he wasn't the dude to look at newspapers or television for news or listen to anything on radio except what he most enjoyed, which was music. Wade felt as if had known Hannibal Dunne for years although the two had never met till now.

"When was this? Friday night, you say?"

"Didn't happen to see her that night, Dunne, did you?"

"She was here when I got back at about seven. I'd been working, if that makes any difference."

"How long did Sabrina Kelvey stay home?"

"I don't know, but she was still here when I left for Brooklyn Heights. That was at about five after nine."

Wade tried not to sound disappointed. "How can you be sure about the time?"

Hannibal Dunne shrugged.

"Did anybody drop in? A friend? A neighbor from a different floor, maybe/"

"Not while I was here. Sab made a phone call not long after I got back. I remember because she took the phone when I was expecting to hear from a girl friend." Still another girl? Probably. "She had told me she'd be quick and she was, but it did take up time."

He sounded aggrieved at the memory of not getting exactly what he wanted.

Wade said, "If you want to do anything for Miss Kelvey, you'll be a lot more believable as a witness in court. I can give you her lawyer's name and phone number."

He realized even while talking that Sabrina Kelvey hadn't wanted to give her friend any trouble, so she hadn't mentioned him. That was typical of her, Wade was beginning to think.

Spring rain had been reduced to annoying drizzles next morning when he and Veronica climbed into their navy blue Volare and picked up Robyn and his grandson from the hospital. He tried to make some talk with his son-in-law, a computer nerd who could only talk to non-hackers if their words were chosen carefully.

By mid-afternoon, he and a twittering Veronica left Robyn to her immediate family at the tip of the Bronx in Riverdale. Veronica was holding a hand in his right arm by the time they got home.

"I expect I'll be back before dinner," he said, letting her out of the car in Manhattan's Yorkville section. Veronica looked up alertly, her smile fading when his voice became lower. "I've got to see if I can get a favor out of a friend."

"Somebody on the Job?"

"Who else would want to do anything for me?"

"If it's a once-in-a-lifetime favor, Wade, I suppose I can talk to you about the Kelvey case," Detective Karl Heywood agreed. "But let me ask you something first."

They sat over scalding coffee and flabby doughnuts at Max's Square Diner a block from the terminally ugly precinct station house where Wade used to work and Heywood still did.

"What do you want to know, Karl?"

"Well, it's not about that case or any other, but in a way it's about all of 'em put together. Phyllis—you remember my missus—wants me to throw down my papers next year when I reach sixty-two."

"You've earned it, fella, after twenty years. Just like I have."

"I suppose so, but what I want to know is how you spend all your time."

Wade was willing to exchange one sort of information for another and told him calmly about his current life-style of theatre-going, frequent vacations, a senior center afternoon once a week to study tai-chi, and his belated attempt to earn an M.B.A. degree at his own pace from Hunter College. He made it plain that he was enjoying the new career to which retirement had given him a passport.

"My turn for information now," he said over Heywood's long jagged sigh. "I want to know what kind of a gun killed Quentin Napier."

"Gun? Oh, yeh, right. It was a .357."

"A Magnum?" Wade sat up. "Isn't that a big number for a slim girl like Sabrina Kelvey to be lugging around?"

"The facts say different. Sabrina Kelvey was identified on a show-up line by a two-bit wiseguy out of lower Manhattan as having bought one during the last week."

"Could be a mistake. There are plenty of young girls who fit Kelvey's description."

"Her prints are clear on the handle of the weapon."

"Any other fingerprints there?"

"There are smudges we can't identify, Wade. Probably hers."

"Have you got a motive for her?"

"Not yet, but a little more investigation will probably bring it out. Maybe an affair went wrong for her because Napier wouldn't ditch his wife."

"'Maybe' isn't enough."

"We don't really have to worry about a motive with the prints as good and unmistakable as those"

"When the D.A.'s guy loses this case, you can tell him that nobody had to worry, which is why it all got settled perfectly from his point of view."

Sabrina Kelvey almost ran to the chair opposite him in the familiar visiting room. She stared wide-eyed through the fine mesh between them.

"You wouldn't be here unless something new had come up."

"One thing that came up is that I heard about the gun at long last. Now you can tell me more."

"Are you talking about the gun I bought for Quent?"

"The gun that killed him. Same gun."

She looked down rather than make some protest about his rough manner. "I didn't know what killed him until now. Nobody told me, and I was too upset to ask. It seemed beside the point."

"It's not. How did you come to buy the damn thing?"

"Quent asked me to buy a gun for him on the street instead of his having to go through official channels. He always said that if the average man had to do something one way, he'd do it differently."

"What made you buy it for him?"

"Quent had been very kind to me back when I lost my job and couldn't find any footing."

Wade reminded himself that she could have come to him, but had obviously refused to ask him for anything except in this emergency. He appreciated her not saying it in so many words.

"What did Napier do for you that was such a help?"

"He hired me to work in a separate part of his office. He paid me a decent salary and never tried to make a pass. He was a good and thoughtful employer, and I'm not surprised his workers liked him very much."

"But you left him?"

"I thought that he was giving me some make-work chores to do, and my old job opened up again even if it was at half the salary. I remember I had to wait till he was feeling better and stopped breathing so hard before I could bring myself to tell him I was leaving."

"So when he asked you for a favor to buy a gun on the street, even though you weren't working for him anymore, you did it." He waited till her nod before asking, "When did you bring it to him?"

"I didn't. He asked me to mail it and I did, of course."

"Do the cops know that? They don't?" He nodded and stood. "If I can get evidence to clear you before the trial, you should be going free very soon. I think there's a good chance now that you won't be found guilty."

"Mr.—Mr. Coffey, I'm, ah, grateful for your help." It galled her to say those words, but she struggled to make every syllable clear.

"You know why I'm helping," he said roughly and walked out.

Using the cellular phone in his car he picked that awkward time to bother Sabrina's lawyer as he himself had been bothered not so long ago. That done, he called Detective Karl Heywood with a suggestion.

Except for the presence of Sabrina's prints on the gun, the prosecution's case in court was brief. Hannibal Dunne, Sabrina's lover-roommate, testified about being unable to give her an alibi, hurting her case while behaving as if he was wasting his own good time as a witness. Other testimony seemed even less useful.

The prints were the heart of the prosecution's case. An expert identified the gun as the one which had been used, and another expert identified Sabrina's prints on its handle. An old man with a criminal record linked the gun to Sabrina by swearing she had bought it from him on the street. The jury was looking grimly purposeful by the end of the prosecution's case, flawed though it was.

Dr. Herbert Greene, the first defense witness, had been Quentin Napier's physician for years. Sadly he told the Court that Napier's perpetual weariness and coughing were symptoms of the esophageal cancer which would've killed him with agonizing pain in three more months at the most.

Marlin Pollard, the dead man's longtime secretary, testified that Napier had talked about getting a gun illegally. Mr. Napier hadn't been much for channels, the loyal Pollard added, sounding proud of his late boss. The dictatorial Mrs. Pollard, in the audience, brusquely gestured him to be less emotional.

Sabrina testified, in the main, that she had mailed the gun she bought at Napier's request. Her cross-examination was surprisingly brief, the assistant D.A. sensing a verdict against him in the wind.

Detective Karl Heywood, called for the defense, testified that he had searched the dead man's home office for a second time at the defense's request. (He didn't mention who had made the request.) Behind books on the lowest shelf, where it must have fallen carelessly, Heywood had found a mailing envelope big enough to hold a .357 Magnum, and with Sabrina Kelvey's name and address in the upper left hand corner in case the envelope had to be returned in the mail.

Sabrina's lawyer, the youthful David Kaplan, cannily suggested to the jury that Mr. Napier had wanted to kill himself with a gun illegally acquired. Napier didn't care who might be accused of murder as long as his wife obtained his ample insurance money and, most likely, control of his other assets.

The prosecution tried to argue that the gun had been found far enough away from the dead man to cause anyone to question the idea of suicide. The jury seemed no more convinced than the judge. Wade Coffey, listening impatiently at first, suddenly sat up in his chair....

The judge eventually summed up with care, but he wasn't able to hide his bias in favor of the defense.

Sabrina Kelvey won the benefit of any remaining doubt in the jurors' minds, and was found not guilty.

Wade wanted to approach Marlin Pollard as soon as court was dismissed, but the autocratic Mrs. Pollard was arguing that he'd been too carried away on the witness stand. When they left the room the self-controlled but unusually indignant Pollard walked into the men's room.

Wade, following, drew his attention when the man finished. "I wonder if Quentin Napier, knowing you were loyal to his interests, offered money for you to shoot him."

"Don't say that!" Pollard looked around frantically. "I'm not going to admit anything."

"I suppose the money is in a separate bank account, and you'll be leaving your wife with your savings and starting all over again."

"Tonight," Pollard agreed hoarsely after a long look at Wade's non-judgmental features. "I'm already packed."

"Thank you for what you did this time," Sabrina said quietly when he stopped. "You hurt me awfully once, but now you gave me back everything I can still have. That makes us as even as we can ever be. It makes us quits. You'll never hear from me again."

Sabrina, who had stopped him on the way to the elevator, may have meant every word. But she was a girl who gave her confidence to selfish wasters like Hannibal Dunne, to ruthless men like the late Quentin Napier, men who used her. Similar relationships were certain to follow, some with dire consequences.

How could he doubt that she'd have to call on him again and he'd have to respond by putting his well-earned life of leisure on the garbage heap and rushing to help her? Always he had believed that a man who lives a decent life earns solid benefits as a result and receives what he has deserved. But a years-ago mistake had saddled him with an obligation which could never be discharged, from which he could never be free, which would weigh him down periodically in actuality and in memory for every day of the balance of his life.

Slowly he went home to wait until he would hear from her again.

DISTANT RELATIONS

Nord Venters was up to the eyes in trouble. He found himself with higher gambling debts than ever before, having smoothly talked his usual contact into extending credit beyojhnd the liits of good sense. That contact, furious, was now threatening to have Nord sent to his forebears in bite-sized chunks almost immediately if Nord didn't pay up.

Which is why he said blandly to his wife one summer morning, "I think I ought to go and see Aunt Miriam."

He assumed that his only other relative hadn't forgotten the relationship and forgotten Nord's name into the bargain,. Everything else seemed to have been slipping the old woman's mind. No wonder he hadn't been to see her in years.

Unlike his wife on occasion, though, Aunt Miriam wasn't likely to be critical or to ask awkward questions.

Kate nodded when he suggested she go with him and make the visit more like a family event.

By the time they got to Aunt Miriam's town and home, the daylight hours were drawing to a close. Aunt Miriam hurried out of her little house, reading glasses askew, and embraced the two blurs who turned out to be her nephew and her niece by marriage.

"We just happened to be passing," Nord said right away, looking out of the corner of his eyes to see Kate's delayed nod of agreement. "We thought we'd come over and see you. That's the least we can do."

His aunt didn't remember to offer tea or coffee to the unexpected guests a little later on. Nord settled down to make his pitch, skillfully pointing out that he and Kate needed money to—uh, start a family all their own. He didn't notice Kate's astonishment, followed by a slow nod.

"I've never asked for a loan before this," he finished was an aw shucks smile that would have stunned his fellow gamblers. "You can be sure I'll pay it back."

"You wouldn't have to, Nord," Aunt Miriam said, "If my trust fund hadn't been arranged to give me only four hundred dollars a month. My heir, meaning you, will get much more."

Under his breath, Nord cursed the memory of his late Uncle Heber, whose foresight had kept money from a mayfly like Aunt Miriam. She either smiled in regret or because she was squinting. Aunt Miriam probably hadn't changed glasses.

He glanced at Kate, silently urging her to do what he'd told her in advance.

Still gulping at the notion of having a child after twelve lonely years of marriage, Kate said enthusiastically, "I'd like to see some of Nord's baby pictures. You told me you have them."

"I suppose you want to get an idea how a child of Nord's might look," Aunt Miriam smiled. "I'm not sure where I keep them."

"In the second floor guestroom," Nord said.

Aunt Miriam led the way to the stairs. Nord, with a super-genteel remark about having to use "the facility," stepped inside the bathroom and flushed vigorously. No one was in sight when he left.

Under the cover of prolonged flushing from aunt Miriam's toilet—she hadn't remembered to fix it after all this time—Nord hurried up the first steps of the stairway. There he spread and firmly knotted a section of twine he had foresightedly brought. Affixing it on the staircase posts at the third step from the top, he saw that the strong twine was light to be made out by him, let alone his weak-sighted aunt.

Returning to the stairs after a dull half-hour, Nord walked in front of his wife and behind his aunt, which kept Kate from seeing set a palm against the small of Miriam's back and then push.

Aunt Miriam certainly made contact with the twine, but a crack in the step, a crack she had warned Nord against some years ago and never had fixed, held her in place long enough to grip the near railing. Forgetfulness alone had saved her.

As she proceeded slowly down, helped by a suddenly bustling Kate who was already being maternal, he got rid of the inefficient twine.

"I think you ought to go to bed for a while, aunt," he said, thinking quicker than ever before. "You've just had a terrible experience."

Aunt Miriam slept on the ground floor. She allowed Kate to help her into bed and fluff her pillows.

"Let's leave Aunt Miriam to get some rest," Nord said in a stage whisper. "The outside doors around here don't need to be locked and we've got a long drive ahead."

He led the way into the hall, then said in a real whisper this time, "Wait for me in the car,."

He hurried into the kitchen as soon as Kate was out of sight. He poured a glass of water over a gas jet and turned it on to work its damage, thinking he wasn't doing badly in a spur-of-the-moment plan.

He left by the kitchen door, discovering in the car that his wife had occupied the driver's seat for the trip back home. "I have a strong hunch that things are going to work out right for me after all."

He didn't look back at the house, which would before too long be destroyed with a sleeping Aunt Miriam inside.

"Jus'a minute dear," Miriam Venters said wearily. She put down the phone which started ringing just after the sound of gurgling water waked her to find that the floor was simply drenched.

"It's me, Kate," said her anxious-sounding niece by marriage. "I wanted to be sure everything's all right after what happened on the stairs."

Everything was not all right. The toilet had overflowed again, as it did when it was flushed too hard. Running to the broom closet nearby, she realized she must have absent-mindedly left a gas jet open in the kitchen. Her arms still ached from having thrown the window wide open.

Tactfully she decided against mentioning the havoc that Nord had wreaked in the washroom. "I'm all right. I'm fine. Tell Nord I'm fine, too."

"Nord will be glad to hear that when he gets back. He left the house almost as soon as we returned, wanting to bring champagne. He's talking as if our money worries are suddenly over. I don't know what he means, but he keeps insisting that he has a whole lot to celebrate."

THE WRONG MAN

Two of us had just come out of the swimming hole on the northeast end of the family farm. It happened to be a seasonable Sunday in the beginning of May. Crops had been planted, so there wouldn't be another eighteen-hour day for any of us guys until next month's harvest. It was a time to rest, to play games, to think to talk idly.

Bert, one of my older brothers, joined us on the grassy bank. Sunbeams glanced off the water behind him. We were just a few yards from the nearest neighbors' property.

"Foreigners," he complained, looking over there. "They never even show up for church on Sunday."

He sounded a little self-satisfied about that. Maybe he guessed that our new neighbors weren't sure God wanted to look at anybody who wasn't American.

I had to put in my own two cents, if only to rattle Bert's teeth a bit.

"Those people must know by now that a lot of folks are dead set against them, so you can't blame 'em for not showing themselves around more."

The "Foreigners" had bought the property the Donaldsons and their parents and grandparents had farmed for generations. A combination of hard times and bad weather and debts and interest-costs had ganged up on them. The Donaldsons had gone into the heap, as my father said grimly. Going into the heap was the worst thing anybody could do.

Bert pushed away a calf that wanted to take a chew at him.

"You always stick up for everybody, Gene."

I said something to make the claim that I was as nasty and short-sighted as anybody else from Piper's Ride to Wedwind, the county seat. Still, my brother Lloyd looked at me and said, "I don't see you mooching over there to say hello, much as you stick up for 'em. You don't really feel different from anybody else. Admit it."

Anybody who has ever had brothers will know how that conversation finished up. A dare was made and it had to be taken. A boy has to convince others he's brave as a lion, tamping down the shivers deep inside him.

It was two hours shy of supper when I started out. I was really leery by this time. Father and Mother hadn't moved a muscle to make these people feel welcome. Father sometimes looked down at his Credit Union bills and asked how those foreigners had got up enough money to buy the Donaldson place. Mother sniffed that Piper's Ride was getting to be like New York.

I'd hardly got under way, it seemed before I was at the northeast end of our property.

Inventing an excuse to be there didn't take more than another minute. There was a mulberry tree with a shabby tire hanging by a thick rope from its biggest limb. That was where we kids and the Donaldson boys used to play when we didn't want to swim or miss baseballs. The new people hadn't taken it down, although everybody knew they didn't have kids of their own.

A dust-free old tractor was inching its way along the field. I'd been too busy thinking to notice it until a shaft of setting sunlight struck its side.

I pulled back and wished I was somebody else. The tractor, halfway down the soy7bean field, stopped cold. Whoever was driving it had noticed me.

By squinting from under a raised hand, I made out strong features and wide eyes, and a handkerchief around the head. It must be a woman.

The next move was up to me. I waved a hand.

The tractor edged up closer. The woman was looking to my

right and left and past me. Did she think I had come out with a posse?

Somebody had to talk first, to show feeling, to imitate friendliness.

"I'm one of your neighbors," I called to her as she climbed down. "I'm Gene Fisher from next door."

She didn't answer until she was satisfied there wasn't anybody else with me.

"I am happy to meet." Her voice was deep, but not a bit mannish. "Do you like to have some milk?"

"Yes, I'd like that very much, ma'am, thank you."

I didn't stay scared for long, probably because their house wasn't as cluttered as ours—not as good, so to speak. The furniture I did see was very clean, very neat. I could look at a smaller image of my face in a shiny table.

The man of the house was drinking steamy tea from a mug when I came in. He was big, with a sleek beard and smoky eyes. The woman talked to him in their native language for a minute, probably letting him know what had happened outside.

Listening to them, I spoke without thinking. "Hungarian is a funny-sounding language," I said.

Somebody had told me they were from Hungary. The looked wonderingly at each other, then he remembered to be hospitable and turned to me. I asked for tea instead of milk because it looked like strong stuff. It was—and so hot it paralyzed the roof of my mouth for a while.

I found out that he was named Sergei and she was Olga. We didn't talk about anything much, all of us in different ways practicing our English. When it was time to go, I said I'd come around again. I never mentioned the tire swing that I had figured to use as an excuse for coming in the first place.

My brothers, when I told them what I'd done, spent only a few minutes calling me a liar. After that, they hung on to every word. Lloyd, the practical one, made the sensible suggestion that I shouldn't tell Dad or Mother about this caper, as he called it. Bert made me promise to tell him everything I saw or did at the Donaldson, which is how we still referred to the place, if I went back.

I didn't hesitate about dropping by again after school in the middle of the next week. Sergei and Olga seemed glad to have such company as I was able to offer. A lone child among childless adults gest plenty of fuss made over him, and I was anxious to be treated along those lines.

It turned out that Mr. and Mrs. Ketlerov—that was their last name, and don't think it didn't take me a long time to say it right—hadn't come from Hungary at all. They were Russian.

Sergei didn't talk much about his life back in Russia. One time, though, he said he had known someone over there he would like to hammer down on. His smoky eyes narrowed and his jaw grew tight. Both hard hands turned into fists. Olga stood with her hands on her hips, glaring at her husband as if she suddenly didn't like him a bit. I was so embarrassed I ran off when they started yelling at each other in Russian.

But I went back—and saw how gentle Sergei could be when he had to put a sick calf to sleep. I had gone over to say I was sorry for having left so quick last time. (Manners are the happy way of doing things, as my mother never got tired of reminding the whole family.) Olga suggested gently that AI wait with her in the kitchen until the chore was over. Given the choice, though, I decided to be where the man's work was being done.

Sergei buried the animal as quickly and simply as Father ever did and I heard him mutter a few words in his native language over the grave. It surprised me. Everybody knew that Russians aren't religious. In at least that way he must have been different from most of them.

Sergei was silent until we had walked back to the house, then he said only a few words to Olga in Russian with annoyance on his face. Olga answered him in the same way and I thought they must have been spoiling to argue again. But Olga caught herself and insisted I sample some more tea. It was high-octane stuff all right, the Ketlerovs' tea. We were soon talking together again, the three of us, but I noticed that although the two of them talked politely to me, their tone with each other had an edge.

By the middle of May I had worked up the nerve to suggest to Father and Mother that the Ketlerovs ought to be welcomed by their closest neighbors.

It was so much wasted breath. Father didn't want anything to do with people who would buy the Donaldson place and that seemed to be his last word on the subject. Mother felt, or said she felt, the Russian man ought to be kept as far as possible from my younger sister, Mavis, but wouldn't say why.

I hinted to Sergei and Olga that I thought it was a shame they didn't know more people. With twelve municipalities in the county, as well as Wedwind, it ought to have been possible for them to find another couple their age they could like. It would have been rude say that some outside sociability might keep them from slashing at each other so much of the time.

That notion went down pretty smoothly with Sergei, at any rate, so I added that they might want to attend church at Piper's Ridge on Sunday. Sergei, who seemed to have some religious feelings, was giving the idea his consideration when Olga started to snap at him in Russian. Another argument was in the works, so I made my excuses and got away quick.

Between that afternoon and Sunday, I saw Olga twice in town, once coming out of the bank and once on her way into a feed dealer's. She smiled and nodded at me, but didn't stop to talk. I supposed her grip on business was surer than Sergei's— he hardly came into town at all....

On Sunday, as it happened, the amiable Reverend Gillis didn't have to welcome the Ketlerovs from the pulpit before going into his sermon. There was no sign of them.

After church, some two dozen families crossed the road on State 107 where it turns into Commerce Street, after obeying the one dusty traffic light in town, and at the Piper Hotel the elders settled down for some worldly pleasures. The women went to the auditorium to enjoy the management's weekly slide show and the men gathered at the coffeehouse to talk about their crops, their livestock, the Production Credit Union, and their conviction that the year's results alone would determine whether or not they could continue at their vocation.

We younger kids played such games as we could, considering we were dressed in our Sunday clothes, while the older boys and girls sidled around each other and flirted.

That Sunday I found myself near the coffeehouse. My brother Bert was being snide about the Ketlerovs nto showing up for church, a possibility which I'd mentioned to him. I suggested that one of them might be sick and got another sarcasm in return.

"Excuse me, young sir."

A man with an accent that reminded me of Sergei's had approached me on the sidewalk. He was about six feet tall and wore the only gold tooth I've ever seen to this day. "I hear you speak of someone name of Ketlerov."

Bert gave me a look and went over to talk with Joylene Shapp. "I am myself Russian," the man continued, "a refugee, you may be sure. I wonder if this countryman of mine is living in the neighborhood. My own name is Yosko."

I minded my manners and asked how he did. Mr. Yosko took that as an invitation to keep talking.

"I have photograph of my friends, which I keep with me as I have not seen them in so long. Here they are."

He passed two black-and-white pictures over to me.

Sergei looked younger without his beard, but there was no mistaking those intense eyes. Olga's strong features weren't muffled by the dark curls at the sides of her face. Neither seemed especially pleased about having their pictures taken. I could understand that. I don't like it myself.

Mr. Yosko read the recognition in my eyes.

"Tell me where to find them," he said urgently, forgetting his own manners.

I wasn't sure what to do. Sergei and Olga might not like Mr Yosko, for all I knew. But he did carry their photographs around, so there must be some friendly feeling on his side. Plus which, it came to me, Olga would probably be a lot more chipper if she and Sergei were seeing somebody from their native country once in a while. (I didn't realize until much later in life that as a youngster I somehow saddled myself with an overwhelming desire to help make other people's lives come out right—a way of thinking of no use whatever to a farmer.)

"I'll tell you how to get there," I said.

I remember feeling good when the man left, even though he was in such a hurry he forgot to thank me. I guessed he was that eager to see his friends again.

I was figuring to stop over at Sergei's and Olga's eventually to let them know I'd been the one to direct Mr. Yosko to them. I'd be very modest about it, and imagined being invited to share some vodka with them for the first time, they would be so grateful to me for what I'd done. But there wasn't any time those next few days to consider the Ketlerovs. Father had decided he'd waited long enough for the wheat fields to dry after a heavy rain and we started cutting.

The old combine worked through the first and second fields. Wheat poured from the harvester to the grain truck, which Lloyd was driving because his feet reached to the floorboards. I rode with him. Bert was with Father in the combine. It didn't look like too much rain had lodged our wheat down to a point where the combine couldn't reach it, but some of it was bound to be wet after those rains and Father expected a dockage fee at the grain elevator in Wedwind.

Nevertheless, he looked grim when he saw the amount of dockage listed on the grain-elevator price ticket Mother brought back. Still, the corn was tall and beginning to tassel some weeks ahead of the normal season. Father said that if the corn and soybeans and milo behaved themselves, and cattle and hog prices weren't too bad, the season might turn out tolerable after all Mother said grimly that after the last few seasons she was almost afraid to think it was possible.

Before going to sleep the night after all the grain had been accounted for, I turned on the small radio in my room. There was a news program on the half hour, which it seemed to me the station put on to keep you from enjoying the music too much.

That was how I heard about the disappearance of a Russian named Mischa Yoskovlev.

It seemed that Mr. Yoskovlev was visiting the U.S. with a farm delegation from Russia. Three days ago he had gone off for the day in a rented car and hadn't come back. The car had been found crashed a little of U.S. 24 not far from Wedwind. There was no sign of Mr. Yoskovlev. It was possible that his body had pitched into the nearby river. Anybody with information was asked to phone the state police at a special number.

Yoskovlev? He had to be Mr. Yosko! I was so surprised and agitated I had to get up and pace the room. He had lied to me about being a refugee and about his name.

I had to let the state police know about him. But even before that, I must go over and tell Sergei and Olga what I was duty bound to do. The state police would want to talk to them, and I didn't want my new friends to be frightened because they didn't know the reason for it in advance.

I slept very badly.

Luck was on my side in the morning in that there were few chores to be done. As soon as I could get away, after lunch, I headed for the Donaldson place.

As I approached the house, I noticed the Ketlerovs' combine in the sun. It had belonged to the Donaldsons, and one of their kids had once told Bert that its air-conditioner had conked out and they couldn't afford to have it fixed. Keeping the machine in the sun was sure to make it hotter, so I went up to test the heat on the metal—maybe it hadn't been in the sun long.

I pulled up short.

Stains were coloring the sickle bar—stains that hadn't been there only a few days ago, strains of the sort I had seen many times, caused by the blood of animals. It seemed very unlikely that such stains would have got onto a combine, even as far down as the drive chains, or that the combine would have been left in the sun for any reason except to fade the stains enough so they were not unmistakable.

Vividly, I imagined what must have happened not long ago.

A man had been knocked unconscious, then carried outside and the combine brought into action. Its steamboat-like reel would pull against the sickle bar, but it wasn't stalks that were being cut this time, not stalks that were spun back against the threshing machinery inside the gigantic harvester. Later on those insides would be cleaned—by which time the machine's fresh contents could have been disposed of in nothing larger than one bloodied garbage bag.

And hadn't Sergei said there was one Russian on whom he wanted to commit violence?

I told myself not to think about any of that again.

I decided not to stay, but just as I turned away I heard the screen door of the farmhouse open. I looked and saw Olga step out onto the porch as if she was walking on air, her face lit with a radiant smile. For the first time in my recollection, Olga was happy.

The smile disappeared as soon as her eyes registered my presence—and almost in touching distance of the combine's drive chains. She actually pulled back and drew a hand over the lower half of her face, as if to keep from being recognized.

And then I heard the voice of a man inside the house. Without knowing a word of Russian, I was sure that his words would have translated into the simple question: "What's wrong?"

Olga's rushed answer was just as clear to me: "Everything is all right."

But her voice was quavering, and she hurried back as if to block the door. Why, I wondered, would she want to keep me from seeing Sergei?

But I think I knew even before the screen door was flung open from inside.

The man who stood there was not a complete stranger, and he saw from my reaction that comprehension had dawned in me, and winced. After all, I did know now why he had really come this far, why he had committed a brutal murder with a type of farm tool he must have used for years, and why he wanted the world to think he was dead. It was plain that not only did he love

Olga, but that she in turn loved him to distraction.

Looking at him, I knew the whole truth. And that included the fact that I was one of the few people in the county who had ever seen Sergei alive.

I have never run as fast in my life as I ran from there.

THE MYSTERIOUS MIRROR

Mr. Squire said disdainfully "The supernatural is a toy for children and old women. And, I'm sorry to say, for too many younger women."

"Such as myself?" Mrs. Squire asked with a smile which changed to a wince as the carriage swayed briefly from one side to another. She smiled again and gestured past the white flanks of the horses. "Look at the hotel to which we're going and tell me if you don't think that it has at least the look of a house that has *been* haunted at some time in the past."

Mr. Squire was prepared to dislike any haunted house, so-called, on sight. This one was a mansion about as long as a city block. It was set away from the street and upon the Bayou St. John. Along the front of it, which was all that Mr. Squire ever wanted to see for as long as he lived, was a handsome veranda supported by pillars the color of cigar ash, and on which some rose vines were growing with a tropical lack of discipline.

"This place looks as if Abe Lincoln—God rest his soul—had built it out of logs," Mr. Squire said irritably. "When we're at home in New York, Gertrude, you insist on the finest accommodations—and rightly so, in my opinion. When we travel by train, you insist on having an entire car to ourselves—and again I am in full accord with you as to the desirability of that. But the first time we visit New Orleans for this infernal orgy of theirs, you insist that we stay in a place like this."

"Let's inspect the lobby, at least, and then we'll decide."

"You can't tell anything from a lobby," Mr. Squire said,

snorting. "By all means, however, let us 'inspect' it or I never will hear the end of the matter. And after the 'inspection,' we can go to a sensible hotel rather than to a Phineas T. Barnum idea of a haunted house."

He allowed himself to be helped off the carriage when it came to a halt in front of the place, but he helped Gertrude down, himself. Gertrude's flowered hat had become a little rumpled during this carriage ride from the station, and she patted the thing as if it was a human being who'd been hurt. Mr. George Lombard Squire, banker and sometime-alderman from the wealthy Harlem district in New York City, touched his luxurious black handlebar mustache with a thumbnail, and sighed.

"We'll walk up the stone pathway and not soil our feet on the grass," he decided firmly. And to the coachman he said with crispness, "Leave our luggage where it is."

The lobby of this place wasn't any more business-like than the outside of it. The place was large enough, but cold and dusty. Furthermore, the calendar against one wall had been intended for use only in the year 1902, and Mr. Squire let out a truly Gargantuan snort when he saw that.

Behind his back a man's voice said softly, "Time, *monsieur*, means different things to different people."

Mr. Squire whirled around. "A calendar that is two years old means that anyone using it is not businesslike. I take it that you are the registration clerk."

"The owner, *monsieur*," the man said bowing. "Mait' Favreau at your service."

"I am George L. Squire and this is my wife. Mrs. Squire has conceived the notion of staying at your hoten for a few days during the what-do-you-call-it festival."

"The Mardi Gras, perhaps, *monsieur*?" Mait' Favreau smiled toothily. He was in his sixties, white-haired and thin. His right hand had been amputated and replaced with a wooden one that had a gleaming hook at the end of it. "If you are curious about the hand, *monsieur*, permit me to tell you that AI was wounded by a Minié ball from a Yankee cannon at Vicksburg."

"Umph," said Mr. Squire.

"As for your staying at this hotel during Mardi Gras, *monsieur* and madame, I may assure you that this place is not a hotel." Above Mrs. Squire's shocked protest, Mait' Favreau said lightly, "Not, that is, in the usual sense of that word. This was one, as you can see, the home of a truly wealthy person. It fell into disuse after the war because the master had been killed in battle. The mistress of the house simply wasted away, as it is called—"

Gertrude nodded sympathetically.

Mr. Squire asked acidly, "What has this old-wives-tale got to do with me? All that my wife and I are seeking is a place to stay for a few nights."

"I was going to say, *monsieur*, that the mistress of this house died in the part of it that is no longer inhabited," Mait' Favreau went on. "Indeed, half of the mansion is locked solidly and the windows are barred. Therefore, one can expect no spiritual unpleasantness of any type."

"Hang that spiritual nonsense!" Mr. Squire rasped. "With all due apologies to you, sir, I feel certain that I would dislike such an untidy accommodation exceedingly."

"I can assure you, *monsieur*, that the rooms are well furnished with excellent antiques." Mait' Favreau correctly interpreted the scowl on Mr. Squire's face. "There are modern improvements, too. I have had the placed wired for electric bells so that you or any guest can call for service without difficulty. I have seen to it that the mansion is piped for gas lighting."

Gertrude said, "You may recall, George, that I asked you to telegraph ahead to Mr. Favreau for a suite of rooms, and we *do* have an obligation. Besides, George, at Mardi Gras time it won't be easy to get any rooms at all anywhere in New Orleans."

"Very well, very well," Mr. Squire said irritably. "I certainly have no intention of chasing up and down this city like Mark Twain's *Tramp Abroad*."

Gertrude turned to Mait' Favreau. "We want your dankest, darkest, most romantically haunted suite of rooms."

"No!" Mr. Squire trumpeted. "Your best and brightest and warmest. Otherwise I will turn right around and take the next train back to New York City."

Gertrude gave in with a sigh. Mait' Favreau rang the electric bell for a boy to take the Squires' luggage up to Suite 201. Mr. Squire signed the registration book and made a point of being first to follow the gangling young porter upstairs and along a dark low passage. The young man's name was Darcy and he spoke with a French accent that was even heavier than Mait' Favreau's.

While Mr. Squire gave the lad a ten-cent piece "for your trouble," Gertrude was crossing from the dainty mahogany table in the living room over to a long pier-glass mirror. Womanlike, she stood staring at it and touching its borders as if it were the eighth wonder of the world.

"Do you realize how many things this beautiful mirror has seen?" she asked him in awe, still staring into it. "Perhaps the mistress of this house passed away in the mirror's view, with jewels on her body and calling out her husband's name before the end. How thrilling!"

"How childish!" Mr. Squire walked past the living room and the small dressing room, then over to the parlor. "Speaking of jewels, I hope you'll wear yours tonight. That sort of thing generally makes you happy."

"Indeed, I'll wear them." Mrs. Squire walked into the dressing room and lifted a pearl necklace and a diamond clasp out of the jewel case. She paused, then put four rings on the dressing room table. The last one was a huge opal that changed color under one's very eyes.

"My bad luck ring," she said. "Ought I to wear it, George, and tempt the fate?"

"Please yourself, my dear." Mr. Squire was looking outside past the garden wall and across the bayou to where part of a thoroughfare could be made out. "If you're going to tempt the fates, do it in a restaurant in the heart of town."

Mr. Squire paced the parlor for a while and finally went downstairs to smoke a cheroot. Rather surprisingly, he found himself talking to Darcy, the young porter. Or rather, Darcy talked to him about how to catch fish and the "science" of angling.

Mr. Squire, who couldn't possibly have cared less, was glad to be left alone by the young porter until his wife signaled downstairs with the electric bell. The signal meant, of course, that she was ready to leave for the night; but she rang the bell a number of times more than was necessary.

When Mr. Squire had traversed the dank passage and gone back to his suite, he found that Mrs. Sqire hadn't yet put on her jewelry. Furthermore, she was in a state of high agitation.

"They're gone," she said frantically. "Vanished into thin air."

"What are you telling me, Gertrude?" he demanded. "What's wrong?"

There was a chill breath of air from the window, and the gas-jets flickered. Mrs. Squire looked up in terror and had to take a deep breath before she could go on.

"I was about to put on my opal—I'm sure it was that which caused the supernatural event to happen—when I heard revelers coming past from the outside."

"Ah, yes." Mr. Squire had heard some of the noise down-stairs while Darcy had been yammering about fish, and even after the young porter had left. "Well?" he prodded. "Precisely what happened then?"

"I ran out of the dressing room to the parlor because I wanted to see the parade, the torchlight procession and all. When I came back—come here, George, and see for yourself if the supernat-ural is a child's toy."

She led him to the dressing room. The small table on which she had put down her jewels was now more bare than he remem-bered it.

"The jewels have disappeared entirely. Don't you understand that?"

"Nonsense! There's been a strong wind here, and I suppose they fell off the table."

Mr. Squire hunted over the room and he looked into the other rooms as well. He examined the floor in front of the huge pier-glass mirror, and even inspected the luggage. While he was at it, Mrs. Squire watched distractedly and made some remarks about the power of opals and the power of some ancient mirrors to take shiny objects to themselves and thereby increase their own perpetual shine.

"It was either that, or the former mistress of the house stole these jewels," Mrs. Squire said. "Every woman, even the spirit manifestation of a woman, must crave jewelry."

"Nonsense!" Mr. Squire said again, fiercely striking the electric bell. "I can attend to this, instantly."

Mait' Favreau himself arrived a couple of minutes later, his old face looking polite.

"There is a thief in this hotel," Mr. Squire said promptly. "Mrs. Squire left her jewels on this dressing table and they were taken while she was in the parlor."

"I vouch for my entire staff," Mait' Favreau said easily. "Is it possible that the jewels have been accidentally mislaid?"

"Not possible any longer," Mr. Squire said with simple dignity. "I searched in every likely place."

"Then we shall now absolve my staff," Mait' Favreau said, quietly but firmly.

It took only a little time before the staff of Mait' Favreau's mansion were in the Squires' suite and looking wide-eyed and innocent. Mait' Favreau asked the questions with more sharpness than Mr. Squire would have thought was in the man, and then let them leave the suite one by one.

The commotion attracted a pair of other guests at the hotel, Mr. and Mrs. Weaver. Mr. Weaver hailed from Georgia, and he was talking business with Mr. Squire in a very short time, while Mrs. Weaver spoke sympathetically to Mrs. Squire. The men looked up shortly afterwards when Mrs. Weaver let out a slight squeal.

"It *must* have been a ghost," Mrs. Weaver said. "No one can doubt that any more."

Mr. Squire put in, "I doubt it very much. In fact, in my

opinion it's a lot of poppycock!"

"But the door was locked," Mrs. Weaver protested. "The dressing room door was locked all the time."

Mr. Squire wheeled around to face his wife. "Is that true, Gertrude?"

"It's true, but I didn't mention it before," Mrs. Squire said. "When you left to go downstairs and wait for me, I locked the outer door and then I locked the dressing room door. I don't know why I did it, George, unless I was afraid of what might happen. And justifiably, it seems."

"Nonsense, nonsense. Somebody on the hotel staff obviously opened the outer door with a key and then walked to the dressing room door and unlocked that also."

"I'd have heard him," Mrs. Squire said stubbornly.

"There was a parade going on, my dear," Mrs. Squire reminded her.

"It was rather far away, George. Besides, the lock on that door is impossibly noisy."

Mr. Squire reached for the key and tried it in the lock. He had to agree, because the lock made a sound as if some chained presence lived inside the door. Mait' Favreau, who had been listening, winced.

"It shall be attended to," he said. "The lock will be oiled."

"Not until I ask you to oil it," Mr. Squire said peremptorily. "First of all, I want the police to see this place and everything in it. Maybe they can figure out an explanation that makes sense."

Mait' Favreau, as usual, arranged matters. The sheriff of the Parish arrived personally, a dark-complected man with thick hands. Two assistants came with him and began tapping the walls with their hands while Mr. Squire spoke.

"There are any number of cutpurses in our fair city at Mardi Gras time," Sheriff Delacroix remarked finally. "It was no doubt one of them who made off with the jewels." He excused himself for a moment and talked briefly with his men. His face had changed when he rejoined Mr. Squire and that gentleman's new acquaintance, Mr. Weaver.

"It had occurred to me," the sheriff said somberly, "that some cutpurse didn't have to lock or unlock the door because he—or she—came in by the transom above the dressing room door. The transom, as you can see, is slightly open. But it's dusty at the edges, which indicates that it hasn't been moved; and the opening is far too small for a human being to squeeze through."

Mr. Squire had been facing the table from which the jewels had been taken, but now he turned slightly to his left. The door was at an acute angle to that table and he measured the distance with his eyes, telling himself that it had been done *somehow*. The jewels could not have simply walked away.

"It occurred to me, too," Sheriff Delacroix went on, "that the cutpurse may have avoided a door at all and simply used a secret passage to enter the room, take the loot and leave. However, *monsieur*, my men have tested the walls carefully and assure me that they are solid. There is no secret passage, *monsieur*. It is, frankly, impossible for me to understand how the thief entered and left. A human thief, that is, *monsieur*."

"So you believe in this supernatural poppycock, too?"

"*Monsieur*," said the sheriff. "I prefer to think that the good lady, your wife, has been careless and has somehow mislaid the baubles. That is what I *prefer* to think, of course."

The sheriff could say nothing more that was useful, and he asked Mr. Squire to contact him in case of any new occurrences. In company with the helpers, Sheriff Delacroix then took his departure.

Mrs. Squire said in awe, "Angels of Mercy! A genuine ghost has visited us right here!"

"Nonsense!" Mr. Squire said, and wheeled savagely on Mait' Favreau. "What are you doing?"

The owner of the mansion had bent over the table and was wiping it with a handkerchief that had once been spotless. He straightened up with a sigh.

"Carelessness, all carelessness," he said, dusting his suit with the hand that had a hook. "There has been a slight scrape on the tabletop. A careless maid using her fingernail, I would assume."

Mr. Squire glanced at the scrape which looked like a half-moon but wasn't more than half an inch wide.

"You never saw it before, sir," he said. "But do you know for a fact that the 'ghost,' so-called, didn't make that scrape?"

"*Monsieur*, you may be certain—" Mait' Favreau began, then stopped. "I can give you no facts on the matter and the offending servant would deny having done the mischief," he said. "However, I will send up another scarf."

"Another what?"

"Another scarf to be put on the table and to serve as a doily," Mait' Favreau said patiently. "There has always been one on this table until your wife reported that her jewels had disappeared."

"*What?*" Mr. Squire jumped as if he'd been galvanized. "Are you implying that this ghost of ours not only steals jewels but doilies as well? My Godfrey, but he must be an interesting specimen!"

Mrs. Weaver said faintly, "One shouldn't laugh at the supernatural, Mr. Squire—if I might say so."

"Indeed you might," Mr. Squire said. "Yes indeed!" And for once he was almost genial. By all means, Favreau, put a new doily on the table. *But leave the lock as it is!*"

Mr. Squire rubbed his hands gleefully when Mait' Favreau had left, and changed the subject of conversation. He talked about dinner with the Weavers and then proposed some sightseeing about the city. "Without shopping, I hope." The Weavers agreed to join forces with the Squires for this evening.

In the lobby afterwards, Mr. Squire glanced again at Mait' Favreau instructing some of the help. He turned to his wife and said loudly:

"I can assure you of one thing, my dear. I place so little credence in this ghost of yours that I am going to lay out *all* of your jewelry on the same table tonight, the very same table, and I wager a pretty penny that it will all be there tomorrow morning."

Mrs. Squire looked shocked and the Weavers seemed appalled. But Mr. Squire was smiling. He paid gladly for the horse-and-carriage that took the foursome to Anatole's restaurant just off Bourbon Street, where they ate some of the fish that young Darcy at the hotel may have trapped in the recent past.

Of their wandering about town, Mr. Squire never retained much memory. He could recall torchlights, *papier-maché*, colors, and people dressed to illustrate mythological themes. There was a wheeled flatcar drawn by mules, and dancers and musicians in various stages of undress, and there was talk about King Comus or King Rex and the next day's parade along the three-mile route.

Mr. Squire, perhaps, saw far too little of these goings-on, for he was discussing the current state of the stock market with Mr. Weaver while looking at buildings with a banker's shrewd eye for real estate values. It is possible that, after his fashion, Mr. Squire enjoyed himself hugely.

Once returned to the suite at Mait' Favreau's mansion, Mr. Squire insisted on going through with the program that he had previously outlined. Mrs. Squire tearfully laid out her remaining jewels on the new scarf that had been put down across the dressing-room table.

Mr. Squire locked the outer door and walked through the foyer to the dressing room. He locked the dressing room door from the inside, noticing thankfully that it hadn't been oiled. Mrs. Squire was watching him from the entrance without a door that led to the rest of their suite.

"I suggest, my love, that you go to sleep," he said, checking to make sure that the huge pier-glass mirror would reflect the dressing room table. "I plan to wait for some 'ghost' who can make a knick in a wooden table."

Mrs. Squire surprised him. "Do you mean Mr. Favreau? Do you think that he stole my jewels and made a cut in the table while he was picking them up inside the doily?"

"Your explanation doesn't require any belief in the supernatural, which is a pleasant change," Mr. Squire said. "But it does substitute some questions of a different and quite puzzling nature. Why should Mr. Favreau scoop up the jewels with the aid of some mechanical device when he could use his hand and run no risk of leaving any signs of his presence? And last—but not least, my dear—how did he gain entrance to the room?"

"Oh, *fiddle*," Mrs. Squire said, shaking her head. "It's too much for me. I'm going to lie down, but I'm sure I won't get a wink of sleep all night."

Mr. Squire heard the last gas jet being extinguished a few minutes later. He sat by the other entrance to the dressing room and at the right of the pier-glass mirror. There was an unlighted cheroot in his mouth, but he didn't make any sound with it.

Not till dawn did he hear a noise in the direction of the dressing table.

He had been dozing briefly in spite of himself, and now he sat up rigidly and stared into the pier-glass. In the first faint dawn rays he could see that the new doily had been moved slightly. He could also see beyond any question that there was no human being in the room.

Mr. Squire did not panic. He remained sitting in his chair and gazing fixedly at the dressing table. There was a slithering noise. *The doily had been lifted slightly at one end.*

For the first time he could remember, Mr. Squire felt as if a bayonet was being touched to his spine. He shifted his weight in the chair, determined once and for all to charge into the dressing room and give any ghost what-for in order to keep it from ever disturbing his wife again.

Only because he leaned forward in the chair while looking into the huge pier-glass mirror did he see any sign of a human presence.

With a bellow of rage, Mr. Squire charged into the dressing room. He swerved from the table and ran directly to the door, unlocking it swiftly. There was an enormous clatter outside as he opened the door, and Mr. Squire put a hand on the collar of the fleeing miscreant.

"You ruffian!" he yelled, shaking his captive again and again.

"Please, *monsieur*, don't, *monsieur*," said the porter, young Darcy.

"I saw the reflection of one of his hands in the mirror at the gap of the transom," Mr. Squire was telling his wife for the tenth time as they rode in the carriage on the way to the railroad station. It had been a pleasant trip as far as sight-seeing was concerned, and from Mrs. Squire's point-of-view, rewarding in its shopping excursion aspects.

"Yes, dear," she said tiredly. "I know what you saw."

"The scalawag unlocked the outer door with a key he stole from Favreau. Then he got up on a stepladder and joined the ends of his fishing pole together. He straightened it with his hand, I suppose, and after that eased it through the transom. He kept one hand on it in case of any further difficulty or to prevent it from making a noise.

"He caught the hook on one end of the doily—leaving a nick in the table the first time—then snagged the other end of it. With the jewels inside the fold, he lifted it through the air and back to himself. Not difficult for a good fisherman. And by no means a *supernatural* phenomenon."

"It would have been better, perhaps, if it had been," Mrs. Squire said thoughtfully. "The supernatural offers a release from the everyday. Belief rather than knowledge. Fear and uncertainty rather than fear and pallid certainty."

"Do you mean you would have been happier if no sensible explanation had been found? But why? It makes no sense to me."

"Because there is already far too much truth in the world," said Mrs. Squire.

THE DIAMOND DINNER

Without too much mechanical exhaling of black-tinged smoke, the automobile, a shiny black Gas-au-Lec forty-five horse-power model, parked gracefully next to the wide curb. One of the back doors opened and a portly man in a fur-collared winter coat over an ice-cream suit with a straw boater to match, eased his way down past the running board to the gray sidewalk.

He moved with lighter steps than expected from such a heavy man, not even relying on his sturdy but decorative Malacca cane. The door of O'Dowd's Restaurant was opened noiselessly for him by a smiling doorman.

"Welcome, Mr. Brady," the headwaiter beamed.

At the sound of the well-known name, at least one of the diners looked up, eyes widened. A flurry of whispers started up. *It's him, all right…now we'll see something nobody will ever forget!*

The diners who were positioned to look down a long hall to the cloakroom entrance were witnesses to a memorable but not unexpected sight. Brady, having gracefully handed over his cane and hat and fur-collared coat, was seen to be wearing diamond rings on a finger of each hand as well as on his necktie pin, collar studs, cufflinks and belt buckle.

The cloakroom attendant, a small irritable man with pinched lips, stared and said, "If my helper sees your rig, Mr. Brady, he'll likely never look at anything else while he has a breath in him."

"As long as I can pay for 'em, I'll wear 'em," said the former salesman known up and down 1904 New York City as Diamond Jim. "You keep an eye on my duds while they're in here."

He walked to the dining room to greet the other members of his party, who had hurried out of the car onto wintry Twenty-Third Street and Fifth Avenue before joining him. Miss Lillian Russell, glamour queen of the musical theatre went to the cloak-room and then the retiring room to freshen herself up. She was followed by Miss Anna Held, the petite star of the Ziegfeld shows. Dan Griffen, the utility outfielder for the New York Giants baseball team, was already waiting for Brady to lead the way to their table.

There was still another guest, a man who was dressed awkwardly and who stared around him at the expensive restaurant, the serene diners, and the large smooth tables, as if he'd never before seen such wonders.

Brady said heartily, "Swell place, Austin, ain't it?"

Austin Zoland nodded. He had been introduced to the other celebrated members of Brady's party as a buyer from "some" Canadian railroad, and Brady, the ex-salesman, still wanted his firm to land an order of pressed steel to help construct safer undersides of Canadian trains. Brady had become a large stock-holder in the firm that made the best quality pressed steel and wasn't above trying to help the business along.

Walking swiftly but not clumsily, Brady led the others to that big round table in the exact center of the dining room, the table he had asked for in advance. Zoland, slender but awkward, started for the chair that Brady was easing himself into. He swerved to the facing chair only to find Lillian Russell making her ample form comfortable, and shrugged elaborately. Griffen, the sturdy baseball player, poined a thick forefinger at the only vacant chair. Zoland hurried into it, avoiding everybody else's amused eyes.

Some nearby diner whispered, "Now it stars and you won't believe what you see."

Lillian Russell was saying with regret, "I won't be able to eat much this time, Jim. I have to be on stage later tonight and food can be bad for the vocal machinery."

"I'll take care of your eats, too," Brady said cheerfully.

A pitcher of orange juice was set down in front of him. He drank slowly, never gulping, never speeding, until he had emptied the pitcher.

Zoland, staring, looked up when some diner whispered loudly, "He's off to quite a start."

"Wait, just you wait."

A second filled pitcher was carried in for Brady at the same time as a large plate of Manhattan Roast Oysters. Zoland, the only diner not used to Brady's eating habits, looked from Brady's diamond rings to the vanishing two dozen oysters and back again, as if nothing else existed in the world. He ate half an oyster himself, with difficulty.

A tureen of sizzling pepper pot soup was brought for Brady while the others, even Lillian Russell, made do with ordinary soup bowls. A dish of salmon fillets with lobster sauce and mashed potatoes was set before each of the others at table. Brady, served a triple portion and dispatching it with his usual good manners, ordered a fourth.

Austin Zoland, who had been looking stunned at the almost athletic play of Brady's ringed fingers with the knife and fork on a dish of sweetbread cutlets bordered with steamed carrots and peas, jumped to his suddenly shaky feet.

"Excuse me," he said with difficulty, a palm hovering on his thin lips. He turned and ran in zigzag toward the Gentlemen's Lounge.

Brady paused in his talk with Anna Held about her producer as well as her great and good friend Florenz Ziegfeld, and looked at Zoland's temporarily vacated chair. "A fella like that, he can't move quick or smooth," Diamond Jim remarked philosophically. "You know why? 'Cause he eats so little he ain't got enough to come or go on."

Zoland returned shakily several minutes later. He offered an apology to which nobody paidf attention. Sitting down gingerly at the edge of a chair he asked for water and drank eagerly. His eyes were studiously averted from Brady's fresh plate, but he could probably smell sizzling braised beef almost drowned in mushroom sauce and accompanied by lima beans.

At another table somebody said, "The man isn't going to survive this!"

"He'll eat tonight and live to eat another night," somebody else at that table responded.

Anna Held, who had been perfectly comfortable, excused herself and made for the Ladies' Lounge, going in the opposite direction from the one that Zoland had taken. That unfortunate, his water glass back on the table, sneezed. He did it some half a dozen times, more vigorously than he'd done anything else, and apologized abjectly each time.

A woman looking in awe at Brady, said fearfully, "He'll explode!"

At that moment an explosion of sorts came from down the hall, somebody shouting. Anna Held returned and asked if anybody knew what was happening.

Brady put a friendly but strong hand on Dan Griffen's arm just as the baseball player, with a swift look toward the kitchen, was getting to his feet. "You run around this place raisin' Old Ned and it'll take till Christmas of '05 before the rest of the eats get here."

Making himself a model for others, Brady finished this course without showing the least curiosity about what might have taken place somewhere else. He wiped his mouth gently and settled back, well satisfied.

After ten minutes, no fresh course had been set down before him or the others. He frowned.

"All kinds 'a talk is goin' on out there instead of work getting' done." He squinted at the hallway. "I see some blue uniforms near the cloakroom. Police."

He didn't care about Austin Zoland disgustingly blowing his nose in one of the restaurant's cloth napkins. His interest now was in the headwaiter, and he attracted that functionary's attention.

"They questioned me," Benvenuto whispered in response to Brady's solicitous inquiry. "The police, I mean."

"Ask the policeman in charge to come over and talk to me," Brady said. "I'm sure I can deal with him."

The headwaiter hurried off, his place taken by a slender but far-from-confident looking offer. "Sergeant—uh, Perley, my friend Dan Griffen over here, the Giants utility man, asked me to send you a pair of tickets to the first game of the next season soon as they get printed up.... You're welcome, sergeant, as welcome as a winter's day in hell. Now, when will we be able to finish our meal?"

"As soon as I straighten out what went wrong here. A Mr. Krinkle, the man in the cloakroom, got hit on the skull. I'm sorry to tell you that he's dead."

"Do you think that Benvenuto, the headwaiter, did it?"

"No, but he saw the killer leaving that cloakroom. It was the kid who worked under Mr. Krinkle, that devil's spawn. He did it!"

"I suppose you're looking for him here. If he has any sense he's sure to be out from underfoot by now."

"No, he's been taken in charge, and I'm getting' statements from other staff members."

"And that's why we're not getting service?" Brady considered. "I can't believe a criminal would wait around after a murder so he could be picked up. Bring the kid over to me and I'll let you know right away if he did it or not. You won't waste everybody's time by rousting the kid."

Lillian Russell put in, "Jim Brady can always find out what he wants from people."

The sergeant flushed and stumbled off. While waiting, Anna Held talked to Lillian about the Amberol phonograph records, which were actually more than four minutes in playing time, but had to be used on one of Mr. Edison's new machines.

A scared looking freckle-faced boy was brought over roughly by an irritable Sergeant Perley. Zoland, trying hard to breathe regularly through his nose during the first words between Brady and the boy, went into a fit of coughing, instead.

"What I'd like you to tell me, Waldo," Brady said affably, having already determined the boy's name and that he was an orphan living with three brothers in the nasty section of the city known as Five Points, "Is just where you were when that rotten thing happened."

"I ran out 'a the cloakroom before there was anythin' wrong, and I didn't see or hear any unusual noises beforehand," young Waldo Stark insisted. "Mr. Krinkle called me to come back, but he just sounded annoyed the way he usually did. I didn't go back, and that's all I know, mister. Honest."

"Where were you when you got out of the cloakroom?"

"Near the end 'a the hallway leadin' to the dining room." The boy gulped. "I wanted to watch...."

Brady, of course, understood what the boy couldn't bring himself to say. He threw back his head and laughed.

It was Lillian, with a heavenly look as if she was going to sing her well-known song, *Come Down, My Evening Star*, who put it into words. "You wanted to watch Mr. Brady eating."

"Yes, that's right, Miss. I'd heard about him, but I didn't know if what I'd heard was true."

Over Austin Zoland's deep relieved breath at not having coughed or sneezed for as much as a minute, Brady asked thoughtfully, "And what did you see me eating? What kind of foods, can you say? Come on boy, tell me what you saw me eating. Don't be backward 'bout coming forward."

"Well, there was a lot of—of orange juice and a whole catch of oysters, it looked like, all for you. There was soup, and I think I saw beef with a lot of water on it. I don't know more because that's when the blue boys—I mean, the police, came over to me."

Brady said crisply, "Well, no jury would believe that a human being could do that awful thing and look at anybody eating up a storm right afterwards, and remember what he saw, too. The real killer is somebody else who's had the sense to get away from here, and the staff can go back to work and keep the customers happy."

Perley had nodded unwillingly at the mention of a jury's likely reactions. He pushed the boy toward the back of the establishment, only releasing him at sound of a warning rumble from Brady's throat.

During the next minutes, Diamond Jim joined in the general conversation, listening courteously while Griffen predicted the winner of the next Kentucky Derby. He drank orange juice in the meantime, not realizing until a little late that no fresh pitcher had been deposited in front of him.

Sergeant Perley offered a distraction, approaching hesitantly. When he arrived, though, he wasn't apologetic.

"Mr. Brady, I think we ought to have a private talk for a few minutes."

Brady, unwilling to leave the table before dinner was finished, said cheerily, "You can come around to this side of the table and whisper. Nobody will hear a word."

He was wrong about Zoland, who had nothing else to keep him busy because he couldn't contribute any substantial comments about sports or the musical theatre.

"You know that the dead man was hit with something hard and it killed him." Perley, who had started by talking too loudly, cupped a hand at the right of his lips and spoke too softly until Brady looked up.

"What about it?" he said, as Zoland became glassy-eyed, and seemed numb.

"One of the canes that was checked in is missing and—well, I guess I'm the one who's got to tell you—it's yours."

"A cane? What makes anybody think it's mine?"

"A cane was checked in with your fur-collared coat and straw boater, and it isn't there anymore."

"Somebody could 'a put it in a different place."

"The boy, Waldo Stark, he says that Krinkle would keep all canes with coats during the winter and fall seasons."

Dan Griffen, edgy at having sat for so long, got to his feet.

"I'll go with the sergeant and look around the coat room to see if your cane isn't really there. It'll be easy enough to identify, being yours."

Lillian Russell, as absorbed by the rituals of comfortable dining as Brady himself, said encouragingly, "If the next course comes in before you get back, Dan, we'll make sure that the kitchen keeps one portion warm for you."

Perley, offering senseless encouragement to a man of influence, said, "Nobody could 'a taken the stick far from here. It'll be found in two shakes of a lamb's tail."

Brady scowled at Perley's back when the sergeant turned away. The police department's representative had blundered into the act of withholding Brady's dinner in effect, the only unforgiveable sin in Diamond Jim's book.

From the corner of an eye, Brady noticed that diners at other tables, no longer able to gawk at his prowess by the festive board, had lost interest in him for a while at least. For that much he was grateful, not liking to be looked at as if he was some kind of a freak.

Anna Held had been murmuring to Lillian, and now the latter nodded as she looked across the table. "Jim, you haven't left the table since the meal started, so not even Sergeant Perley could seriously think you did that wicked thing, no matter whose cane was used."

"'Course not," Brady agreed. Zoland nodded rapidly in further agreement, as if he thought his support mattered.

A fresh pitcher of orange juice was brought to Brady only after he started hitting a glass irritably with the side of a spoon to attract attention.

Because he was looking up impatiently, Brady noticed that Waldo Stark had approached the table hesitantly.

"Excuse me, Mr. Brady, but I heard that you're wanting to know what happened to your cane."

Brady didn't bother to correct him. "Tell me what you've heard."

"Yes, sir, that's why I came over. One of the kitchen helpers just ran back from the alley. Before he could take off his winter coat again he told everybody that there's a cane in the garbage can outside. It had been put in real quick without being hidden very good."

"And nobody was seen doing it, I bet."

Dan Griffen returned to the table with very much the same news, but not offered so breathlessly.

"Well,the police can sooner or later give it to some charity," Brady said. "Maybe a loner on the Bowery is soon gonna be traipsing' around the streets with a good Malacca cane dangling from his fist."

Griffen said, "He'd better scrape it off first, Jim. There are a lot of catsup stains on it." The ball player suddenly drew a hand across his lips in shock at the possibility he had just raised.

Which was the worst time in the world for the next course to arrive. Even the master diner came close to flinching at sight of an O'Dowd specialty, Baked Maryland Chicken enhanced by a steaming tomato casserole with cabbage. Brady kept his eyes from the fresh luscious tomato after the first look. He paused before reaching for fresh cutlery.

Once he started to eat, though, old habits came back into play. He chewed each mouthful with care and deliberation, not talking till he had swallowed and often washing down the food with a fresh dollop of his favorite beverage.

Aware of Lillian's tawny eyes suddenly narrowed on him, Brady turned. "What's on your mind?"

"Do you realize how important it is, what the boy and Dan just said?"

"Uh-huh," Brady responded only after he had sent another morsel of Maryland Chicken to its reward and washed it down. "I figured that out, too, what it means."

"So, Jim, what are you going to do?"

Brady said, "You'll see." The boy, Waldo Stark, had removed himself to stand edgily near the dining room exit, eyes riveted on Brady or Brady's stomach. Calling him over needed only a brisk gesture.

"Son, you can do somethin' for me now. Find Sergeant Perley and tell—no, ask him to come over. As a favor to me."

The chicken had been dispatched by the time Perley lumbered across the room."

"I don't know if Dan Griffen over here told you about it, but I kept a blue-and-white diamond on the ring near the bottom of my cane."

Brady didn't have to tell the sergeant, let alone his friends, that he carried one of his decorative canes on social occasions or that, if necessary, he could use it to stun and wound a thief who might come close to him.

"I'm pretty sure that Danny Boy mentioned it," the sergeant said, referring to Griffen's nickname in the newspapers and causing the player to wince at that inappropriate familiarity. "As a matter of fact, I'm sure he did. I'm having my men search up and down for it."

Brady looked almost balefully at the finished dish in front of him. The restaurant's usually efficient staff had been too busy with police questioning, he felt sure, to work. Maybe the next dish hadn't even been prepared.

He realized that Perley was taking even more time by blowing his own horn for the benefit of a few celebrities. "You can call off the search," he said. "It's not really necessary."

He saw Lillian nod in agreement.

"You'll pardon my saying so, Mr. Brady, but there's no call to be so generous."

"My diamond is gonna be found very soon now," Brady said serenely.

Lillian didn't often interrupt a gent who was talking, but she made an exception this time. "Jim, when I said that about what it meant that the cane had been found I wasn't thinking about your diamond."

"Like I told you, Lillian, I know what you were really saying and I think you're right."

She apologized, after a fashion. "You were so busy plying the knife and fork that I wasn't sure you'd caught up."

"Trust me about that." Brady turned to Perley, disregarding the puzzled stare that had lodged itself on the sergeant's features. "I think we could make a deal, you and me, Sergeant. Like a business deal. My part is that I tell you who to arrest and see that you get the proof so you can be sure to bring that person down to Centre Street before the night is over."

"Who do I put the clinkers on, Mr. Brady?"

"Not so fast, Perley! Your part of the deal is to let me and my guests finish our eats. The one who did this rotten thing won't get away in the meantime."

"I'll keep men in front and back of the place to make sure about that."

"If you do, some perfectly innocent diners who are finished with their meals won't be able to leave." Brady smiled like one friend to another. "What you can afford to do is to sit back and rest till I let you know I'm ready."

Griffen didn't let himself sound even slightly critical until the sergeant shambled away, muttering under his breath before he asked, "Did you have to fix everything so we're too upset to eat?"

"You might be upset, but not me." Brady patted his stomach affectionately. "I came here to eat and that's what this party is about. For everybody."

Lillian spoke of her biggest worry only after the broiled partridges had been served up, each on a bed of fresh moist lettuce. Then she asked, "Do you suppose I'll be able to get out of here in time for my show tonight?"

"I never thought 'a that." Brady was so startled he hesitated with fresh cutlery in hand. "Nobody wants the crowds comin' to see the show called *Hoity-Toity* without its star attraction being there."

"One 'a the star attractions, Jim." Lillian knew very well the exact degree of her professional importance.

Dan Griffen promptly changed the subject, asking about Brady's new Gas-au-Lec automobile and looking impressed when told about the forty-five horsepower, four-cylinder touring car.

"Do you mean to tell us, Jim, that a horse fancier like you are is going to ride up for the races at Saratoga in an automobile?"

"You can bet all your wampum on it." Brady nodded impressively. "It looks good."

Austin Zoland, plainly feeling he had a duty to join in, said that he wished he had enough money to afford a touring car, and meanwhile looked a little sadly at Diamond Jim Brady's gleaming cufflinks.

Brady wasn't so out of sorts that he didn't notice Perley come to the dining area in hopes of catching the great man's attention as a silent reminder of the deal between them. Brady shrugged massively, then gestured the sergeant to come closer.

Lillian said, "Jim, I sure appreciate what you're doin' for me." No one else at the table except Griffen realized that he'd be interrupting a meal, at the very least, to help her.

The waiter, appraising Brady's mood, suggested, "I can bring over your cigars with the fruit and coffee."

"Don't bring over nothing else," Brady forced a smile. My sawbones, he says I got to cut down on some things. It ain't enough that I never touch any rotgut."

Smiling no longer, he turned to one of his guests just as the sergeant finally came in earshot. "I wanted you to finish a good meal, as much of it as you could handle, so you'll know what you're missing for the rest of your life."

Instead of responding directly, Austin Zoland burst into another spasm of coughing.

"This man wanted money," Brady said as Perley planted himself back of Zoloand's chair. "He made believe he was on his way to the jake a while ago, but instead he went to the cloak-room. It must 'a looked empty, so he hurried inside. He had got his paws on my cane when Krinkle, the guy who took coats, showed himself. Zoland turned on him with the cane, which is easy for somebody to do; I've had to beat off footpads in my time. Zoland committed murder, maybe not intending to. But he did it and he'll pay for that."

Griffen said, "For a minute I thought you were going to say *I'd* used the cane like a baseball bat."

"You were at the table when it was happenin', Dan, just like me. Anyhow, Zoland hurried out to the dark alley, where he took the three hundred carat diamond off my cane from its place in the ring near the bottom. He dropped the cane into the garbage can and dropped a few things on top, but not enough."

Lilian Russell, glaring at Zoland, said, "And being outside without a winter coat and hat and gloves gave him the coughs and sneezing fits he didn't develop till he got back. Something a lot like that, Jim happened to me just before I was to audition for W. S. Gilbert's show, *H.M.S. Pinafore*. That's why I said it was important where the cane was found."

Zoland protested, "I'm not the only one in this place who left a table during a meal."

"You're the only one who came back with a diamond because he couldn't possibly have found a place to hide it."

Zoland jumped out of his chair and ran past the sergeant, who called out. It was Waldo Stark, the boy who had been watching from a distance, who brought Zoland down.

Perley and two of his men half-carried the frantic Zoland back to the table. An insect-buzz of sound promptly broke out among diners at other tables.

"Good boy," Brady said heartily to Waldo. To Lillian he said more quietly, "Next week I'll try and get Old Andy Carnegie to give that kid one of those awards he hands out to people who've done something considered as brave. Young Waldo might get pretty far if he's got five thousand green paper spondulics in his kick."

Perley had already found a jewel in Austin Zoland's wallet. "There's a rip in the wallet," he told Brady. "The man might 'a made it himself in case he was asked about it. He'd call it a decoration, like one 'a yours."

"That little trinket is mine," Zoland protested, "and it's not a real diamond."

"It's real and it's mine," Brady snapped, having looked

closely. I keep thirty sets of diamond accessories at home and I know my property when somebody sticks it under my nose."

"Can you prove it's real?" Perley asked carefully. "Otherwise I won't be able to hold him long enough for an expert to get here this late at night. That's the law, if you can't prove this is real."

Brady didn't hesitate. "I sure hope nobody ever asks me to do anything harder than that."

He stood without having to put a palm to the table. In the deepening silence, he walked lightly to a heart-shaped mirror against the northeast wall. Jewel in hand, he leaned over. Perley couldn't see what he was doing. When he straightened, the letters JBB had been carved into the mirror at the bottom.

James Buchanan Brady had proved that the diamond was real because it could be made to cut glass.

ACKNOWLEDGMENTS

"Dangerous to Know" by Morris Hershman was originally published in *Hardboiled Magazine* #39, January 2009. Copyright © 2009, 2013 by Morris Hershman.

"The Lady Confesses" by "Arnold English" was originally published in *Mike Shayne Mystery Magazine*, October 1964. Copyright © 1964 by Renown Publications; Copyright © 2013 by Morris Hershman.

"Payback Time" by Morris Hershman was originally published in *Hardboiled Magazine* #29/30, 2003. Copyright © 2003, 2013 by Morris Hershman.

"Rumble for a Blonde" by "Arnold English" was originally published in *Trapped Detective Stories Magazine*, April 1958. Copyright © 1958 by Crestwood Publications; Copyright © 2013 by Morris Hershman.

"Too Much Law" is published here for the first time. Copyright © 2013 by Morris Hershman.

"A Snare and a Delusion" by Morris Hershman was originally published in *Hardboiled Magazine* #24, 1998. Copyright © 1998, 2013 by Morris Hershman.

"Peril in Paradise" is published here for the first time. Copyright © 2013 by Morris Hershman.

"Knight's Move" is published here for the first time. Copyright © 2013 by Morris Hershman.

"Distant Relations" by Morris Hershman was originally published in *Hardboiled Magazine* #43, April 2011. Copyright © 2011, 2013 by Morris Hershman.

ABOUT THE AUTHOR

MORRIS HERSHMAN is the author of some ninety novels, including mysteries, science fiction, romances, gothics, and many others, a number of which are being published or reprinted by the Borgo Press. He lives and works in New York.

www.ingramcontent.com/pod-product-compliance
Lightning Source LLC
Chambersburg PA
CBHW022009010726

47494CB00003B/958

VICIOUS CIRCLES

Gabe Manton's been acquitted of the horrific crime of raping a fourteen-year-old girl. But although the law has washed its hands of him, others in town are convinced that he's guilty—and Gabe begins receiving harassing phone calls at all hours of the day and night. Gabe reports the threats to the authorities, but they can do nothing except suggest that he GET OUT OF TOWN. But when a sniper shoots him in the back, he decides that he has to take action himself. So he makes the girl's family an offer they can't refuse!

Eight rough-and-ready tales of urban life and crime, yanked from the pages of the pulp magazines of the 1950s!

Borgo Press Books by MORRIS HERSHMAN/LIONEL WEBB

The Blackbirder
A Knife for My Love and Further Mayhem
Rogue Slave
Sebastian
Seeing Is Deceiving: A Gail Brevard Mystery
Silent Treatment and Other Stories
Sparhawk
Stop at Nothing: Classic Crime Stories
Vicious Circles: Classic Crime Stories

VICIOUS CIRCLES

CLASSIC CRIME STORIES

MORRIS HERSHMAN

THE BORGO PRESS

MMXIII

VICIOUS CIRCLES

FIRST EDITION

Published by Wildside Press LLC

www.wildsidebooks.com

VICIOUS CIRCLES

CONTENTS

GET OUT OF TOWN

"Phone call for you, Gabe."

Manton had been bent over the water cooler. He rose, nodded, wiped his lips with a handkerchief and walked back to his desk. He was careful not to annoy any of the other workers or look twice at the pretty girl typists.

"Hello, Manton?" A quiet phone voice, the words almost whispered. "Manton the rape-artist?"

Gabriel Manton looked hurriedly around him. The other workers were busy. He turned back, staring down unseeingly at the prongs that held the receiver when the phone wasn't in use.

"You were acquitted and you think you can wait around till another fourteen-year-old girl strikes your fancy," the voice said with whispered venom. "Well, we don't want you in this town."

Manton hung up, then purposely put his hands behind his back. In time, he finished the day's work, and walked out to the gray wintry street. He stepped into a bar for a drink, heard the silver from his hands clink down to the table and took his usual night's walk home. His hands were firm by now, his steps quick.

As soon as he reached the small two-story home on the outskirts of Midvale, he had to answer the phone.

"Manton, you damn rape-artist, get out of this town: Nobody wants you here."

He hung up very quickly, doubled by sudden pain and trying to catch his breath. He looked up to see Marge watching, an apron around her waist, eyes wide with fright.

"Was it another one of the calls?"

He nodded, then caught himself. He rubbed savagely at the crow's-feet under his eyes.

"I don't know what you mean."

"Calls by a man who whispers that you have to get out of town because of—of that trial."

He said gruffly, "Don't answer the phone from now on."

Marge ran a hand hopelessly through the bright-red hair twisted in a doughnut at the back of her neck.

"Don't answer the phone, don't leave the house, don't buy the papers, don't talk to anybody. We might as well be dead. We'd both have to die, that'd make the whispering man happy. We've never hurt anybody."

Manton sank down on a chair, head in hands. "That damn girl! You don't understand how it was. I'd see her every day and she'd walk past me with her nose in the air and swish her tail, and I'd look after her and I'd wonder—Marge, I would have *wanted* to do it, do you know that?"

He smiled weakly at his reflection in the full-length mirror at his side. "The craziest ideas come to you. You think that by the time she's a full-grown woman you might be dead, you know you'll be no good to her at all, and you think that while you've got anything to give...you know, I'm a damn fool."

Marge's face was very serious. She looked down at her short nails, at the house apron she wore and at her legs made stubby by the advancing years. She flushed.

"When the girl accused you and said you had raped her, Gabe, you actually felt guilty, didn't you?"

The phone rang again. Manton hit a fist so hard against his palm that it turned red. He looked up at his wife. The two of them stared at each other as the bell jabbed at their nerves with inhuman precision. Finally Manton approached it.

"You're going to get a phone call like this once an hour, you raping bastard, *till you get out of town!*"

Another voice this time. Manton hung up on profanity.

"Don't answer the phone from now on, Marge," he repeated. "I mean it."

Marge asked slowly, "What are you going to do about this?"

"I guess in a way I deser...no, I'm just feeling guilty, like you said. I'll think of something."

Manton awoke cheerfully, though. He rubbed early morning frost from the window of his bedroom and went downstairs for the mail. He always saw the mail first. In a letter with an advertising firm's imprint, he found a block-printed message:

"Get out of town, rapist. Nobody wants you here."

He shredded it to pieces and threw them into a wastebasket. When the phone rang, Manton hesitated, his eyes on the receiver on top of the prongs. It had rung during the night, but neither he nor Marge had answered. Seven times it rang before he approached carefully and picked it up.

"Did you get the letter this morning, you raping...?"

For a moment only, he listed to the even low-voiced profanity. Words trembled on his lips. He put down the phone, his head hanging. Then he grew embarrassed, looking up suddenly as he sensed Marge's presence.

She asked heavily, "Don't you want to fight them? They've got no right in the world to pester us."

"I—if we moved out of town, we could start all over again...." He looked away, turned toward the phone. He picked it up decisively and made an appointment with his lawyer. When his phone rang again an hour later, he and Marge smiled palely at each other....

In Harley Fox's book-lined brown-paneled office Manton sat in one of the leather chairs, and crossed his legs. He had notified his office that he'd be out for the day.

"I came to see you about something that's been happening for a few days now," Manton told the lawyer. "It grows out of my case. A jury cleared me, God knows. The judge said that Gloria Keene is a dangerous liar, although she's only fourteen years old. You know about it, you defended me."

Manton talked quickly. Occasionally his voice leaped into a higher register.

Harley Fox sat stiffly back of the desk; even his clipped iron-

gray hair was stiff.

"It might be that the Keene family is doing it to you," he said when Manton had brought him up to date.

"The girl's parents? Why?"

"Their daughter's good name has been hurt. Every day you're in town, you're a living insult to their kid. You called her a liar, and a court backed you up."

Manton leaned forward, brows drawn. "But all I want to do is forget the whole nasty business!"

"*They* can't forget. If you quit town suddenly, the Keenes could always tell their friends that you must have been guilty or else you'd have stayed to face your neighbors. They'd convince a lot of people."

Manton mumbled, "Sure it's convincing."

Harley Fox, dry-washing his hands, scowled. "And don't forget that they actually believe the kid, not you. The sooner you get out of their hair the better for them all around."

"You would think they'd be glad their kid made up that story, but they'd rather the kid had been raped than told a lie." He shrugged. "I guess all can do is get out of town."

"You might have them arrested," Fox said, and Manton's eyes widened. "But it'd be hard to prove they've been pestering you and besides, it'd be as good as re-opening the whole business all over again, and you don't want that, either."

When the phone rang, Manton drew back perceptibly in his chair. Fox, noticing it, quirked a steel-gray eyebrow and, deliberately slow, answered.

The low, even profanity didn't disturb Fox's bearing at all. Manton watched him hang up. The noise of typing in the next room was suddenly very loud.

"The police can't stop it short of arrests," Fox said, "and the Keenes or friends of theirs will find other ways to keep after you, as it stands now."

Harley Fox rose and walked over to the window, then said irritably, "They never wash windows in this damned building."

Manton said weakly, "Thanks a lot, anyway, Harley. I guess

the only answer is to get out."

"The hell it is!" Fox snapped, his voice rising in volume. "Don't you want to fight back? When they curse you, curse them back. Ring them up and call them names before they do it to you, Meet old man Keene in a park for a knockdown drag-out fight, if you have to. But don't let them get away with running you out of town on account of a lying, trampy little girl."

"But you don't understand...."

He broke off as a secretary came into the room, set some papers down on the desk and, her small bottom swaying from side to side, left slowly, pausing at the door to smile at both men.

"When that girl swishes her rear," Fox said suddenly, "sometimes I dream about cornering her back of her desk and ripping the dress off her and...did you rape that girl, Manton?"

Not once during the trial had Harley Fox asked that question. Manton shook his head.

"I swear I didn't."

"Even if you were tempted," Fox said slowly, "you never touched the girl, and the Keenes haven't got any right to hurt you. Think it over and you'll see."

Manton rose awkwardly and left. He started to walk home, pleasantly surprised that he wasn't working at this time on a weekday. He walked briskly with hands in pockets.

He heard the clap! Sound as if from far away, then felt pain knifing his back. He stopped, frightened, and put up a hand to his coat. He discovered a small, jagged hole.

Staring up, he saw the small man running to a car, a small untidy looking man. He recognized Art Keene's back.

Manton turned to where a cab stood. As soon as he opened the back door, the driver folded up his newspaper and threw down his flag.

"The Midvale Hospital," Manton directed slowly. "I think I've been shot."

From a doctor he soon learned that he had sustained a flesh wound, nothing more. The bullet had nicked his right side and lodged somewhere else. He'd be able to leave, he was told, as

soon as he answered questions for a cop who was waiting.

"If I tell you I know who did it," he said, "that means I've got to prefer charges and I can't prove anything."

His face grew hard, his lips set firmly.

"No sense in shooting me," he muttered. "I didn't *do* anything."

The cop persisted, "If you'll give me the name...."

"If I left town, they might even come after me," Manton muttered. "I won't be safe unless I do something."

"*Who* might come after you?" The cop's patience was stretched thin. "All I want to know is who you think might've done this to you."

"I—I don't know."

The cop's face was red. "A little fairy, maybe."

It took a little more talking, during which Manton came close to losing his own temper. Finally he told the cop warningly:

"And I don't want my wife to know what happened, you hear?"

The bandage along the right side of his back was making him fidgety. He finally left the hospital. He had been there an hour.

Outside the cold of early evening made him walk irritably, eyes almost closed, hands deep in his pockets. His lower lip trembled in anger.

He could remember the last few days vividly, in all their aching lingering pain.

Suddenly he turned and raised a hand. A taxi passing by, stopped twenty feet down.

"Skytop Road," Manton told the driver when he reached him. "1800."

The Keenes lived at 1825.

He had no idea exactly what he would do or say when he got there, but he was angry. He sat with hands folded, staring out the window.

The cab finally pulled up in front of a small street of narrow houses, most of them two-story. Manton paid, pulled his collar around his neck and stepped out. Cold wind chilled his body

and ruffled the hairs of his mustache. His coat bellied out as he walked.

Approaching 1825, he halted suddenly, then stiffened as he walked up the wooden porch and rang the doorbell. His hands, though rooted in his pockets now, were so cold that he could feel chill at the tips of his fingers.

Gloria Keene stood in front of the door. Manton fell back almost against his will.

"Your parents in?"

"No."

They must've been delayed downtown, perhaps so that each built up an alibi, if that should be necessary later on.

"I'll wait. I want a heart-to-heart talk with them."

He turned his back on her. He blew into his gloves, stomped the porch in his efforts to keep warm. Finally he turned and knocked on the door again.

"I'll wait inside."

Gloria hesitated, then stood off to let him come in and close the door back of him. He turned.

"Do you know what your folks have been doing to me?"

Gloria looked away. She was a chubby girl with thick legs. Her face was attractive, though, and her breasts well-shaped. She wore dungarees. A shirt could be seen, on it a large button marked in red letters, I Like Elvis.

"Well, Gloria, do you know?"

She faced him finally, chin thrust out. "Yes, and I've been helping them."

"Why?"

She blurted out, "I can't stand you! I hate your guts! I can't stand you!"

Manton's fingers moved, almost as if over invisible piano keys. He clenched both hands, looked down at them.

The house was warm. From somewhere close by, steam hissed and spat.

Manton undid the top button of his coat. "I've decided not to wait around for your folks after all." He undid another button.

"You can give them a message for me, though. To start with, tell them I won't quit."

Gloria sniffed. "I bet you will! You look so jumpy, so nervous."

Manton stared at her for a very long time. His head jerked up, suddenly. Footsteps outside hesitated in front of the house, then passed by and faded down the street.

He said suddenly, "And they believe what you tell them, don't they?"

Again Gloria looked away. One of her hands fondled a button on her shirtfront.

"Isn't that true," he prodded softly....

"I told you once, didn't I?"

"You'll tell them I was here," Manton said softly. "You'll tell them we were all alone here. You'll tell them that, won't you, Gloria?"

"It—it's the truth."

She walked back a couple of steps, ran a hand nervously through her hair. A bobby pin tinkled down to the floor, rolled into a crack.

"Tell them I'm suggesting a deal. Their part of it is to stay out of my hair."

"I—I'll tell them. If that's what you want, I'll tell them every word."

She stood near a drop-leaf desk, eyes wide. Watching her, Manton was reminded of an early movie heroine talking to a villain. He smiled very wide.

"It takes two to make a bargain, Gloria. In this case, two sides. On my side, I guarantee that I'll leave you alone in the future."

"But you never—oh, all right."

"Tell them everything, Gloria. And make it as convincing as you can, to show them that I mean what I'm saying."

Hands outstretched, he walked softly toward her. He felt no elation now, no sense of an expectant thrill. It was something that had to be done now, and it faintly surprised him that he

could ever have wanted it.

Gloria screamed.

IMMORTAL ENEMY

Burton Carlin smiled as he listened to the verdict, then stood up and began putting papers quickly but carefully into an expensive leather briefcase.

At his right, the former prisoner said, "That was real close, Mr. Carlin. Did you ever think I might have actually been guilty?"

"I haven't thought about it at any time," Carlin said. He finished with his papers and reached for the gold-headed cane that lay against the flaking wooden counsel table.

"You mean you always thought I was innocent?"

Carlin adjusted the gray homburg on his head, saying while he was at it, "The way you widen your eyes and let your mouth hang open so flabbily is your best acting trick. Speaking as a criminal lawyer, though, I wouldn't advise you to employ it very often."

"All I want to know is whether you really think—"

"A lawyer is an officer of the court, and doesn't have to wonder about what the court is going to decide," Carlin said, controlling his patience with difficulty.

As he turned, he saw a couple of jurymen talking uncomfortably with each other. "Shake hands with the jury and thank them," he advised. "A friend or relative of somebody there might be serving on a jury the next time you're arrested for robbery with assault."

Carlin walked quickly through the hall, where the curious smell of sawdust-and-cheese made him want to pinch up his

nostrils. He had paused to check the angle of his homburg as reflected by a pane of glass on the outside door when a green-and-white police car roared to a stop at his left.

A uniformed policeman got out and turned a little awkwardly to look at him. "Mr. Carlin?" he asked.

"Why, yes. What can I do for you?"

"You sure fit your description," the uniformed man said with relief. "Lieutenant Symington asked me and my partner to bring you uptown, if you want to come."

"Did the lieutenant say what this is about?"

"He said you'd know."

"Yes, I see." A pain-filled memory flashed across Carlin's mind, but faded slowly, as it always did. "I'll go along with you, of course."

He sat by himself in the back of the police car, lightly flicking the heel of a shoe with the rubber tip of his gold-headed cane. He didn't glance out the window till the driver reached the East 70's, where he and his wife had lived before—what had happened to her a year ago.

"Can you give me any details about what's been going on?" Carlin asked again.

"I'm sure the Lieutenant will tell you, Mr. Carlin."

The police car stopped half a block from the apartment house where Carlin and Phillippa had lived.

"Let's go upstairs, Mr. Carlin, please," one of the uniformed men said. "It's in Apartment Three E, and the name is Backus."

Carlin walked as quickly as usual, but stiffly, without glancing to his right or left. The apartment living room was cluttered with cigarette smoke, and the rich black carpet which covered four-fifths of the floor looked as if it had been creased near the middle.

"Nice to see you, Mr. Carlin, but I'm sorry it has to be under circumstances that are the opposite of pleasant," a new voice said.

Lieutenant Symington had come in from the kitchen, his right hand extended. He wore a gray four-button double-breasted suit

and a striped button-down shirt; it was second nature for Carlin to notice the sort of clothes that other men put on themselves.

"What's happened?"

"The lady of the house is dead, Mr. Carlin, and it's the sort of case you've asked the department to keep you in touch with."

Carlin looked around him for a chair and sat down heavily, automatically hiking his trousers an inch before he did so. He ought to have guessed, he told himself, that this would be a case similar to Phillippa's. But he hadn't been expecting one, somehow. He remembered that after twenty-two years of marriage to Phillippa, he hadn't sensed at the time that her death was taking place; and though a year had passed since she'd been murdered, that single fact could still fill him with a melancholy that he was powerless to throw off.

"Mrs. Backus, like your wife, interrupted a cat burglar at work," Symington was saying. "Cat burglars are so jumpy that if you crack your knuckles when one of them is around, he's down your throat."

"The cat burglar who killed my wife didn't stop screaming till he was in the electric chair." Carlin looked up at Symington and remembered having cross-examined him once, years ago. In those days, Symington had been a low-ranking policeman who'd had no use at all for the dandified, needling lawyer.

"How did this one do it to her?" Carlin asked.

"The saw way it happened a year ago to your wife." The high-ranking police officer drew his hands together in semicircles.

"Strangled?" Carlin asked from a dry throat.

"We nailed the hood who killed Mrs. Carlin, but this kind of thing keeps happening," the police officer said.

Carlin took the time to relax his grip on the cane before asking, "Who was it? Do you know?"

"Not yet, but we will. There are neighbors who saw the killer on his way up the building, and we'll run an identification parade with known cat burglars. All we need is one identification that holds up."

Carlin wiped his forehead precisely with a monogrammed handkerchief. He knew that his eyes were narrowed, but he couldn't seem to make out anything in front of him.

"I'm glad someone saw him," Carlin said, getting to his feet. "I'll be at the station house to watch the line-up. I'm grateful to you, Lieutenant. I guess you know how I feel about this kind of human viciousness."

Burton Carlin sat on a hard chair in a big stuffy room. The people next to him were talking to each other at the sight of the seven men on stage who blinked as the glaring light flooded down over them.

"Well?" Lieutenant Symington asked. "Which one is it, folks?"

A woman's voice exploded almost in Carlin's eyes. "Third from the left. I saw him or his double climbing up the side of the building that day. I looked out of my window and there he was, moving up."

"why didn't you call an officer, lady? That's what they're around for."

"Well, I figured he was part of the maintenance crew, so I didn't give it another thought."

The man she had pointed to, a black-haired and agile looking youngster in his early twenties seemed scared but didn't say a word. He was dressed in a bright yellow suit which hurt Carlin's eyes and outraged his esthetic sense, and "young hoodlum" was stamped all over him.

Lieutenant Symington asked, "Do you other folks feel the same way?"

It took a few minutes to get them to admit the fact that they did. Symington thanked them and they filed out one by one, continuing to glance back at the stage.

Symington was finally left alone in the audience with Burton Carlin. He saidm, "I'll be right with you, sir," and called out: "Take Gruber to my office. The rest of them can go."

The man called Gruber winced as if he'd been hurt.

"His name is Tony Gruber," Symington said when the stage

was empty. "He's a known cat burglar, small and strong enough to pick up this building and drop it in the river."

"I hope you've caught the guilty one and that he burns like my wife's killer did," Carlin said. "I won't disturb you any longer, Lieutenant. Thank you for allowing me to see another one of those rats picked off."

He stepped into the men's room to get some of the freshly accumulated dust off his best suit before leaving the building. On his way out of the building, Symington halted him.

"I wonder if you'd talk to this Gruber," Symington said. "He found out what he's accused of an he says he wants to ask you something."

"All right," Carlin agreed after a long pause.

Tony Gruber sat in the visitors chair in a small office. His handsome young face didn't hold any expressions, but his body seemed to be swaying very slightly from side to side.

"You're Burton Carlin?" he began. "Okay, counselor, I want a few minutes of your time, at least. Number one: I didn't do this thing. I don't care what anybody says, I'm not guilty."

Carlin looked at a point over the young prisoner's head and said quietly, "You'll have to convince a court about that."

"I've got to convince a lawyer first," Tony Gruber said. "Now listen, Mr. Carlin. I'm not the most honest guy in the world and I never said I was. But I'm not a cat burglar any more. I used to be, but I ran into a lot of trouble that way and I'm off it. Those witnesses are crazy. I'll bet it must have happened millions of times before. People say they saw something and they're wrong. Well, those people are wrong this time."

"Get a good lawyer," Carlin said, startled by the young man's vehemence. "You'll need one."

"I'm trying to get one, right now," Tony Gruber said. "I want you to take the case."

Carlin looked at the young man for the first time since walking into the room. Tony Gruber was leaning forward in the chair, one hand stretched out and another squeezing a kneecap.

"I admit I'm only living in one room and I've got no clothes

except what I'm wearing now. But you'll get the money. I promise I'll make it up to you. This is a bum rap on me, I tell you! I never did this thing!"

"A cat burglar killed my wife last year, and I swore I'd never defend any cat burglar in court." Carlin drew a deep breath. "In this case, though, I—well, let me do a little checking around and then I'll let you know."

He heard Lieutenant Symington draw a shocked breath.

Burton Carlin sat at the defense table in the almost-empty courtroom, brushing idly at his $250 British suit. Next to him sat Tony Gruber, dressed in black. Carlin had paid for another suit out of his own pocket for the defendant to wear. He had told Gruber that as a result of his own investigation he believed in the younger man's innocence, but he didn't go into any details.

"I wish it was over," Tony Gruber said, shivering.

Each man looked at the brown paneled door through which jurors would soon be coming. Carlin remembered having once told his wife that by the time a jury reaches the so-called deliberating stage, its members have all made up their minds long before. Jury room time was spent playing cards "to make it look good," Carlin used to say, and because he himself was such a strong believer in impressions he was convinced that it was true.

He didn't realize somebody else was close to him till he heard: "I'm Hogarth of the *News-Intelligencer*, Mr. Carlin. Would you like to make any comment on the case?"

"It's been a fair trial, as far as I can see."

"Do you feel that Tony Gruber is innocent of having committed this murder?"

"Nobody *knows* what happened," Carlin said carefully, "and nobody can prove it. Therefore, a reasonable doubt exists, and any man accused of a crime is entitled to the benefit of a doubt."

"Do you feel that way even in a case where—?"

"I have no further comment," Carlin snapped.

He took off his jacket when the reporter left, and put it on a hanger which one of the bailiffs gave him. Then he sat reading the stock market reports till he realized that the court was

starting to fill up again.

His first inkling that word had gone out about a verdict having been reached came when he heard some woman in the audience saying to a friend: "I'm sure it's be over by half-past three and I'll be home before the kids get back from school."

Carlin glanced around at an old couple walking in with lunch boxes; a young couple arm-in-arm, whispering and giggling at each other while they took their seats; and a woman who swept her big hands over an outfit that looked brand new.

The sight of them convinced Carlin that a verdict would be reached before too long. He put on his jacket again and slid the clothes hanger into a drawer of the counsel table. He was checking the drape of it when the jury came in slowly. The judge followed.

Carlin and Gruber stood up briskly along with everybody else when Judge Applegate swept in and glanced at the assembled jurors.

Carlin sat down again with a swift impatient backward flick of the hand towards the spectators; clothes had rustled. With narrowed eyes he watched a slip of paper being handed up to the Court.

The clerk droned, "Do you find the defendant guilty or not guilty?"

The foreman's voice was low and Carlin so keyed up that he missed the words themselves; but not the meaning back of the heavy sighs of relief coming up from the audience. In a murder case, a not guilty verdict is nearly always popular.

Carlin stood up quickly, brushed at his homburg, gripped the gold-headed cane and took a step toward the exit.

Tony Gruber put a hand on Carlin's jacket. "I want to ask you something, Mr. Carlin."

"You want to know whether I think you're guilty or innocent," Carlin said. "Right?"

"Yes, that's right."

"I must have said so before, but I'll say it again; it's none of my business. I'm a hired fighter, and I was hired to fight for you

and show your side of the issue to a group of people. That's all. I try not to think of the rights and wrongs of it."

"But this situation is different," Tony Gruber said.

"How do you mean?"

"We're talking about a crime very much like the murder of your wife."

"I see." Carlin pursed his lips. "For a little while I had almost let myself forget that side of it."

"You were defending a known criminal with a record for burglary and who was accused of a similar murder. Do you mean to say you didn't have any idea if I did it or not? You didn't even think about it?"

"Yes, I thought about it," Carlin said finally. "I made my decision and acted in the only way that made any sense to me."

"How did you come to decide on my being innocent? You told me at first that you wanted to check up on something and that you'd let me know afterwards whether or not you would act for me. What was it? How did you *know* I was innocent?"

"That's as simple as my knowing from the start that it would almost impossible to catch the real killer with such cockeyed eyewitness testimony."

Carlin got his arm free of Tony Gruber's grip and brushed furiously at the near-crease that Gruber's fingers had made in the material. "You said you only had one suit to your name, that gruesome bright yellow thing, and I made sure you were telling the truth on that one point at least."

"What about it?"

"I could never make myself believe that an experienced cat burglar would go out on a job in an attention-catching horror like that."

ONE FOOT IN THE GRAVE

Sam Fox never seemed to realize that he'd eventually lose his temper as soon as a friendly argument began. On one subject his temper couldn't be seen through a telescope; that was modern police methods and how they differed from the ones used in Sam's day.

"I was a copy twenty years," Sam would say, pronouncing it "twunny." "And I know one thing; the tricks of the trade don't never change. But when a half-smart wrong gee comes along, you gotta think up your own tricks."

And Lieutenant Greg Palmer would shake his blond head. "Not these days," he would say heavily, as if Sam was ignorant as they come. "These days, criminal reactions can be foretold. The policeman knows exactly what to do. Psychiatrists and the science boys can tell you everything about criminals and criminal patterns."

"Patterns?" Sam asked with dangerous calm. "All the wrong gees are knittin'?"

They were walking down a windy though sun-touched street one afternoon. Sam tried his best to keep up with the lieutenant. His temper showed signs of coming out of hiding, but nothing had ever been known to ruffle Lieutenant Palmer.

"We simply do what the science boys tell us, and get our man that much quicker," he said stiffly. "That's how we handle things nowadays."

'But what good are 'science boys,' when you're up against a crook with some brains?" Sam snorted. "A lot of fatheads! They

got charts and things and they think they're hot stuff. But take my word for it, one half-smart crook can blow your whole setup to—what's goin' on over there?"

Not more than ten yards ahead, they saw a uniformed cop walking his beat. Suspicion flared in his face; he had noticed a tall, furtive sort of man carrying a light suitcase while running along the street. Sam and Lieutenant Palmer saw the cop plant himself in front of the man. He pointed down at the suitcase.

"What've you got in there?" the cop demanded, his words windblown to the watchers.

The stranger halted. "Nothing much." A gray hat perched at one side of his half-moon-shaped head. He took another step toward the black Buick on the corner, obviously waiting for him, but the cop held his ground.

"Okay if I look inside and see for myself?" the cop asked.

And then it happened. The stranger whipped out a gun. At first the cop looked surprised; no other expression crossed his face again. Two shots sounded, loud, harsh. The cop tried to get a gun out of his holster. He lurched and slowly, very slowly, fell to the sidewalk.

Lieutenant Palmer said loudly, "Halt!"

The killer started to run a zigzag course down the street to his car. Palmer ran after him a few steps, unable to shoot because the neighborhood was cram-jammed with mothers and children. The car roared away. Palmer took a futile shot at the left rear tire, then ran over to the cop. The cop writhed and tried to inhale. He made a curious sucking noise. He died. Sam, following the lieutenant, came over as quickly as he could.

"I can tell you who the killer was," he said quietly. "His name is Bejan, Mitchell Bejan. An ex-con." He said nothing more.

Palmer looked grim. "I'm going back to headquarters and put in an alarm."

Sam Fox didn't want to get sore, didn't want to lose his temper, but couldn't help staring. "Whyn't you try to follow him or something?" he demanded. "Bejan's still in the neighborhood."

Palmer passed an impatient hand over his hair. "Don't try to tell me how to run my business," he said. "The psych boys would tell you the odds are too heavy against any chase."

But he did go into a nearby candy store to phone a description. Once outside again, he motioned a cruising taxi over to the curb. "Downtown headquarters," he told the driver.

Sam watched with growing fury. Not only didn't he have the energy or authority to do the job himself, but he had to stand by and see it botched. He nearly exploded.

"Why don't you ask somebody what police work is all about?" he thundered. "I'd've had Bejan in cuffs already for hours if I'd been on the job."

"So help me Hannah," he went on, struck by the notion, "I'm going to find Bejan and bring him in myself."

Palmer, one foot on the back seat throw rug, turned his head gravely, "Try if you want to," he agreed, calm as always. "But I'll have you arrested for your own good."

"My own good?" Sam echoed. He was too stunned for a moment to tell the lieutenant off. *"Me?"*

"Nowadays, you're just an ordinary citizen," Palmer shrugged. "If you meddle in this, I may also see to it that you lose your pension money.... I phoned the morgue boys, too, just now. Stay with the body until they come."

The cab moved into the crowded street. Sam swore at everything under the sun. For one thing, it was a cold day and he didn't happen to be dressed for it. He stamped his feet and blew on his hands. The passersby stayed clear of him, not even trying to edge closer to the body. All Sam could do was think. He did.

Of one thing he felt certain, anyhow. Mitchell Bejan hadn't seen him. He'd been walking behind Palmer all the way trying to keep up with the lieutenant. Not having been seen might come in handy. That is, if Sam was going to nail Bejan himself.

And he thought he would. It hadn't been the occasion just now to tell Palmer about the last time he'd seen Mitchell Bejan. But Sam remembered the day Bejan was sentenced to serve from fifteen to twenty years in the State Penitentiary. Before

being led away, Bejan asked to have a short talk with Sam.

"I only got one thing to say to you," Bejan's eyes gleamed with hatred. "You dug up the evidence to send me upstate for this rap, Fox. When I get out I'm going to kill you for that."

Sam had never doubted Bejan would try it first chance he got. Thinking back on it now with wind running up and down his stamping feet, Sam shivered. Not just on account of the weather.

But he was sniffling and sneezing by the time the morgue boys came. Sam would gladly have risked his life against a killer's bullets because he knew the odds, but he didn't like to horse around with his health. He went straight home and called a doctor, expecting the worse. He got it.

"You have to stay in the house for at least a week," the doctor said. "And no arguments."

Sam followed newspaper reports on the case. Palmer had learned at least one thing. The dead cop's casual suspicions of Mitchell Bejan had been justified. Bejan had been fleeing the scene of a nearby holdup. The light suitcase had contained thirty thousand dollars in loot.

But Palmer learned nothing else. Those wonderful lab boys he was always talking about didn't help a bit. They chalked up a nice round goose egg for themselves this time.

But Palmer wouldn't depend on them alone. He was probably trying the usual dodges too. He'd have Bejan's hangouts watched, talk to stoolies and the like. It was a good bet, Sam thought, that the killer had been so busy hiding out as to have no time to carry out his threat and kill Sam. But when things cooled down, there'd be plenty of time.

There was nothing new a week later on Sam's first shaky afternoon walk along the windswept streets. Mitchell Bejan had disappeared. Lieutenant Palmer was stumped.

"This," Sam told himself, "Is where I show Palmer a few tricks."

Once up against the problem, though, Sam had to go about it reasonably. Bejan was the half-smart wrong gee Sam and Palmer had often talked about. He had brains enough to know

he'd be caught leaving town. But he was still at large. It stood to reason, then, that he was in a neighborhood which Palmer didn't think of as a likely one for him to hide in.

If Bejan was half-smart as Sam claimed, he'd hide in the last place in the world cops would be likely to look for him. What place was that? Sam asked himself.

One of the first things a cop learns and one of the last he forgets is to always play his hunches. No matter what they involve; no matter where they take him. That helped to explain why Sam Fox was still alive. In twenty years of police work, he had played all sorts of wild hunches. The one he had now looked like the wildest yet.

Sam knew the most unlikely place in which Bejan could hide; it'd be as near as possible to the neighborhood in which he'd killed the cop.

Sam told himself a few things. He was out of his mind; he was crazy with the heat; he was so full of birdseed it was coming out of his ears. But he spent the next three hours in weak sunshine sitting on a park near Maple and Barstow streets, talking affably to anyone who sat down near him.

Nothing happened until a bunch of kids, tired out from a game of johnny-on-a-pony, sat down on the next bench. Sam worked fast.

He managed to get the talk around to moving into different rooms. A boy of eleven came through with what he wanted. "There's a guy moved into my house a couple of days ago."

"Is that right?" Sam felt the old excitement of the chase stirring in him. But his voice was casual. "Which house is it, sonny?"

The boy pointed to a red-brick apartment building about forty feet away.

It took less than five minutes for the kids to feel perked up good as new, Sam noticed with envious eyes. The kids began a game of Salugee. Sam got up. He sauntered casually over to the apartment house the boy had pointed to, stopping in front of the bells in the vestibule. Each tenant's name was printed in a little

square above his bell. Sam could see which one belonged to the new tenant since the paper on which his name was written had not aged. The name was Martin Bowers.

Martin Bowers or Mitchell Bejan.

Crooks were all the same. This one, like the rest, used the first initials of his name when he needed an alias. Sometimes Sam didn't blame the so-called experts who thought in terms of criminal patterns.

A shadow loomed up before him. Sam turned. He found himself looking into the straight, homely face of his friend, Detective Pete Newlake.

Newlake looked at the tenants' names and drew the same conclusion Sam had. "Good job you did, Sam," he chuckled. "Palmer's going to be very much obliged."

"This Bowers may not be Bejan," Sam said, though he couldn't hope to convince Newlake. "It might be a coincidence."

"We can't find a wanted killer and somebody with the same initials turns up in the neighborhood where we'd least expect to find that killer. That's the sort of coincidence we never get in murder hunts, Sam. You know it as well as I do."

"You been on my tail all afternoon?"

"Palmer was afraid you might get in trouble," Newlake nodded; "he isn't a complete fool."

"Only enough," Sam growled. He eyed the name. "You better tell Bejan to move out of here quick. The 'criminal pattern' boys are gonna be awful sore at him."

Newlake took his arm. Together they went out to the street. Sam knew that Pete Newlake was sympathetic. Newlake was slated to be retired himself in a couple of years.

"Pete, couldn't just the two of us go up there—"

"Even if I didn't remember how Bejan swore to get you when you put him awayk," Newlake rumbled, "I still want to keep my job. I'd better phone Palmer right now."

"He's gonna be sorer than anybody else," Sam predicted with gloomy anticipation. "Bejan's hidin' out in this neighborhood is downright unethical."

They waited in silence for Lieutenant Palmer and his men. Sam was thinking deeply. Even in his active days he had never gotten used to being just a cog in the police machine. Though he knew more about ordinary cases than most, his important credits had been earned on highly unusual ones. Having done so much of Palmer's job on this case, he hoped that the lieutenant would let him see it through.

Pete Newlake, standing near him, broke the silence once. He coughed embarrassedly. "Palmer's a good guy," he said, as though he'd been reading Sam's mind. "He isn't stupid; he just never thinks about the other guy or what makes him tick."

Sam nodded. "I know."

In a quarter of an hour Palmer's men arrived and had blocked all the exits. They'd memorized detailed descriptions of Mitchell Bejan. They seemed to be loitering in the streets. They weren't.

Sam strutted over importantly to Palmer. He didn't have much hope, but he didn't intend to crawl. "Well," he said with an affable grin, "What's the next step?"

Palmer, giving orders, didn't even hear. When he did notice Sam it was with something close to a scowl on his face.

"What can I do?" Sam asked.

"Go home," Palmer told him. "I'm grateful to you, of course, and next time I won't make that kind of mistake. But I've got things to do here."

"You'll need every man you can get when you start upstairs for him and bullets are flying around your head," Sam warned. "Upstairs?" Palmer frowned. "That's the old-fashioned way. Nowadays we know that crooks can't stand being bottled up. Sooner or later they must have out. That's when we get 'em. It's what we always do nowadays in a case like this."

After a moment of stunned silence, Sam Fox discovered strength to ask one question, "You kidding?"

"We can't even be sure the right man is up there," Palmer said. "It could be somebody innocent, for all I know." Sam started to say that if Palmer had thought so he wouldn't have come out with these men. All he could do was click his teeth.

"And most important of all," Palmer went on serenely, "if one or two of my men get behind Bejan and take him in, we won't have any more killings. We never do have much trouble in these cases. I've told you that."

"But this guy knows he'll get the chair, you'll have trouble with him anyhow," Sam finally said. "You gotta hit when all the advantages are on your side, not wait till he's good and ready to kill a few more cops."

"I've managed this kind of capture before, you know," Palmer said carefully. "You can trust me to do a good job. And now, if you don't mind, I'm busy."

Sam looked as though he was going to have apoplexy. The words that trembled on his lips would have brought blushes to the cheeks of Studs Lonigan.

Instead he spoke with menacing calm. "I was standing here waiting for you and I said to myself, 'This time not even Palmer can louse things up.' But it just shows you never can tell. I was wrong. I apologize. I stand corrected; I didn't know there was a police lieutenant in captivity who'd want to catch a murderer by the honor system!" The he roared out, "You dratted numb-skull!"

Palmer walked on a few steps. Sam panted along at his side, still talking. "Bejan can look out his window and laugh himself sick at you. He's probably changed his appearance. No matter how well your boys have got his description memorized—"

This time Palmer's reserve gave way. "I've had enough of this," he said, his voice a shade higher-pitched than usual. Then he turned to Pete Newlake. "Get him out of here, will you?"

"I'll go," Sam said, "but there's just one thing." He took a crumpled five dollar bill out of his pocket and handed it to the astonished lieutenant. "This is my share to buy a wreath for the first cop Bejan kills today."

Pete Newlake hustled him out of there before the lieutenant could reply. They walked along on the next block, Sam in front, Newlake grimly behind him. Sam, seeing the astonished stares of passersby, said, "I'll go along quiet, just take your claws off

me."

After that they walked side by side. The hurt look on Sam's face brought a response from Newlake. "There's no way for me to prevent what Palmer's doing."

"You know as well as I do that young Philo Vance is on the wrong track." He quoted bitterly, "'What we always do nowadays in a case like this.' Gah!"

"That's not the point," Newlake's face twisted with agony. "I just take orders and Palmer's my superior. It's none of my business whether I think he's right or wrong."

Sam's voice hardened. "It's your business whether you like it or not. Bejan killed a cop. If your boss has his way, the street'll be full of dead cops before you can 'criminal patterns.'"

Newlake didn't reply. Dragging footsteps spoke for him.

"Look here," Sam said reasonably. "What's to prevent you from telling Palmer that you put me in a cab and ordered the driver to take me home? Then I can take care of Bejan myself and you'll have nothing to worry about, Pete; you'll be in the clear."

Apparently Newlake was so bothered he was willing to let Sam have a chance, but his first concern was for his job. "What do you mean, 'in the clear'?" he echoed, stung. "How about my future?"

Sam was gentle. "How about some guys on the next block who won't have a future unless you let me go back there?"

Newlake halted. He looked at Sam Fox, perhaps beyond him. "And what about you?"

"Well," Sam said thoughtfully. "Bejan swore to get me; he might do it at that."

"You're a good cop, Sam," Newlake said.

The two men shook hands. Sam muttered about sentimental foolishness. Cops, he grunted, ought to be sensible and know better. But his hand was tight and firm in Pete Newlake's. A long time passed before he thrust it back into his pocket.

"Better wait a few minutes, Pete, before you go back."

Sam headed for the rear entrance of the apartment building.

Luckily, he and Palmer had tussled in front of the building around the corner. The two young plainclothesmen standing alertly near this door didn't prevent him from going in.

His eyes soon got used to the half-light on the narrow staircase. He found himself trying to memorize everything he saw, and shrugged. Near the first floor the smell of potatoes on a kitchen stove assaulted his nostrils. He was breathing heavily. He gripped the bannister to keep from falling. *Age*, he thought. *A fine time for him to feel old.*

Two women came down the stairs, one talking about the trouble she was having with her mother-in-law, the other pretending to listen, but with her mind obviously on something else. A man elbowed his way past him, carrying a shopping bag. A child grinned at him, boy or girl Sam didn't know. He smiled back.

"Bowers'" apartment was on the third floor, to his left. Sam huffed his way to the top of the stairs. He halted to catch his breath. His hands moved heavily along the smooth edges of an empty coat pocket.

He had no plan. He'd just go in, try to catch "Bowers" off guard and then slug him. Old age had altered Sam's appearance considerably since the last time Bejan had seen him fifteen years ago. The odds were good that Bejan wouldn't recognize him. And the killer had probably altered his features deliberately, so that two changed men would soon be facing each other as mortal enemies.

At any rate, he'd take the breaks as he got 'em. A cop learns to improvise. Sam Fox was still a cop.

He rang the bell and waited for the inevitable sound of footsteps padding softly and cautiously to the door. From behind the door a voice asked, "Who is it?"

"I want to talk to Mitch."

A pause. The man behind the door asking himself rapid questions: What does he know? What does he want? Is this a trap? Sam could *feel* the questions being hurled at him in spite of the silence. He stood, watching the knob on the door to see

when it would turn.

"There's nobody here named Mitch," the voice said, lower now. "I don't know what you're talking about."

Sam always tried to win a discussion by shouting down the opposition. "You want me to yell it out here in the hall?" he roared. "Lemme in, for pete's sake, and stop this futzin' around."

A pause. The lock snapped, the knob moved, the door inched open.

Fortunately, Sam remembered that half-moon shaped head or he would have been fooled. Mitchell Bejan had thoroughly changed his appearance. The hair was now raven black. Invisible lenses made the color of his eyes blue. A pencil-thin mustache did its share in the transformation. The very shape of his head, though recognizable, was subtly different. Sam hoped that nature had changed him as much as disguise had changed Bejan.

"I want to talk to you," Sam said urgently.

A strange look passed over Bejan on seeing Sam Fox, and his eyes narrowed dangerously. "Come on in," he said, holding the door wide open.

Sam didn't even ask himself whether Bejan had recognized him as he walked in and looked around. It was an uncared-for apartment and whatever dust hadn't caked on the closed windows hovered around Sam's nostrils. Street noises, in spite of the windows, came through only slightly muffled.

Sam told himself to be quick. Bejan was looking at him so fiercely that Sam could have sworn—he cleared his throat. "You don't know me but we've got plenty of mutual friends," he said. "I'd heard on the grapevine where you were holed up. I was just passing by when I seen cops standing in front of the building. I figured somebody better tell you if you didn't know."

Bejan threw him a sharp look, then strode to the window. Careful to keep from sight of the men below, Bejan looked out. The killer turned back to Sam Fox. That altered face was reflected harshly by light coming through the window.

"Who gave 'em the office?" he demanded.

"You got me," Sam shrugged. His eyes swiftly roamed the apartment. He'd better find something to use for a club.

"Well, I'm not gonna wait for 'em to come up here," Bejan said. "They'll get me, but I want to take a few of 'em with me first."

He went slowly to a bureau drawer from which he took a hefty .45. In Mitchell Bejan's hand, it looked stylish.

The moment Bejan's back was turned, Sam's eyes settled on what he needed. A small but heavy-looking statuette of Mercury stood at his right on the mantelpiece. But he didn't move. Right now he couldn't afford to go near it.

Bejan came toward him again and Sam had to fight the temptation to run. Bejan stopped three feet in front of him.

"I'm getting out of here in a minute," he said, raw hatred in those glass-blue eyes. "But first I want to settle up with you, Fox."

Sam didn't say a word.

'We've both changed," Bejan said, "changed a lot. I wouldn't have known you if I hadn't heard you fly off the handle when you wanted to get in here. The way you always fly off the handle."

"I—I don't know what you're talkin' about," Sam blustered. Edging nearer to the statuette he played for time. "I come up here strictly single-o to do you a favor. This is the kind of reception I get?"

"If you don't like that," Bejan smiled cruelly, "What'll you think of this?"

And he raised his gun.

Sam whirled to pick up the statuette and tried to swing it like a blackjack. The gun exploded in Bejan's hand.

For a moment Sam felt nothing. The force of his swing carried him to the floor. He gasped at sudden searing pain in his stomach—bullet-pain. Sam knew he'd been hit and hit bad.

He saw the contemptuous look on Bejan's face. The killer snarled, "This'll make two cops."

Sam rolled over. Desperately he hoped that the pain would be better if he lay on his stomach. He heard shots, explosion after

explosion. Bejan intended to do a good job this time.

But he didn't feel any new pain, only what he'd felt before. That bothered him; if there'd been any new pain he would have known, all right.

Something heavy fell to the floor beside him. Sam was about to turn when he heard two men come running into the room. Their pounding footsteps came to a sharp halt. Sam nearly sat up straight on hearing the voice of Greg Palmer.

"Are you sure that's Bejan?" Palmer was asking doubtfully. "I'd never have recognized him."

"Has to be," Pete Newlake said briefly. Then, "Here's Sam."

"Phone a doctor," Palmer ordered. He knelt down beside Sam. "You'll be all right," he said lips white with suppressed anger at the killer.

"I—I tried to blackjack him." A tired smile formed on Sam Fox's lips. "That's what we always do in such a case, nowadays."

And he passed out....

The smell of antiseptic not only revived him but keynoted his senses with the word "hospital" even before Sam's eyes opened on a bare room with whitewashed walls. A nurse stood over him. She told him he'd be all right from now on if he did what he was told. He could begin by laying still.

A doctor came to see him, and Sam was kept busy for a while. When doctor and nurse had left he started swearing at himself. He'd botched things up good and proper. It'd serve him right if he lost his pension money now.

He went off into a deep, natural sleep and when he came to, tried to push himself up out of bed only to fall back at the sudden pain in his stomach.

The nurse came in again. A man walked behind her. The newcomer's nose was wrinkled up at the smell. He looked around the room before locating Sam and taking a chair by his bed. It was Lieutenant Palmer.

"Newlake told me he'd let you go up to Bejan's apartment and told me why," Palmer said, answering Sam's question before he asked it.

Sam thought that over, "Did you—do anything to Pete?" he asked cautiously.

Palmer might have seen only that Pete had disobeyed orders and not bothered to look beyond, might never guess that there would anything to find.

"Pete's a good cop," Sam added.

"I just gave him a dressing down he'll never forget and that's all," Palmer said with a curious look in his eyes. "I thought this was a special case."

Sam turned his head to look earnestly at the young man at his bedside. He got the impression that Palmer wanted to apologize, perhaps to apologize in a special way.

After a while Palmer cleared his throat.

"I came here," he said, "to ask you to help me out on something important to do with the job. I—" he coughed—"I have a case that's bothering me and I thought that if I told you what it was all about, you might tell me what you'd have done in my place."

So that was how he wanted it, Sam told himself, feeling a warm glow inside him as he listened to the details. With an occasional push in the right direction, he realized, Palmer could not only go a long way, but eventually become a better cop than Sam had ever been.

And Sam Fox was glad.

ONE HUSBAND
TOO MANY!

Ken Lodge parked his car in the garage and stepped out. He gave a satisfied little look at the two-story house, then glanced at the porch.

For once, Audrey wasn't waiting. He frowned, pursed his lips. Reminded of something else, he glanced up at the nearest home, waved at his neighbor.

The evening air smelled of bird droppings. The full moon looked like butter smeared on velvet, and patches of light gave the bunched grass a sandy look.

Ken opened his door. His nose wrinkled at the sound of a man's voice in the kitchen. He stiffened and walked in.

"Hello, Audrey. I don't believe I know this gentleman."

"You will." The newcomer gave an unhealthy smile.

The man was gaunt, very thin. His eyes darted round restlessly. Hands moved up and down like pistons. His blond hair tumbled over his forehead, not loosely, but in a slide at one side of his scalp that moved as his hair came to.

"And how you will!" he added fervently.

The room was quiet. Air rustled through the curtains. An ashtray on the windowsill pirouetted, then dropped to the linoleum flooring. On the table, a paper bag sheathed a bottle. A patch of liquid appeared on the bag. Audrey swiped a hand at it.

"You'll know soon enough." Audrey gestured helplessly. She ran a hand down over her compact body and then over her black hair. "This is Jake Fair."

Breath keened in the man's nostrils. "That mean anything?"

All his sentences had been short. Talking seemed like hard work to the man.

Ken glanced again at Audrey, sitting at the table, hands folded.

"I'm not used to this kind of theatrical show in my home," he said, almost primly. "You know that, Audrey."

Jake Fair smiled after a fashion. "Try an' remember the name. I'll bet it comes back to you. Audrey must 'a told you about me."

Audrey put out a hand, so close it almost touched Ken's belly button. "Don't you remember? I told you a dozen times, before we got married.... My Jake!"

Ken could feel muscles jumping at the backs of his hands. The words he wanted to say must have hung sharp and stinging in the air.

"All right, I remember now." Angry tufts of hair, suddenly pointed up at the sides of his head, giving him the look of a devil. "You've got some tall explaining to do."

Jake Fair poured himself a glass of milk and drank it down noisily. Audrey watched the milk leaving the glass, almost as if she was hypnotized.

"I didn't know," she began. "I had no idea, Ken."

"Maybe not," Ken Lodge agreed. "Maybe you knew all the time and you wanted a husband with a good job and security."

Ken was on Civil Service, as a Welfare Supervisor. He was proud of his job and his small home.

"There ain't much to tell." Jake Fair wiped the milky mustache on his upper lip. "I was in the Army. Forty-four or so, the Russians got hold of me. I was wearing a German uniform at the time as part 'a my job. They figured I was German."

Ken paused, thumb and forefinger at his stomach, then folded his hands. "They just let you go recently?"

"Yeh. The Russkies never like to let go of what they're holdin'. They never told a Red Cross unit about me. Finally, they let me go along with some Germans. I went to the American consul in Bonn, Germany, and spit out my guts."

Ken had read in the newspaper about a recent return of prisoners, among whom an American was said to be included. He had talked about it to a couple of friends.

"I told the War Department they shouldn't let my wife know I was okay. Wanted to surprise her. I sure did. She kind 'a belted me one, too."

"You're legally dead." It sounded foolish. Ken shrugged. "What'll we do?"

"I dunno what you do." Jake Fair wiped his lips with the crook of an arm. "I want my wife. I had a rough time the last few years, and I'm gonna make up for it, or bust tryin'."

Ken smiled thinly in Audrey's direction. "I hope the two of you will be very happy."

Audrey bit her lip.

Ken said, "I suppose you'd rather stay? I don't blame you. I'm better off than he's ever likely to be."

He was relieved. For a moment, he had seen visions of searing newspaper stories.

"It's not easy, Fair, and you know it." Ken showed a hand, with middle joints of the fingers crooking like claws.

Fair grinned at Audrey. "It was easy before, wasn't it, honey? A half-hour ago. Remember/"

Audrey nodded dumbly, then colored. Her hands went down to her dress, disheveled and with dozens of folds, as if she'd been lying in it.

Ken colored. For the sake of peace, he beat back the first angry words that came to his lips.

Audrey pawed gently at his sleeve tip. "I couldn't help it, Ken. It was practically rape."

"We can talk about it tomorrow." He added reasonably, turning to Fair. "We can talk about all of it tomorrow. I'm too damned tired."

"What happens tonight?" Jake Fair said quickly, inclining his head to Audrey. "She stays, I stay. She's never been married to you."

Audrey threw back her dark head and gave a laugh that

sounded desperate. "We'll have dinner first, Ken. For...for old time's sake."

She bustled around, preparing the meal. Ken took her place at table. Jake Fair slicked a hand through his blond hair, a dirt-streaked hand with more exclamation points of dirt under the fingernails.

Once Audrey said, a little foolishly, "Thursday night, you know."

On Thursday night, Audrey prepared fish for supper instead of meat. One of the rituals that she and Ken lived by.

Over dinner, Ken said, "You'll stay here tonight, Fair. In the guest room."

Audrey smiled uncertainly at Ken, then looked away and bit her lip.

When Fair tried to be pleasant, the effect was jarring. "Welfare worker, huh?" he asked. "A guy like you must pull down a couple hundred a week."

Ken left for the living room. The sound of cutlery followed him. He sat down, his eyes steely, and tried to read through a newspaper. The rustle of soft footsteps told him Audrey was in the room.

"Do you want to go away with him?" Ken asked. "You can, you know."

Audrey said quickly, "I've gotten used to this."

She meant the stability, the certainty. Ken almost laughed.

"You don't want a scandal. I don't want to go." Audrey was grim, but in some control of herself. "I'll find a way."

"How/"

"I'm not sure yet." A tiny pulse hammered in the wall of her throat. "Not sure."

They were soon joined by Fair. The man picked up a news-paper, pawed over it and set it down untidily, torn in places.

It was grotesque. Ken turned on the television set, but walked around the room muttering instead. He could feel Fair's hard eyes on him.

Audrey went into the kitchen to wash the dishes. When she

returned, Fair looked up at her smiling.

"Kid, I'm gonna go into business and settle down. You'll see. A gas station or something. I been thinking about getting me a G.I. loan."

He was tyring to get a smile out of her, some sign of approval. Audrey couldn't keep the froen look out of her face.

"Tomorrow," Fair added, "you and me are gettin' outta here. Right kid?"

Audrey smiled weakly.

Fair said, "We get some shut-eye now. Where do we sleep, kid?"

Ken said something angry.

Fair growled, "A man's got a perfect right to sleep with his wife."

Ken's voice was flat, almost toneless. "I want to be decent about this, but you're pushing too hard."

Fair accented every word by hitting his palms together. "I—want—my—wife! Don't give me trouble, buddy, or I'll beat your brains out."

Audrey said hurriedly, "Let him do what he wants, Ken. It won't be long."

Fair laughed. "That's right, baby. We'll be out by tomorrow."

He rose. Playfully, he pulled her hair. Audrey fought back tears.

The two of them walked toward the stairs. Audrey glanced back at Ken's stony face. At the top of the stairs, Fair looked down and gave a contemptuous little smile.

"Tough luck, fella, but there's only enough woman for one of us, you know what I mean?"

It didn't seem to strike him that Audrey was nothing short of paralyzed by the prospects. She walked slowly, eyes downcast, lips tight together.

Ken Lodge stayed below. The sound of Fair's raucous laughter in one of the bedrooms came through vividly.

He stood with fists clenched, his eyes thin slits. Several times he shook his head as if to clear it.

"Sure, I'm strong enough to do it again, baby. I'll show you."

He faced the window, seeing his straight, handsome figure reflected in the glass, then turned. All the doors and windows were locked. As a rule, he enjoyed checking tidily, and often did it twice.

He bit his lower lip continually as he walked, sometimes wincing and putting on pressure until tears formed at the corners of his eyelids.

A little wistfully, he looked out at the neighbors' places, uniform with his own. In one window, he could see the back-wash of a television set in a darkened room.

He walked the steps noisily and finally into the room he had always shared with Audrey. Down the hall, the sound of a creaking mattress.

He bit his knuckles painfully to set up a counter-pressure.

It occurred to him out of the clear sky that he had treated Audrey pretty badly sometimes. He would have liked to make it up to her. Audrey was a loyal wife.

The sight of black headlines and fuzzy pictures in the newspapers was so clear that he forced himself to listen to the sound of his own breathing to take his mind off it.

His pajamas had been placed under the pillows, as always, but he didn't feel like putting them on. He regretted it later on, in spite of the spring-like weather, because his legs were unusually cold. The big double bed, held down entirely by himself, seemed uncomfortable.

He must have slept. It was much later when he pushed himself into a sitting position. His body was stiff. Sitting up so that his feet touched the floor, he felt his toes tingle.

By craning his neck, he could see a street lamp in the distance. Its light hurt his eyes. The night was blacker than before. A foul taste was lodged in his mouth.

Except for his own motions, the silence was so complete that he was tempted to see if Audrey and Fair were in the guest room instead of having left in the middle of the night.

Footsteps sounded in the hall, slow relaxed footsteps. A

whistled tune bounced hard against Ken's ears.

The door opened. A sudden flash made him cover his eyes. The room was lighted. When he could see again, Audrey stood in front of him.

"Well, Ken, been sleeping comfortably?"

She was cheerful, smiling while she asked the silly question. Her bathrobe was primly closed around her. She wore no slippers; she detested them, except for scuffies when she went to take a shower.

Ken looked past her, at the door, straining his eyes.

Audrey smiled. "Don't worry."

He blinked hard at her. Finally, conscious of his position, put a bathrobe around him.

"You shouldn't sleep in shorts," Audrey said, almost absently. "I've told you that before."

"For God's sake!" He gestured wildly. "What about him?"

"Wild boy, you mean? He won't be coming after you."

"At least he's a heavy sleeper. That's something." He added maliciously, "Probably tuckered out from the night's work."

"Even if he is, it makes no difference. He's dead."

Ken stared, then said slowly, "Are you sure? Did you take his pulse or...or something?"

"I'm sure."

He sank back on the bed. "It's a miracle. Like the answer to a prayer. I've never been what you'd call religious, but a thing like this makes you wonder."

Audrey laughed grimly, but Ken couldn't stop talking.

"Imagine it!" he marveled. "All of a sudden, the man's heart gives out. I feel sorry for him, of course, but you've got to admit, Audrey, it's Providence."

"You don't understand,." She added calmly, as if expecting congratulations. "He's dead because I stuck a knife in him."

"God!" He was rigid for a moment, then gripped her hand. "What did you do it for? Now the police will get you! If you'd had any brains at all, you'd know that I...I can't afford to be caught in the middle of an unsolved killing! I'll have to give you

up to the police. I'll tell them the truth."

"You don't have to, Ken," she said softly.

"I'm not going to connive at murder."

"Listen to me, Ken. I stabbed him in the heart and put the knife so that the tip slants downwards, as if he'd done it himself."

"The cops will see through it."

"Not if you keep quiet, Ken. I wrapped his fingers around the handle, just as if he'd held it all the time."

Ken cracked his knuckles. "But what can we tell them? Why should he want to kill himself?"

"Because he was discouraged. He had expected to find me waiting for him. When he didn't, he asked you to let him sleep her for a night and killed himself."

"I don't know if the cops will believe it."

"We can tell them he was upset by what happened to him in prison camp. His moods changed all the time."

Ken hesitated. He wet his tongue with his lips.

She said, "And there won't be any scandal. Just a few lines in the newspapers, maybe, that's all. No scandal. No long, drawn-out court action, either."

"I suppose not...but murder!"

She shrugged. "You've still got a good servant—that's just about all I've ever been to you—and I've still got a certain standing in the community."

He nodded slowly.

"We'll call the police in the morning and say that we just found the body," Audrey said in a businesslike way. "Meanwhile, we can get some sleep. And I wish you'd put on pajamas, Ken."

"All right."

It occurred to him, as he was changing, that he ought to be very kind, very good to Audrey from now on. If a woman was capable of using a knife one time....

THE OTHER SIDE
OF THE LIMELIGHT

Eugenia Summerhayes hadn't been able to persuade her dear Jethro to go out for an evening's pleasure. Most of four years had gone by since the last occasion, as she called it. Jethro had only needed to explain once that as the third Undersecretary of War in Mr. Lincoln's cabinet, he dreaded attending some jubilation and wondering apprehensively what the soldier in blue might be enduring in those same hours. Loyally, Eugenia hadn't pursued the matter.

But her husband turned absolutely jovial when he was able to tell her that General What-was-it Lee had just surrendered his rebel troops to the Federal Army. Eugenia was delighted for him, sincerely convinced that the accursed rebellion, as he called it, had affected no one as strongly as her Jethro.

Not until the fifteenth of April in this year of '65 did Jethro enchant his Eugenia by agreeing to a night's amusement. Eugenia happily tucked their surviving four daughters into beds shortly after supper and put on a low-necked evening dress for the first time since '60. People in Washington observed her husband while their shiny family carriage drove from Franklin Street to Tenth between E and F over to Ford's Theatre.

Eugenia drew back to let Jethro precede her into the rear of the darkened auditorium. The play, *Our American Cousins*, was already being performed, and the awkward Mr. Lincoln and his undersized wife could be seen sitting contentedly in the State box. The Summerhayes were soon located two boxes

down from them.

Eugenia insisted that Jethro occupy the sole rocking chair. When he asked lazily what was the last play they had seen, Eugenia instantly supplied the title, *Fanchon the Cricket*, and the name of Meg Mitchell, the radiant star of that drama. She became happily aware of his hand relaxing its affectionate grip on her as his breath became unhurried and even. Freed of strain, he needed no whiskey or laudanum to induce blessed sleep.

On the stage, the actress who performed the role of Mrs. Munchingessen, made an exit. She was roundly applauded.

A triangle of light suddenly appeared across the carpeted flooring of their box. A sturdy man in a dark sack suit and riding boots stood in the entrance. He glared, as if poised for conflict.

Eugenia surged to her feet, taking the place between her sleeping husband and the lumbering intruder, promptly keeping Jethro from being disturbed. Not till later did she recall putting a forefinger to her lips, enjoining silence upon the man.

He raised himself on tiptoes, peering over her head and down at Jethro's peaceful features. Having shaken his head he turned, moving like a cat as he started off. Something shone in his right hand, shiny as a pistol.

She made certain that Jethro hadn't been awakened, then gasped in anger when she heard the horrid sound of shouting followed by what she vaguely sensed was a gunshot. Shouting increased until it seemed that every theatre-goer had gone mad.

She never blamed herself, later on, because she might have called out and possibly stopped the assassination. She had been making certain that her Jethro slept comfortably for the first time in heaven knew how long. For many years it had been her constant task to be a devoted wife and, like a soldier, she had been carrying out the assignment. She had done her duty.

PROOF NEGATIVE

Skinner was heaping curses on the air conditioning system at headquarters, for laying down on the job over this mid-August weekend. At the sound of purposeful footsteps, he glanced up. Harry Preston, Chief of Detectives, was striding toward him. In one hand the energetic chief carried a file card.

"There's work for you," Preston said. "go over to see a guy name of Thomas Hardesty at number 18 Claymore Street. Been mugged, apparently. Find the perp if you can."

As Skinner was getting to his feet, the chief remember something more. "Come into my office first. It's part of the deal."

There was an FBI man named Graham sitting in the chief's office. It seemed that the mugging had taken place before twelve the night before, but Graham knew there wasn't much chance of nailing whoever was responsible and had waited till morning to come over with the squeal. The Bureau was forbidden to investigate this (or any) civil matter on its own, though they were involved. The victim was doing key work on a government contract of the sort that might interest undercover people from a foreign country. As a result, an eye was kept out for Hardesty's welfare.

Skinner didn't feel too good about this. The Fed was going to be sniffing around while Skinner went through the paces on this particular case. And he didn't like it. He didn't like *him*.

Graham allowed himself one look at the opened top button of Skinner's shirt and hardly talked directly to him again. FBI guys didn't sweat, Skinner supposed wryly....

Eighteen Claymore Street was a newish two-story building with a garage in back, just the sort of place Skinner would have liked to buy for his wife and kids, if he could ever get ahead of his expenses. Finding a parking space for the squad car took ten minutes. Graham, who had followed in a four-wheel yacht, nodded at a heavy man sitting in another huge car at the curb. Apparently, Mr. Thomas Hardesty was in at least fair condition by now.

Skinner was first at the door. From inside, a hesitant voice asked who was there.

"Police. For Mr. Hardesty."

"Oh. Well, put your I.D. card up against the peephole where I can see it."

Graham, coming up behind Skinner, called out. "It's all right, Mr. Hardesty."

The door was opened slowly. Hardesty turned out to be a small, thin man with a full, brown-grey beard. His story was quickly told: He and his friend had been home, the latter "downstairs, like she is now, watching some idiot program on the tube," when somebody knocked on the door. After opening it to a man he'd never seen before and couldn't coherently describe now, Hardesty had been hit several times and left writhing on the floor. The mugger had been alerted to a possible interruption and ran off.

"It could hardly have happened at a worse time," Hardesty added. "I'm in the last stages of a job involving a section of new heat-seeking target finders over at Darnell Systems. This baby ought to make *Star Wars* equipment as old-fashioned as a water pistol."

"Please, Mr. Hardesty," the FBI man said, but it was an order. "You don't have to go into that."

Hardesty looked frustrated, probably not for the first time, having wanted to brag to some stranger bout his ingenuity. Skinner sympathized. Once or twice in the course of his work, he'd been to the Darnell buildings, and, he remembered, his every step had been as closely supervised as the way this snotty

Fed was overseeing Hardesty right now. It was no surprise that a proud professional like Hardesty would be galled by this sort of working condition.

Skinner took advantage of the chance to rub Graham's patrician nose in the dirt. "I'm amazed that you people let this mugging happen."

"Our man came running, but the creep was gone in a minute and got clean away."

"Did your guy get a look at him?"

"There wasn't any time for that."

Skinner nodded as if to say that nobody could expect anything else from a Fed. He turned away to Hardesty, acting as if the engineer was free to make up his own mind.

"A picture of the perpetrator might be in our violent criminal files downtown, Mr. Hardesty. Can you come with me and take a look?"

It was Graham who decided that, of course. "Tomorrow morning ought to do it. Mr. Hardesty has a lot of work to get done now, and he's feeling better. A few more hours aren't going to make much difference."

Skinner had to give in. Next morning, at a call from Records, he hurried over there. The Department artist had just about finished drawing a sketch from Thomas Hardesty's description of the mugger. Hardesty, looking as if he was sitting on eggs, leafed through a photograph album of mug shots. Near the end of the book, he looked startled at the sight of one picture.

Rausch, the top honcho at Records, followed his gaze and said, "That's Marty Tolliver, a local strong-arm man who only works on assignment. Got an alibi for this caper, though. You'd better believe it!"

The FBI man who was with them, somebody Skinner had never seen before, looked up questioningly.

"Tolliver was found dead this morning, near the Meck," the Roach answered, using the local term for the river tributary five miles east of town. "Not our jurisdiction, but I did get a report on it."

Skinner pursed his lips. "Murder?"

"I don't know, good buddy."

Back at his desk, Skinner put a call through to a friend and colleague, Detective Dan O'Malley, in the city of Korit. O'Malley sounded rushed, but took the time to help."

"Someone fought with Tolliver and then he had a heart attack on top of it," O'Malley said, after the shortest explanation Skinner could make. "Very appropriate for a strong-arm. He's been dead for a day, at most. Probably it happened close to where he was found."

"Had anything been taken from his pockets?" Skinner asked, after a moment's thought. "Could you tell? If he got mugged in turn, like you suggested, Dan, it seems possible."

"As a matter of fact, about half of his pockets had been turned inside out."

Thoughtfully, Skinner went back to Records. The room was empty, though Roach came back in a minute. Hardesty and his FBI escort had left at the latter's insistence.

"I'm bringing them back here," Skinner said, mulishly. "Both of them."

He managed to get Preston's agreement without having to say exactly what was on his mind. The chief enjoyed bugging the FBI, although there were some agents he happened to like. A phone call to Darnell Systems got the information that Mr. Hardesty wouldn't be available until eight o'clock that night.

"I'll stick around till then," Skinner promised grimly. "Ask the FBI people to have Graham come out with Hardesty, will you, Chief? I particularly want him back if it's at all possible."

Preston asked a Fed he knew and liked if that could be done. It sounded as if both men were so glad to inconvenience Graham that neither one asked Skinner what was going down.

Hardesty and Graham reached headquarters at about eight. The chief set up a meeting in his own office, which was so quickly crowded another chair had to be brought in.

"I'll make this as short as possible," Skinner said. "I know what happened last night and why."

Graham, biting his lower lip, looked everywhere but directly at Skinner, as usual.

"Mr. Hardesty is carefully watched so that the Russians, say can't possibly get to him while he's doing this particularly important government work. Last night, a mugger came to his house, hit Mr. Hardesty, and was caught outside by the Bureau guard or guards."

"Prove it," Graham snapped.

"Whoever was on the job hustled Tolliver into a car, made sure that a replacement agent came on duty, and then he or they took off with the mugger. The Bureau wanted to know if somebody had hired Tolliver to do that particular job, or if the mugging was part of a scam in which Mr. Hardesty would actually give valuable papers to the representative of an Iron Curtain country. Mr. Hardesty would have to act in some unusual way if he wanted to get the stuff out, right under your eyes."

Hardesty nodded grimly, a man who clearly hated the continual tension under which the Bureau supervision was forcing him to live.

"I suppose Tolliver was taken to the nearest quiet spot, then hauled out of the car and searched for the papers or microfilm. When only half the job was done, he saw an opportunity to get away. A fight resulted. The stress brought on a heart attack and he died. Rather than make an embarrassing report to civil authorities, the agents just left and scattered. In the morning, most likely because Mr. Hardesty would be sore that the holier-than-thou Bureau people didn't hesitate to cover up a crime, a selective report was made to the local police. From your point of view, then, the innocent Mr. Hardesty gave away too much when he saw a mug shot of the guy who had victimized him."

Hardesty, who had nodded through Skinner's reconstruction, at the mention of his name nodded once more.

Graham looked at Skinner for once, a small triumph. "And what do you think you can do about it?"

"Nothing," Skinner admitted. "The Bureau can truthfully claim that the country's interest is vital and what happened was

accidental. But I want you to know I wasn't fooled for long. Mr. Hardesty, in his turn, might be interested in another proof of what some of his firm's contracted agents really think of him."

Graham was talking to the chief again. "I'd appreciate two minutes of your time. Now please."

Preston had no choice.

"Ask your detective to escort Mr. Hardesty out to the anteroom and wait for me," Graham added.

Preston's look reinforced the suggestion. Skinner, getting to his feet, wondered if he'd ever get enough ahead of himself financially to tell them all what to do with their jobs.

He led the way into the wide anteroom. "Nice to have met you, Mr. Hardesty."

"Likewise." Hardesty's grip joined Skinner's as the men shook hands. "And I'm not surprised to know what the Feds, some of them, think I'm capable of doing. In fact, I'm damned well sick of most of them."

Skinner made a fist of his hand as he withdrew it, swiftly put the hand in his pocket so as not to lose the microfilm that had been handed over; the microfilm that he'd soon bring to those people who would be paying heavily for it. The idea had worked, bringing Hardesty to headquarters where the stuff could be passed along. It had cost him the future services of one of his best informers, Marty Tolliver, but everything had its price.

The two men were standing awkwardly in the anteroom when Graham opened the chief's door and came out. There was a smile on the FBI man's lips. He had used some muscle with the local and got an agreement that was perfectly satisfactory. In his exultation, he even smiled at the detective who had behaved as if he was putting one over on him, and the Bureau as well. He wasn't surprised at not getting any kind of smile in return. All locals were a bunch of soreheads.

SIX MILLION MURDERERS

"But where do you get money to buy drinks?" the kid asked.

Blair didn't answer his son. He turned and staggered toward the bathroom. Once he had started cold water flowing into the sink, he nerved himself to pull his head under the tap. Water coursed through his hair and down his face as well as bunching into rivers and dropping down small circular holed in the grating.

When he drew up his head and wiped it quickly, he heard Harry's voice again. "Where *do* you get the money?"

"It don't matter." Blair's own voice was husky and deep. "You shouldn't worry. All you do is go to work in the daytime, and school at night. What else is there to think about?"

Harry shrugged and picked up the briefcase that held his High School books. As soon as he heard steps descending the stairs, Blair began making preparations.

He was slow as always, drawing the scarred round table to the center of the room. Then he drew up three chairs and three glasses, and filled a pitcher with iced water. The last job took time because his hands were almost too shaky to pry out cubes from the tray in the refrigerator. He had barely finished when the doorbell rang.

He opened the door on two boys, neither of them older than seventeen. Behind them stood a fair, slim young girl.

Blair hid his surprise at the sight of her. Not a word was spoken until the door swung shut again and a key clicked in the lock. The girl looked around, sniffed, and then glanced inquir-

ingly to one of the dark-haired boys. He gestured to the scarred round table.

"Okay, baby, you want to know what the story is." The boy looked proud and a little cynical. It was unusual to see him without contemptuous curves at the ends of his lips. "Easy enough, but it ain't the kind of thing every Joe Blow thinks up. This guy here, he's Nails Blair."

Blair's teeth clicked at the sound of the old-time nickname. To distract his energies, he patted down the thinning gray tufts at the sides of his head.

"Nails here, he used to be a big shot," the kid went on. "Then he got nailed—ha!—for not kicking through on Uncle Sammy's taxes. When he came out of the pen, he tried to go straight. No dice! Who'd want him? And the cops were always on his tail. So he gave up and started living off his son."

It was all true, and the words hurt as much as if it had all happened recently. Blair made fists of his hands.

"What he does now," the boy said proudly, "is easy. He works for the Kings."

"For you?" the girl asked, wide-eyed. "For your gang?"

"Sure, baby. For instance, we want a job planned. So what happens? We come here, two of us, and we hand over some of this stuff." The boy gestured down at a package in one hand. "Nails, he figures out all the angles. Oh, here!"

Almost carelessly, he opened the package of three bottles of muscatel. He was perfectly satisfied, and he sneer seemed to have fixed itself even more firmly on his smooth face.

"Well, Wolfie." Blair was mild. "What's the set-up this time?"

"It's a big one," Wolfie answered. "I'll get to it in a minute. First off, about this trim here. The broad, I mean. She's named Miriam. She'll be here every time from now on."

Miriam moistened her lips with the tip of a tongue so white that Blair caught himself just short of recommending a laxative. It was hard to take seriously the fact that these kids were criminals.

"I—I need to raise some money for myself and for Wolfie

here. "I've been good at picking pockets and I'll keep it up unless there's a better grift for me."

Blair said slowly, "Shoplifting. That's the answer. You can sell the stuff later at Iggy Bly's on Hammond Street. A good deal, there."

"How do I work the boost/"

"Any number of possible ways. The stuff you grab, you might put away in heavy elastic bloomers and hold it there till you get out of the store."

"Then I'd be walking too heavy," Miriam said, shaking her blonde head. "It'd look bad to the store dicks."

"You might carry a package with a spring lid that bends inward, so the goods can be shoved into that."

"It'd take too much time to have one made for me."

"There's another way. If one of the—" he had almost said kids—"men can get a department store dummy, you can cut off one of its hands. Then put a glove on it and a pocketbook, and set it to hang from a coat sleeve."

"I'll have one hand free," Miriam nodded. "Not bad at all."

She smiled at him, then at Wolfie. The other boy in the room suddenly said, "Okay, there's a big thing to take care of, now."

He was a small slim youngster who kept himself neat. Even on a night as warm as this one, he wore a suit, white shirt and tie. His fingernails were immaculate, and always trimmed perfectly. His hair was combed back from a high forehead. He was called Shim.

"Yeah, that's right." Wolfie drew out a package of cigarettes, set them on the table and took his time lighting one. When he had blown a couple of smoke rings, he was ready to talk. "The Kings have decided to pull another stick-up."

"Where?"

"A place that's always got plenty of loot. Merrit's."

"The supermarket?" Blair was stiff. "A hard job. I wouldn't suggest it."

Wolfie said sharply, "Don't tell us what jobs to pick—just how to carry 'em out! Besides, what are you so hot and bothered

about? It cuts no ice with you."

Blair kept his eyes lowered. It wouldn't do to show any of the fear that had become part of him now. He would try to behave as if he'd forgotten that his son, Harry, worked daytimes at one of the two checkout counters in Merrit's.

But he began hesitatingly, "Well, the job ought to be done at night."

"Ixnay on that." Wolfie shook his head. "More loot during the day. Around two-three o'clock is right for it, because that's when money's being set for a last-minute bank deposit."

Blair started to protest. "I don't think it'll work," he said. "In fact—"

Wolfie cut him short. "Never the hell mind what you think about it. The job's gonna be done, so get used to it and do some talking instead."

There was a pause while Miriam asked for a cigarette and Wolfie shoved his pack across the table toward her. He watched carefully to see that no more than one cigarette was taken. Blair had pulled over a seat for himself, and now he poured a half-glass of muskie. He stared at it as though to tell himself he had the willpower to keep from pouring the stuff down his throat. Then he drank, and let out a long sigh before giving hints.

"Well, you know the usual things to do. Dark suits and hand-kerchiefs over your faces. Get a car. After the job, leave the car someplace, and wipe it clean. The wheel, the doors—that's where fingerprints show."

"Anything else?"

'Write out notes in block printing, and don't talk at any time in case the voice can be remembered." Slowly he added, "One thing more, whatever else you do, be sure to bring along some-thing that looks like a gun. Keep it in a suit pocket. If you don't take it out, nobody can see it's not for real."

Wolfie drew his head back. "Did you flip? You know there are six guns in the club. We stole 'em because you said they'd come in handy for jobs."

Blair remembered. It had been gone over in detail. He had

drilled the young hoods on where to stand, what to do, how to move in emergencies. He had stressed how important it was always to keep one peeled for entrances.

Now he gave in on a point. "If you've got to use guns, don't load 'em up."

Wolfie flared, "Why the hell not?"

'Get caught with loaded guns, and you're sent up for stiffer jolts. Load up the gun with blanks if you have to. Blanks can hurt at close range, too, but they don't get you a murder rap."

"You're kidding." It was Shim, the quiet one, talking now. "We might need to fire a bullet into the ceiling—just to make with a scare. Blanks are no good for a guy in this business. And if he's good, he won't be caught."

Blair shrugged. "I used to think so, too," he said.

Wolfie said ruthlessly, "You're old and sick and useless. Except to me, sometimes."

Blair poured himself another glass of muskie and drank it down in a gulp before he said, "My kid's there."

"Huh?" Shim looked up, startled. "You mean that's what he does for a living? A fine idea this is, coming down to a rum-dum whose kid—"

"Hold it!" Wolfie showed his teeth. "You don't like the way this outfit is run, Shim, you can help yourself or get the boot or get your head handed to you."

Shim muttered, but drew out an emery board and began filing down his fingernails. Miriam smiled faintly, then sat back and folded her hands exactly as if back at school. Wolfie's lips quirked.

"Okay, now we all know what the score is. Your kid works at Merrit's, so you want us to go easy. Well, we're not going easy, and your kid had better not give any trouble."

"I'd tell him," Blair began quietly, "but he doesn't know—"

"So the kid has no idea you're mixed up with us," Wolfie said quietly. "Okay, that makes it a little rougher. But nobody wants any trouble, and the caper won't be stopped tomorrow."

Wolfie turned and walked toward the door as if leading a

parade. Blair didn't look up at all. He poured himself another drink and downed it in a gulp.

At two o'clock the next afternoon, Blair was sitting across from Merrit's Market. He was on a bench in an island between the streets. In front of him was a newspaper, but he didn't look down at it.

He had spent a rough morning trying to persuade Harry to stay away from work. Harry had refused pointblank. He had not attempted to conceal the way he felt. Nor had he paid much attention to last-minute advice on what to do in case of trouble.

"If there's a robbery," Harry had finally blurted out with bitter sarcasm, "I'll give all the money to any friend of yours who wants it."

Once the kid had gone, Nails Blair had been on the verge of calling the police. But he forced himself to forget that idea. Cops would come armed. In any gunfight, the worst might happen.

So he sat across the street from Merrit's Market at two o'clock of a sun-soaked afternoon, and he waited. He didn't have to wait for long.

The car that pulled up was a battered old Ford. One boy walked out, then another. Each in a dark suit and hat, and with handkerchief tied conveniently at the neck. Four to do the robbery, and one to drive the stolen getaway car.

Three minutes passed. Blair could easily imagine the speed at which it was being done. Now the notes were being thrust over the counter, now the money was going into a bag—

A shot.

Blair lurched to his feet, his face ashen. But he managed to control his agitation, his eyes darting in alarm to the neighboring bench-sitters.

Somebody said, "Either a flat tire or a gangster program on television. Nothing else could make that kind of noise, for sure." But others were staring at him.

Under the continued suspicious scrutiny, Blair sank as if falling into water. He reached for the last of yesterday's muskie bottles. Just as his shaky hands jerked out the cork, he heard the

second and third shots.

They were very loud and followed each other so closely that they probably had been fired from different guns. For the second time, Blair wobbled to his feet.

He was staring straight across at the supermarket when the run-out started. The young hoods emerged one at a time and piled into the battered old Ford. The third boy out was carrying a legal-type portfolio, which he held tightly clutched to his chest.

Blair started to cross the street. A car passed directly behind him, and warm air whistled against the nape of his neck. He leapt back toward the raised threshold of the sidewalk, and just as he did so a woman ran out the front entrance of Merrit's. She stood just beyond the curb, swaying unsteadily. Her dress had been torn down the front, and her hair was disarranged. She cried out wildly, "Robbery! Murder! Help, for God's sake!"

She collapsed backwards against Blair, holding on to him and sobbing, her face pressed tightly against his chest.

Blair wasn't able to move far enough to peer inside the store. But he did manage to pull out the sheath of a police call box.

Five minutes later, a P.D. car arrived on the scene, spewing out uniformed cops who swiftly cleared away street bystanders.

Blair was pushed around because he looked so seedy. Strangely enough, he didn't resent it any more. He expected it. But he didn't know anything more about what had taken place inside the store when he walked off. He moved as quickly as he could. In the saloon which he usually went to, he wasn't able to borrow a dime to put through a phone call to the supermarket. After twenty minutes of trying, he groped his way home to the apartment he shared with Harry, who looked white and shaken when he opened the door.

Blair stared at the lad for a second, then asked dully, "You—you're all right?"

"What did you expect? To find me dead?" Harry ran a head across his fair skin, mussing up his red hair. He looked very much like his mother and a stab of remembrance and grief made Blair wince. "Nothing happened, son?" He was pretty much

ashamed, for some unknown reason, to call Harry by name. "No trouble of any kind?"

The youth spoke very slowly and deliberately. "It'll be in tomorrow's papers, so you might as well hear it now. There was a robbery at the place and the manager was shot and killed."

He paused an instant, then added. "I've left supper in the refrigerator, and I'm going to school."

Blair stayed in his own bedroom and drank down the last of the wine. As usual, he threw the bottle out the window. When he heard footsteps leaving, he got up and walked to the refrigerator. He was finishing a dish of cream and cheese when the doorbell rang loudly.

Even before he arose to answer the bell his heart began a furious pounding, and his agitation became even more pronounced when he saw that his callers were the two young hoods and the blonde girl.

For a moment he simply stared at them, swallowing hard. Then he looked up and down the hall and stood to one side.

"The kitchen," he said, pointing a gnarled forefinger, and then switching on a light. He walked first, straightening his back a little when he heard a sneer behind him.

Wolfie sat down in the dim-lit kitchen. He was carrying a package this time, but it looked much smaller than the usual. Its outer wrapping was soggy with stains of a sweaty hand. He was sneering again, but now nervousness made his lips twitch slightly.

Shim was jumpy, too, drumming his fingernails continually against the table top. Only Miriam looked calm, applying makeup to her lower lip with the red-smeared little finger of her left hand.

"Didn't expect you tonight," Blair said abruptly. "How did the job go?"

"Okay," Wolfie answered, "except for one thing."

"The manager?"

"Naw," Wolfie said contemptuously. "He was just a goddam fool who didn't know what to do when he saw somebody

pointing a gun. He deserved what he got."

Miriam said in a level tone, "I wish I'd been there. I've never seen somebody killed."

"You will, baby," Wolfie nodded. "Real soon, it could be." When he turned back to Blair, his voice was harder. "That's what I'm here about."

Wolfie's eyes hardened. "I'll make it short and sweet. Something went wrong. There was one witness to the killing— somebody who saw me and could put the finger on me."

He explained that he'd tripped over a carton and the handkerchief-mask had briefly slipped below his nose before it could be put back in place. There had been no time to handle a second rub-out, for the carefully calculated schedule had already been riddled to pieces.

Wolfie talked fast, and to the point. This was a kid witness who could easily trip up a grown man, and send him to the electric chair.

Blair suddenly gripped the creaking table, and swore under his breath. "Who was it?" Blair asked. "The witness, I mean."

Shim said, "Some young squirt about seventeen or eighteen."

"What color hair/"

"Couldn't tell. He wore one of those hats that all the people in Merrit's are supposed to wear. He worked at the checkout counter."

All of the color had drained from Blair's face. The description, he realized, fitted both Harry and another young clerk who worked at the next checkout counter.

"*Which* counter was it?" he asked quickly. "What number did it have?"

"Who the hell could notice and what difference does it make?" Wolfie rasped. He narrowed his eyes. "It might have been your kid, huh? That'd be funny, coming here to ask you how to bump off your own kid."

Blair started to speak, then thought better of it. He moistened his lips and shook his head in silent protest.

Wolfie suddenly crashed a fist against the table. "Listen, you

goddam rum-pot! Don't ask no more questions! You just give answers. You hear?"

He placed the package on the table and quickly opened it. Beneath the wrappings was a bottle of whiskey—a fifth of Paul Jones.

"Here's your fee," Wolfie said. "For figuring how to do a kill job—you get whiskey this time. Ain't that a good deal?"

"No, I don't want it." Blair spoke in a hoarse whisper.

"Is that so? What don't you like about it? It's good whiskey, isn't it?"

Wolfie had been holding a palm on the label. Now he slid the bottle straight toward Blair. It began to topple, and would have rolled over to crash on the floor if Blair had not caught it in time. He held it in one shaking hand, a look of desperate pleading in his eyes.

"Well, we got something settled," Wolfie said, smiling coldly across at Shim. Shim nodded, and broke an emery-board in half. Miriam's blonde head moved in a nod before she folded her hands on the table.

"Not yet," Blair protested. "I won't do a thing for you unless I know—"

"Let's get something straight," Wolfie said sharply. "I might be in a bad mess unless that goddam witness, whoever he is, gets rubbed out. You understand?"

"Go ahead."

"There's a chance that maybe it's not your kid. A fifty-fifty chance. No more, no less. If it isn't your kid, that don't mean your kid will have it so easy. He'll get a bad beating out of it, anyhow—with everything in the book from tire chains to bottles."

"Why?"

"Because his old man didn't want to help us," Wolfie said lightly.

"I see."

"And on top of that, he'll be told why it happened, and that his old man tells us how to do heists. So we've got a deal, right?"

All Blair could manage was a nod. His eyes were squeezed closely together, as if to hold back tears of frustration. There was a fifty-fifty chance, after all, and maybe some way out could be figured....

"Okay, then," Wolfie said. "How do we get rid of this witness?"

"Get a guy from the other side of town—a guy who isn't part of the gang." Blair talked almost automatically, as if fearing the self-destructive power of his thoughts. Words alone, he felt, could not destroy him. They could be repudiated later on.

Shim held up a hand. "That's out," he said. "The Kings take care of their own problems."

"Well—that isn't too hard. Get one of your own men to follow the witness. Then let the witness try to pick up Miriam in the street. She can handle that by giving him the come-on."

Miriam flushed with pleasure at the prospect of setting up a man for killing.

"After a while, she says she's just noticed that the witness is being followed. He becomes scared and manages to 'ditch' the shadow. But he's simply disappeared at a signal."

Shim was aping the table with a fresh emery-board as he leaned forward. "And what happens then?"

"Miriam brings the victim to a place that's just right for the job. I'd suggest somewhere off the beaten track and quiet, like—"

"We'll take care of picking out a place," Wolfie interrupted quickly. "Nobody wants you to find out too much in a special case like this."

He whirled around and started for the door. Shim looked undecided for a moment, then got to his feet and followed him. Miriam was the last to leave. She paused to glance back once before the door closed.

Blair looked down at the bottle and knocked it off the table. It rolled for a dozen feet, dusty but intact. He buried his head in his arms and left it lying there for a moment. Then he arose slowly, bent and picked it up.

It was evening when he woke up. The smell of the room alone was enough to tell him that at least fifteen or twenty hours had passed. For almost a whole day, he had been out to the world. His temples were pounding and he experienced difficulty in getting to his feet and opening a window.

Suddenly he stopped, cocking his head slightly in a listening attitude. Sounds were coming from the next room. There were shuffling footsteps and the sound of running water. He walked to the door and looked in. His face brightened in relief. Harry was getting dressed.

Harry looked up—then down and away. "I wish you'd fix this tie for me, but your hands are dirty," he said.

"I'll wash 'em," Blair said eagerly, grateful that the boy was here.

"No, never mind. Thanks, anyhow."

"The knot is supposed to become narrow toward the bottom." Blair hesitated. "Going out, son?"

"Sure."

Nails Blair stood against the wall to keep from swaying. "Maybe you shouldn't go. There's a lot of things to do around here." He gestured around the unsightly room. "A lot of cleaning up."

"*You've* never done any," Harry grinned. "Start tonight—if you feel that way about it. I've got an important date."

Blair looked steadily at his son. "Nice girl? Known her long?"

"Met her last night." A frown darkened Harry's face. "Why are you so damned curious, all of a sudden. I've taken out girls before."

"Kid, listen!" Blair took a step forward, swayed, and then fell back again. "Listen, kid, and find out a few things. The girl you're taking out—she's a blonde and her name's Miriam. Isn't that right/"

"How do you know?" Harry demanded. Suddenly his eyes blazed and he said, "So you were up for part of last night, after all. You saw me walking her home—"

"No. I didn't. But here's more of it. She encouraged a date

with you tonight, and you're probably thinking that she looks like hot stuff."

He hesitated. Never had he talked frankly with his son about the differences between women. How much could Harry know, after all? If he had a few facts to go on, he must have picked them up in the streets.

Blair said, "It's all right to make a fool of yourself over a broad, but not when it's a life-and-death matter."

That wasn't entirely fair to the kid, and Nails Blair knew it. But his respect for other people always cracked under the impact of liquor. He could start drinking in a cheerful frame of mind, and in a few hours he'd be in bad shape, and hating the world.

Harry blurted out, "I don't know what you're talking about."

"She told you you were being followed, and you saw somebody, for sure. Then that guy was ditched. Like hell he was!"

"What?" Harry blinked, but he couldn't bridge the gulf by talking honestly. He sounded a little dazed.

"That's crazy! I don't know what you're talking about."

"Listen here," Blair said. "The girl's a shill for a mob. A mob of kids, sure, all about your age. But they're after you so as to get you dead. You'll be taken to some out-of-the-way place and finished off."

Harry said, "I still don't know what you're talking about. Honest, I don't!"

"You didn't see the face of the hood who killed the manager back at the supermarket? It isn't true that you can make an identification?"

"How do you know?" Harry asked, going white. "Nobody's supposed to know. It can only mean—you were in on it."

Blair turned away and faced the wall. "Kid, all those cracks of yours might be coming. More than I've got coming. But all I want right now is to keep you from getting killed."

The only answer was the crash of the door behind him. For a full minute, Blair stayed still. In a way, he felt sorry for himself. But self-pity had to be shaken off. His son's life was at stake,

and it could only be saved by somebody who knew the way hoods acted and thought. There wasn't even time enough for him to get over an all-day drunk.

Because he realized the importance of haste, his actions took on an aspect of unreality. He nearly tumbled down the apartment stairs, and out into the warm deserted street.

There wasn't a uniformed cop in sight. Blair managed to beg ten cents for a phone call, but when he dialed his fingers shook so that he had to ask the operator to get the number for him.

"Twenty-Eighth precinct. Hendrickson speaking."

"You've got to help me. My son's going to be murdered."

A heavy sigh. "Your name and address, please."

"There isn't any time for filling out forms, or any kind of delay. My son's name is Harry Blair. He works at Merrit's Supermarket. Yesterday he saw an armed robbery and killing there. He saw the killer's face when a mask dropped. That killer is out for a second scalp, tonight."

The deep voice asked patiently, almost casually, "But where can your son be found, Mr. Blair?"

"I don't know. He's out with a girl who's a shill for a gang that will stop at nothing. They've killed before—so they have nothing to lose."

"And how do you know that, Mr. Blair?"

Blair hesitated, fearing that if he attempted to explain he'd be taken for a crackpot, and nothing would be done.

"—I just know, that's all."

"Where does your son live, Mr. Blair? We'll send a man around."

"But he's not home. Don't you see? There's no time and every second counts."

"Sure it does," the big voice soothed. "Don't worry about a thing."

The phone was hung up gently. Blair started to say that he hadn't given the address, but there was no point in torturing himself. In spite of his best efforts, he hadn't been believed. That couldn't be set right by a trip down to the precinct, but he

needed to set himself a goal.

He walked down to Silver Street, the main drag in this section. He walked into a movie theatre and left a painstakingly written message for the kid. Between pictures, Harry's name would be blared out over the loud speaker system.

He had repeated the procedure at two other movie houses when he passed Conley's Ice Cream Parlor. Abruptly, he turned and walked back. Boys and girls stood in front of the place. Some of the kids were dressed well, but for the most part they wore dungarees and sports shirts. They were smoking cigarettes and tapping their feet in rhythm to rock-and-roll music from a nearby amplifier. The song was just finishing when a brunette turned very quickly and smiled at Blair.

"Hello, Handsome!"

Next to her, a boy of sixteen or seventeen had whirled around, but his face cleared when he saw how old Blair was. He grinned.

"My girl likes you," he piped. "She thinks you're cute."

The group around the store had halted to see what was going on. At first, the eyes trained on Blair were large and unblinking, almost all of them. But ripples of laughter soon started. A girl took stock of the situation and called out, "You send me, daddy!"

Blair focused on the dead-white skin and close-set eyes of the familiar-looking little brunette who had first spoken to him.

"I need some help," he said. "I was wondering if you might want to help me."

"No loot here, daddy." One of the boys drawled the mocking title, and spread out his hands palm up. "Besides *we're* working this side of the street."

"Never mind."

Blair walked to the door of the ice-cream parlor, and opened it slowly. He was met by a sudden blast of cool air, and the impact of fifty or more conversations going on at the same time. Youths sitting or standing in attitudes of hoodlum-like bois- terousness, girls as callow and noisy in their behavior as their escorts. Waiters threaded back and forth like so many robots, occasionally stopping to swear at each other, or at the soda jerk.

Only one of the bright, grinning faces meant anything to Blair. Over in a corner, and wearing his usual neat outfit, was the King's second-in-command. Shim was leaning a little forward, using his hands expressively as he talked to a girl with her hair in a pony-tail. The girl was drinking a soda.

"You ought to try some of the hard stuff, kid," Shim said. Then he saw Blair and his eyes grew glassy. "What do you want?"

Blair, standing rigidly by the table said, "A little talk."

Shim shrugged and turned back to the girl. "Go powder your nose, will you?"

The girl gasped. "What did you say to me?"

"I said, scram. Go jump on your scooter and don't come back till you get the office, or you'll get clobbered. Understand?"

The girl stood up, turned on her high heels and walked off. Shim gestured toward the table.

"Sit down and speak your piece," Shim said.

He was as mannered as a movie gangster. To him, this soda-fountain took the place of an older man's tavern. Shim would probably haunt the expensive drinking places in a few years—if he lived long enough to grow up.

Blair settled into the seat which the girl had vacated.

"I want to know where my kid is," he said, his eyes steady and probing.

"Don't look at me, old-timer. There's nobody up my sleeve."

"You're going to see him later on tonight. The whole gang is going to help kill him."

"That's how the ball bounces, if it's true, old-timer. If you're just here to waste my time when I could be making out with some broad, then you can crawl up on a cockroach and get out of here."

"So you want to make tough talk." Blair sighed. "I'm pretty good at that. At least, I used to be—back when I was a young punk. If you want to hear something instead, then quiet down."

"Okay, I'm quiet," Shim said seriously. "This had better be good."

"All right, here it is. How would you like to get rid of Wolfie?"

Shim's eyes narrowed, but he said quickly, "It's your dime."

"There's never yet been a lieutenant who didn't want to be captain. You can do it, Shim. You can take over the Kings."

"I—" Shim paused, then ran a wet pink tongue over his thick lips. "Old-timer, you've got Benzedrine in your yogurt. That's what hops you up."

"You mean you're not even interested? All you'd have to do to get help out of me—and I'm the one who knows the gimmicks—is to help my kid out of a jam. That's all there is to it."

"Maybe that's all. And how do I know you aren't handing out a snow job?"

"I'd have nothing to gain by it."

"Oh no? Suppose you got sent around here on purpose? Suppose Wolfie wants to know who he can count on? Where would I be if that's the score?"

It was only to be expected that the pattern of kid gangs would take its cue from those of grown-ups. Always expecting trouble, always super-careful.

Shim added furiously, "I wouldn't trust you with a wooden nickel. You're a lush, a rum-dum! You've got a bottle on your back."

Another loss, then. Blair set his hands down flat against the checkered tablecloth and got slowly to his feet.

"Maybe I can take care of the job, myself. Thanks for nothing, Shim. You missed a good chance for a payoff."

But as he started for the door a little of the strain went out of his face. The fact that Shim was here at a corner hangout was proof that the Kings weren't ready for the night's action. Not yet. There might still be time.

Blair was walking a little more quickly when he closed the door firmly behind him. As he might have expected, the sudden heat was almost paralyzing. The first person he saw was the young, narrow-eyed brunette who had called out to him in front of the ice-cream parlor fifteen minutes earlier.

"Well, it's handsome again," she said, holding her arms

akimbo, and rolling her eyes at him. "You don't like any of the girls in there, so you came out to pick me up?"

Then something curious happened. She touched his arm, and her smile widened. "Isn't that right, handsome dear?" she cooed.

Blair asked quickly, "Do you know a ki—a fellow named Harry Blair/" He looked around. "Any of you people know?"

No response. All the faces went dead, closing him out. Because he was in his late fifties, he was the Enemy.

The brunette turned to glance at the boy who had been talking to her before, and who was now paying attention to another girl. Suddenly the brunette's voice grew louder—so loud, in fact, that all of the others turned to stare at her.

"You shouldn't do that to me! You shouldn't!"

Blair moved a step back. He was just starting to turn away when he saw the blue uniform of a young cop coming toward him.

"Anything wrong here?" the patrolman demanded, looking straight at the girl.

The brunette said loudly, "This disgusting old man tried to take liberties with me, officer."

"Okay, okay," the young cop said, closing in on Blair. "Come on, buster. You've got a date with the wagon."

Blair said quickly, "Now look here, this is all a mistake!"

"Yeh, sure." The cop's strong grip had crushed into an arm. He was being led. There was no sense in fighting it any more. Two decades ago, he'd have put up a furious protest, but that had been back in the days when he'd been learning a trade that had only brought trouble.

He did manage to glance back toward Conley's at the young brunette, however. She seemed familiar now, and he suddenly realized just how and why he had been framed. The brunette was tied in with the Kings, and now she was talking to Shim. Shim had probably gestured to her, indicating by an obscene motion what he wanted her to do, and then had sent somebody out the back way to get hold of the patrolman.

The wagon was a black affair with four gray steps that led to

a barred compartment with a dim light at the far end. Because he couldn't move fast enough, he was pushed inside and landed on the floor. A moment later the wagon started to move.

At the station, he was taken into a small room to be questioned by a heavyset detective who remembered the name and stared down at him with a grimace of disgust.

"So this is what becomes of a big-shot crook," he mused aloud. "Turns into a bum—gets picked up for molesting kids."

"That girl was lying. She lied her head off."

"What were you doing at Conley's, in the first place?" the detective demanded.

"Looking for my son," Blair said, a sudden firmness in his voice. "He's in a bad jam. He works at Merrit's Market and yesterday he saw the face of the guy who killed the manager.

"Well?"

"The killer is after him. A kid named Wolf Paris. He's called Wolfie."

"How come you know this Wolf Paris?"

"He's the head of a kid gang called the Kings. They raise money by doing stick-ups and small crime. They ask me for advice and I—I tell what I know."

The detective's expression hardly changed at all. The coldness, the hardness remained, visible not only in his eyes, but in the continued tightness of his lips.

"There was no other way I could make anything at all for myself," Blair went on. "When I came out of the pen I was broke and no one would give me an honest job—no one. There are six million people in this city, and they tried to blot me out."

The copy looked away. "All right, forget that for now. How do you get paid by your employers?"

"In wine. Muscatel. Three bottles of the stuff every time except—well, the last job. And look out for a girl, a blonde named Miriam. She's the shill...."

When Blair had finished, he searched the cop's face. Disgust was gone, at least, but the man's level gaze was otherwise unreadable.

"I had a note on this from Sergeant Hendrickson," the detective said. "He took the call when you phoned in. It's being checked on right now."

"And in the meantime, my kid may be shot down by a vicious young punk. You don't really care. Nobody cares."

"Sorry for yourself," the detective muttered. "Isn't it as much that as concern for the kid?"

"Isn't there anything I can do? If I'm let go, I give my word I'll come back."

"No," the detective said heavily. He walked to the door and gestured to somebody outside. Blair was booked and directed to a narrow cell. It held two small cots and a sink and toilet. His cellmate was a small, skinny sad-eyed youngster of about twenty-two.

"I'm in for a stick-up, if you want to know," the cellmate said arrogantly. "How come you've been collared? It's getting real unusual to see an old duck in stir these days."

Blair shrugged and walked toward the lower bed. Before he could reach it, his arm was gripped tightly from behind and he was wheeled around.

"You don't go into that pad, jocko. That's the one I use till I get sent upstate."

Blair nodded resignedly. He wouldn't be able to climb a five step ladder to the upper cot. If he stayed long enough he's sleep on the floor.

He turned to the sink, falling against it. With shaking fingers he un-wrapped the cake of soap that had been provided, and raised it to his lips. He drew the soap into his mouth, and champed his jaws tight. Then he pretended to swallow the small, oval cake, briefly lowering his Adam's apple.

The cellmate had been watching. Now his eyes widened. "That soap's got lye in it, jocko. You'll be sick as a dog. "You might even—God! You're going to cream yourself."

He turned and rattled a tin cup against the bars. "Guard, guard, come here fast!" he shouted. "This guy's trying to kill himself."

The sounds grew louder. It was a shame, Blair thought, to be both young and stupid. He smiled briefly, then opened his mouth and caught the cake of soap in his right hand. With a deft motion, he threw it under the lower cot.

The youth finally caught the attention of the cell block guard, who lost no time in phoning the hospital unit. Blair was lying in the lower cot by this time, writhing and twisting like a dying man. He groaned loudly with pretended pain.

In a few minutes, a guard and a hospital orderly arrived. The orderly listened, nodded, and then turned to the guard.

"Can't do much for a lye-poisoning case here. The city doesn't give us enough money to establish the needed facilities. We haven't even got a stomach pump. We'll give him some preliminary treatment, then rush him to the hospital. He needs hospital care, and he needs it fast."

"Okay, then. You won't need an extra guard to go along, will you? We're understaffed as hell."

Blair waited and groaned. It took some time before a stretcher deposited him in a gray ambulance.

The intern asked him why he had tried to kill himself, and became angry when Blair refused to talk at all.

"You don't want me to hold your hand," he snapped. "I'll sit up front with the driver."

That, too, suited Blair very well. He didn't expect to be hampered too much by the opening and closing of the partition-slat and the occasional appearance of the driver's hard blue eye. No doubt the intern and the jail guards would be in for a rough time later on, but the anger of prison officials had a way of simmering down when the blame was too widely distributed.

The escape was easy. At a pause for a red light, Blair simply got off the bed and softly opened the ambulance door before stepping out into traffic. The noise and closeness of moving cars seldom bothered him, but now it was unnerving. He walked in a duck-waddle to the sidewalk.

The street was jammed with people. Blair made himself as inconspicuous as possible and headed for the Cable City Park.

Like everyone else who lived in the city, he disliked parks at night. No park was safe. It was hard to get used to the fact that the sight of two teen-age boys dressed informally could make a grown man cringe.

Nails Blair walked slowly, his eyes exploring the greenery and level lawns to the left and the right. In the shadows of a bronze group of World War I infantrymen, a young couple sat necking and the boy's hands moved purposefully.

All his years must have given Nails Blair a sixth sense to reveal the presence of the enemy. It happened when he had trudged through half the park. Scattered in an irregular semi-circle, but fairly close together, a dozen couples sat on a hill. The boys and girls held on to each other, but all eyes were riveted on the path below.

At intervals, a boy would lean forward to turn up a radio. A chill went through Blair when he realized that the reason for that was probably to drown out screams.

All the gang members stiffened at the sight of him. Blair stood very still for a moment, his lips tightening. Then he walked slowly toward them.

"Hello Johnny, Pete, Roger." At the mention of each name, he nodded. Nobody else reacted. "I suppose it's going on in there," he said, gesturing toward what looked at first to be a pile of rocks, but must have been a cave in which there'd be room enough for what the gang felt had to be done.

"I'm moving in," Blair said.

A boy said sharply, "The hell you are! Goddam stew-bum!"

From inside the cave a voice rose in pitch. Somebody leaned forward to increase volume on the radio.

"Look at it this way, Pete," Blair said reasonably. "If you and the others try to keep me moving on, that's not going to end it."

"Huh?"

"I might go to a police call box, and give a report in detail."

He heard the rustle of grass on both sides of him, and knew that he had been encircled by four or five of the Kings. The unmistakable *snick* of an opening switchblade knife rose above

the radio rock-and-roll.

"Or I might get myself killed. But if that happened, I wouldn't be around to give any help on future jobs. Better thank that over."

"Who'd miss you!" Pete said scornfully.

"Nobody's been caught yet. The cops haven't latched on to a single man in this crew since you've all been using the gimmicks I've talked about."

Someone else said worriedly, "That's right."

Blair didn't smile. "Or I can manage to delay you—like this!"

He never knew how he managed it. Nothing could have been more unlike him. But he turned abruptly and smashed his foot down on the portable radio. The music halted in the middle of a wail. He was just turning when something hard crashed against his skull. Pain seared his flesh, and he sank down with a groan and rolled over on his face.

How long he remained unconscious he had no way of knowing. But it could not have exceeded a few minutes because when he was revived he was being watched by the same people. And somebody else. Shim had come out of the cave and was staring down at him.

"What do you want here?" he demanded.

Blair started to sit up, but a foot kicked into his side.

"You answer when somebody talks to you," Shim said sharply. "Hear that?"

Blair fell back. He looked up at the stars and then down to his right. Patches of the city's skyline could be seen far away, diffused through a glimmer of lamplight.

"Well?" Shim's foot was raised again.

"I want to stop this killing."

There was a pause. Then Shim said mildly, "You're in good shape to stop it, you are."

"Let me talk to Wolfie."

"You did, remember?"

"Let me try again. My own kid is in there!"

"Big deal!" Shim was cool. "If I got rubbed out, my old man

wouldn't say a word one way or the other. Why should an old rum-pot care what happens to his kid?"

Blair didn't know what words to use in saying that he'd always tried to be good to his son. There was no sense in saying it, anyhow. He blinked when Shim turned to one of the others.

"Bring the old rum-pot in there. Might be good for a few laughs, anyhow."

Blair was told to stand up, and walk slowly. The last sound he heard on the outside was Shim's harsh warning.

"The rest of you—look like you're loving it up out here. We don't want any cops sneaking up on us."

Blair bent down to walk into the cave and then straightened. He wasn't prepared for the feeling of coldness that suddenly came upon him. Candlelight threw long shadows against the stone and dirt. Harry sat huddled against the far wall. His lips were bleeding and there were dark welts on his throat and chest.

"Sorry I didn't hear you out a little earlier," he said.

"That's all right, son. Are you in pain?"

Harry said thinly, "It only hurts when I laugh."

The old joke had been a favorite of theirs back when Harry had been ten years old. Harry didn't ask questions. He must have taken it for granted that because he was in trouble his father would be here. Blair found himself standing very straight.

A sneering voice came out of the shadows.

"It's the old rum-pot, all right."

Wolfie had been standing well away from the light. Now, as he walked forward, a switchblade gleamed in one hand. His smile had softened to something like friendliness.

"Probably I could take both of you at the same time. Want to see me try?"

Harry said sharply, "Leave my father out of this!"

"Oh, he's making terms!" Wolfie grinned. "Like a prime minister, now. He's giving orders."

And the knife blade cut against Harry's cheek.

Blair called out, "Leave him alone or you won't have another easy minute as long as you live. That's a promise you can bank

on."

"That so?" Wolfie spat on him, then swung back toward Harry. "You, kid. You think your old man has got your interests at heart. Well, that's wrong. He's the guy who figured out how to handle this job—and plenty of others, too."

Harry tensed, looking from Wolfie to Blair.

"That's where you got the liquor money," he said. "I was pretty sure about the other times—but I never thought you'd—no, I don't believe it."

"Bottles of muscatel or whiskey—they're what buy the old man," Wolfie said, satisfied. "You got sold out for a fifth of whiskey."

Blair said urgently, "Harry, sometime I'll tell you why it had to be done."

He felt fingers under his chin, forcing him around to face Wolfie.

"A real prize, you are." He spat full in Blair's face. "Nobody's old man is any goddam good."

Finally Harry said, "It can't be."

"Still don't believe it?" Wolfie grinned. "I've been playing around too long, but there's an easy way to prove this."

Wolfie turned slowly. "Hey, rum-pot! You still got any of that whiskey left?"

Blair shook his head.

"How about another bottle of the stuff? Six bottles, rum-pot. Half a dozen bottles of prime-quality whiskey, and all you gotta do...." he extended the knife with hands out, "...is kill him."

From back of them, out of the light's circle, came a chuckle of high girlish laughter. "That's good, Wolfie. Awfully good."

The girl was Miriam. She was sitting on a newspaper, with her feet crossed in front of her.

The bone-white knife handle was pressed into Blair's fist.

Slowly he drew his palm around it.

Wolfie's voice seemed to be coming from far away. "Finish the job old-timer, and you get the whiskey."

Blair walked two paces forward, hardly seeing his son at all.

Harry called out, "No!—No—!"

Blair raised the knife and brought it swiftly downward. He stepped back. For an instant, brief as a dropped heartbeat, Harry stared, wide-eyed, unbelieving. Then he shuddered convulsively and pitched forward on his side.

Nails Blair brought a hand to his cheek and cried out in anguish.

Wolfie said quickly, "Let's blow."

He looked at Blair for a long moment in complete silence. Then he turned and left. Miriam and Shim followed him out of the cave.

Blair walked out slowly, last of all. He saw that he was being avoided now. For that much, at least, he was grateful. Nobody would notice or care when he fell behind and vanished into the shadows.

In a few minutes he'd be doubling back to the cave. He'd have to bandage up the boy so that Harry could testify in court.

The knife had been plunged into the right shoulder, where he'd known it would do as little harm as could be managed. It had been a matter of knowing which spot was exactly right—

Nails Blair's criminal years had helped an honest cause for the first time. And when most of the story broke in the newspapers, maybe some honest man in this city of six million, maybe he'd help a guy who needed it real bad.

WILD HOUSE PARTY

Rock drove the jalopy intently, eyes on the road. He paid no attention to the rest of the crew. Some of the girls sat on guys' laps. The gurgle of liquid out of a bottle could be clearly heard.

"Good section 'a town we're in," somebody said. "Look 'a them houses, will you?"

Rock glanced briefly. Good-looking private homes, mostly two-story, with gardens and garages. Most of them well-lit. In a house here and there he saw the gray glow of light from a television set.

"When *we* want to have a party," Rock said bitterly, "we got to go someplace to find an empty lot. Them pigs live like they were God."

From the back, one of the crew said something quietly and a girl covered her mouth over sputter-noises. Another girl started to laugh, but was quieted down.

Rock's jaw hardened, but he didn't say anything. He didn't like to get angry when he was driving. Without a word, he pulled over to the side of the road.

"Sorry, Rock," Hal said, from the back. "Didn't mean to hurt your feelings."

A girl giggled. One of the fellows said irritably, "Knock it off! You too, Hal. Forget it."

Rock wanted to say something angry this time. He glanced at the crew-members riding up front with him, then suddenly snapped his fingers.

"I've got an idea," he said eagerly. "A good one. About what

to do. We don't want to throw a party in an empty lot, so we won't."

"Too cramped here," Hal piped up. "And I think somebody's rented the White House already."

The laughter was general.

Rock smacked a palm into a fist. "Now, you listen here, all 'a you! We're gonna do just like them pigs out there. You don't suppose that *they* haven't got decent places for their brats to throw parties for other brats."

"You want to use a house for the party?" Norm asked. "Whose?"

"We'll come to one," Rock said grimly. "Any house that's empty."

"You kidding?" Norm shot back. "The people come back in the middle of it, they scream their heads off."

To the muttered chorus of agreement, Rock said contemptuously, "Chicken talk!"

"Well, it'd have to be the right one," Hal said slowly. He ran a heavy hand against his girlfriend's legs, and she giggled. "What's 'a matter, honey, am I going against the grain?"

In the burst of laughter, comfortable remarks were made. Rock remained looking back for a full minute, then turned to face the front. At his side Molly smiled shyly at him, then looked pointedly out at the road.

Some of the crew sighted houses that might do, but Rock turned them down without even looking out towards them. He himself picked a house he saw first.

"This'll do."

He found a parking spot in a grove of trees. The crew climbed out slowly, pulling out bottles and sandwich spread. Moonlight washed the girls' hair and whitened the guys' faces.

Finally the comments and little whispered jokes stopped, and every face turned to Rock. Smiling, Rock stepped out of the car and gave orders.

"Me and Hal, we'll go in first. The rest of you sit on your hands till you hear from us."

Somebody laughed, "If they don't see Hal, they can't see anything or they're not home."

Patiently, Rock said, "When you finish with the wisecracks, maybe you'll listen." At the tone of his voice, silence fell quickly. "Like I told you," he finished belligerently, "we'll let you know."

Hal turned to Gloria, his girl, stood at attention and saluted. Gloria smiled and waved at him as if he was leaving forever. The crew laughed. Even Molly smiled a little, then glanced at Rock and covered it.

Rock led the way. Back of him, Hal's footsteps were heavy in the dirt. The house was the usual two-story affair, but it stood by itself. No nearby house could be seen.

First, Rock walked around it. All windows were closed. A hall light burned, as well as one in the bathroom—its window was smaller and the only one with frosted glass.

"What's the next move, Hal? You're a big man with jokes, but what's the next move?"

"I dunno, Rock."

"Sure you don't. All you know is jokes." Rock put his hands on his hips before noticing Hal's look, then put them down quickly. "The lights were probably left on so as to scare burglars. We'll find out."

"Suppose they're home/" Hal asked. "Then what?"

"You talk to 'em. Tell 'em jokes."

He approached a window and set thumbs and forefingers along the right angles made by the wooden frames.

"Okay, it's locked," he said finally.

At his nod, Hal looked around for a big stone, and threw it. Glass crashed down into the house. Carefully avoiding the shards that remained in place, Rock climbed through.

After fumbling for his pocket flash, he pulled it out and lit it. He laughed when Hal, following him in, cut himself, and when Hal's big shoes cracked glass on the floor.

The bathroom door was closed, and no sound came from inside. Rock nodded at Hal, who slowly approached and opened it, then looked in.

"Nobody," Hal whispered. He cleared his throat. "We got it made, I guess."

"Let's check."

They walked into every room, flashing their lights around. Upstairs, in one of the bedrooms, Rock's light struck a cleanly-made bed.

"Goddam 'em," he muttered. "Hal, did you ever see the pig pen *I* sleep in?" Purposely he sat down on the bed then lay down. The heels of his shoes made sharp marks on the bed linen. "That'll show 'em. They'll know I was here."

Suddenly Rock turned and flicked on the overhead lights. He blinked pain away from the eyelids.

"Call 'em in," he said.

Hal's lips quirked unpleasantly. He opened a window and waved his fat arms, crossing and uncrossing them.

Rock and Hal went downstairs together, turning on lights as they went. It took time because they had to adjust to furnishings and layout.

In the big living room, Rock rubbed his hands and took in everything. Wide, airy. Log fireplace, couches. He walked around, kicking pillows or dropping them on the floor.

The crew came in slowly, quietly, except for some of the girls whispering among themselves.

"How do you like it?" Rock asked, his hands outstretched like a host's. "Sweet little place."

As the crew walked into various rooms, the girls grew more admiring, the guys more surprised. Voices became louder, friendlier. One girl found the victrola and some dance records. She grabbed her guy by the hand.

Rock saw Molly in the kitchen with two other girls. They talked about prices, and tried to guess at the cost of utilities.

A girl changed the subject, sighing, "Imagine bringing your fella up to a place like this!"

Rock put up a hand. Molly said something to the girls and stepped out of the group to join him. On their way to the living room, he asked: "You like?"

"It's a very nice place," she said carefully.

He was bitter. "You think I was all kinds of a damn fool to break in?"

"I'm sure you're not a fool."

Two girls came out of the kitchen, one carrying a tray with candy and chocolates. Dancing had started among most couples. Lights were lowered in the living room and logs burned in the fireplace.

Rock watched then turned abruptly to Molly. "Come on, kid, let's do some dancing."

The music was soft, pleasant. Molly danced closely, her head resting on his shoulder, her small fingers at the back of his neck and climbing into his hair.

Hal appeared, talking very loudly. In his hands he carried three whiskey bottles. He blew the dust off them and reached for one of the cocktail glasses on a tray.

"Let's have an orgy," he crowed. Everybody laughed. "This kind, too."

Rock held a cocktail glass. Loudly, over the laughter, he said, "We'll do it like in the movies: after you drink, you throw the glass into the fireplace."

The strong whiskey brought tears to his eyes, but he wiped them furtively, using a hand to cover what he did. Glasses crashed into the fireplace with crackling noises.

Molly excused herself to join some of the other girls in the kitchen. She was almost running, so as to get away faster.

He glared after her, then wandered around, taking half a drink from a glass and breaking it against the fireplace.

"Wouldn't the neighborhood drips want to be here!" he said more loudly than he wanted to.

He glared at the sight of Hal sitting with Gloria, while the girl giggled or bit his ear.

"Hey, blubber, I want to see you!"

She said lazily, "Can't it wait?" At silence from Rock, he turned slowly and stood, then gravely saluted. Gloria raised her cocktail glass to them.

Hal joined Rock in the far corner of the room.

"What do you suppose they've got upstairs?" Rock said slowly. "I mean, clothes and things."

"You want to rob 'em?"

"It don't make no difference any more, what we do," Rock said. "While we're here, what's to lose if we look?"

Hal nodded slowly. "If you want. I'll tell Gloria we'll be gone for a while."

As they started up the stairs, a girl's voice called out from the kitchen:

"Steaks coming up in five minutes."

Rock said bitterly, quietly, "I ain't had a steak in years. My old man wouldn't know what to do with one. A lousy cook, he is. I don't remember how my old lady was, but I guess she wasn't much better."

The living room sounds were like faraway echoes when they reached the bedroom. Rock cleared out closets. The man's hats, coats and suits were too big, but they fit Hal.

"What do you think he paid for a suit like this?" Rock asked, holding one on its hanger. "A hundred? Two hundred?"

"Search me."

He dropped the suit to the floor, and turned angrily to the drawers. The shirts wouldn't fit, of course, but he took two ties after first asking Hal's opinion about them. A tie pin, too, something in the shape of a pirate's cutlass. The sight of it made him uncomfortable, though, and he finally threw it out the window. Hal didn't take anything for himself.

From downstairs, the sounds of dance music stopped as a needle skidded off a record. Somebody rang a cow bell.

"Midnight supper!" a girl called out. "Come and get it!"

Rock turned to the top of the dresser, where a picture frame showed a man and woman with heads together. The man looked young and heavy, with weak eyes.

"I guess that's them." Rock tapped the picture frame with a dirty thumbnail. "Are they going to like the house when they

get back!"

He spat on the bed sheet. "Something extra!"

Hal chortled. "Any friends 'a yours, Rock," he began.

"What's so funny? Cut the jokes. Nobody wants to hear jokes." He scowled down at his watch. He wanted to say something about Molly, something off-hand and casually cruel, but the words wouldn't come.

Hal hesitated, then asked, "You want me for anything more, Rock? Then I'll go downstairs. If I don't keep an eye on Gloria, she's liable to make eyes at another rooster, you know what I mean?"

Rock nodded and began pacing the room. He hit a fist into a palm, then opened drawers and purposely cracked them down to the floor.

He followed Hal downstairs a little later. From the third step he stared down at the crew. Most of them had become quieter. On the couch Hal and Gloria struggled; something Hal did brought giggles out of Gloria. Dishes had been used, then broken against the fireplace, like most of the cocktail glasses. Knives and forks were scattered around, all of them stained.

In the kitchen he saw Molly sitting morosely, her eyes red from crying. She sensed that he was close by, looked up and flushed.

"You don't like what I do, kid," Rock said flatly, "so drop dead, kid."

The sound of renewed sobs followed him out to the living room. He glared down at Hal and Gloria, frowned at the others, then suddenly clapped his hands twice.

"Okay, you! Time to scram outta here."

He repeated it. Soft words of protest came back at him. Hal said mockingly, "All of a sudden we've got a Scout master." There was some laughing.

Rock stepped over to the couch, prodded Hal and Gloria till they separated. He kicked the fellow on a blanket stretched on the floor. "Come on you, move!"

When he heard that the crew was moving, he nodded sullenly,

then turned to the kitchen. Molly sat tracing the pattern of silverware with thumb and forefinger. She talked to Gloria, who fixed her hair by a small mirror on top of a calendar.

Rock asked Gloria, "Did you tell her that we're moving out?"

"Sure." Gloria looked sad. "It's a shame I didn't get a chance to go through the woman's closets. Wonder what kind 'a clothes she's got."

Rock tried to smile, but couldn't stretch his lips far enough. "Maybe we'll come back again, sometimes."

Gloria turned back to the mirror just as Molly closed the silverware drawer.

Rock pounded over to the door. The crew was moving slowly, some of them stopping for last drinks or to warm their hands by the fireplace. Most couples gave wistful looks back before leaving. One of the guys upended a bottle of whiskey to see if it was empty and discovered it wasn't. Whiskey smacked his eye and cascaded down over his face.

Rock stood like a host seeing guests out. A girl actually thanked him shyly for arranging the party. She said it was the best she'd ever been to.

Rock turned briefly to Hal. "Stick around with me."

"Sure," Hal said eagerly, anxious to get back into Rock's good graces. "Any time."

Gloria glanced once at Rock but he thumbed her outside. As she left, he said, "Won't be long."

Molly was the last to go. She was erect, eyes front.

The door closed finally. The cheerful murmur of talk grew lower in the distance.

"What's the next move, Rock?" Hal wet his lips. "Wouldn't it be funny if we could take the fireplace with us?"

Rock said slowly, "I get tired 'a your jokes."

"That's the way I am, always joking." Hal fidgeted, scratching his stomach.

"Well, I don't like the way you are. What's more, I been telling you that. You had plenty of warnings."

Hal was dry-mouthed. "'Had'?"

The knife was in Rock's hands, a small gleaming pocket-knife, blade out.

"What are you doing, Rock? You're crazy...."

With a shaky hand, Hal suddenly reached into a pocket. Rock threw the knife. It landed quivering. Hal gasped very loudly. His eyes glazed and he reached out for the wall. He fell heavily. On his stomach, where his position drove in the blade more deeply.

The crackle of fire on logs was suddenly so loud that Rock had to cover his ears for a second.

Rock turned him over. He bent down and felt for a pulse, then nodded, satisfied. With a quick motion he pulled out the knife. He poured the remains of a half-filled cocktail glass over the red-drenched tip. He wrinkled his nose, at the smell, then stalked over to the kitchen tap, where he soaked the blade thoroughly and wiped it with a towel which he left on the floor.

He started out. Looking at the body again, though, he suddenly snapped his fingers and smiled, genuinely for once. Bending over, he lifted Hal on one shoulder and carried him slowly, panting, to the soft chair in the big room. He crossed Hal's left leg over the right, then found a cocktail glass and poured a drink into it. Finally he set Hal's right hand so that the elbow rested on the chair arm. Forcing four fingers into a semicircle and bending the thumb to meet them, he carefully set the drink in the fat dead hand.

"Wait'll they see you when they come in," he whispered. "What a joke, huh, Hal?"

He looked around the room, nodded shortly and started to the door. Slowly, hands in his pockets, he headed for the grove of trees where he had parked the jalopy. The crew had settled themselves, and girls rested their heads on guys' shoulders. One guy had taken a spoon along and waved it as if conducting an orchestra.

Gloria called out, "Where's Hal?"

"Lost him," Rock said shortly.

There was sudden silence, except for a girl, drunk monotonously singing.

A guy asked, "What does that mean?"

"Means he's not comin' back," Rock said heavily. "Means I lost him. Want me to lose you, too? Anybody else?"

Silence, except for a heavy sigh. Molly was sitting in the back, and a glance at the driver's mirror showed her looking with glazed eyes at nothing.

"Okay, he's lost," Rock said. "Forget him."

He turned to Gloria, who had taken a front seat to make up the space Molly had left. He winked. Gloria's eyes widened, then she winked back. She rested an arm in his, and her head on his shoulder.

Starting back, the passed a quieter, more expensive car going in the opposite direction. Rock stole a look at the driver's face, then at the woman next to him.

Rock looked back in time to see the car heading for the garage of the house that the crew had used for the party. Then he laughed.

ACKNOWLEDGMENTS

"Get Out of Town" by "Arnold English" was originally published in *Trapped Detective Stories Magazine*, December 1957. Copyright © 1957 by Crestwood Publications; Copyright © 2013 by Morris Hershman.

"Immortal Enemy" by Morris Hershman was originally published in *Mike Shayne Mystery Magazine*, July 1965. Copyright © 1965 by Renown Publications; Copyright © 2013 by Morris Hershman.

"One Foot in the Grave," by Morris Hershman, was originally published in *Smashing Detective Stories*, June 1951. Copyright © 1951, 2013 by Morris Hershman.

"One Husband Too Many!" by "Arnold English" was originally published in *Sure-Fire Detective Stories*, December 1957. Copyright © 1957 by Pontiac Publications; Copyright © 2013 by Morris Hershman.

"The Other Side of the Limelight" by Morris Hershman was originally published in *Kracked Mirror Mystery Magazine*, [January?] 1996. Copyright © 1996, 2013 by Morris Hershman.

"Proof Negative" by Morris Hershman was originally published in *Espionage Magazine*, August 1985. Copyright © 1985 by Leo 11 Publications; Copyright © 2013 by Morris Hershman.

"Six Million Murderers" by "Arnold English" was originally published in *Mike Shayne Mystery Magazine*, September 1958. Copyright © 1958 by Renown Publications; Copyright © 2013 by Morris Hershman.

ABOUT THE AUTHOR

MORRIS HERSHMAN is the author of some ninety novels, including mysteries, science fiction, romances, gothics, and many others, a number of which are being published or reprinted by the Borgo Press. He lives and works in New York.